SLAYING MONSTERS FOR THE FEEBLE

ANNETTE MARIE

dark owl
fantasy

Slaying Monsters for the Feeble
The Guild Codex: Demonized / Book Two

Copyright © 2019 by Annette Marie
www.annettemarie.ca

Dark Owl Fantasy Inc.
PO Box 88106, Rabbit Hill Post Office
Edmonton, AB, Canada T6R 0M5
www.darkowlfantasy.com

Cover Copyright © 2019 by Annette Ahner
Cover and Book Interior by Midnight Whimsy Designs
www.midnightwhimsydesigns.com

Editing by Elizabeth Darkley
arrowheadediting.wordpress.com

ISBN 978-1-988153-38-4

MORE BOOKS BY ANNETTE MARIE

STEEL & STONE UNIVERSE

Steel & Stone Series

Chase the Dark

Bind the Soul

Yield the Night

Reap the Shadows

Unleash the Storm

Steel & Stone

Spell Weaver Trilogy

The Night Realm

The Shadow Weave

The Blood Curse

OTHER WORKS

Red Winter Trilogy

Red Winter

Dark Tempest

Immortal Fire

THE GUILD CODEX

CLASSES OF MAGIC

Spiritalis

Psychica

Arcana

Demonica

Elementaria

MYTHIC

A person with magical ability

MPD / MAGIPOL

The organization that regulates mythics and their activities

ROGUE

A mythic living in violation of MPD laws

SLAYING MONSTERS
FOR THE FEEBLE

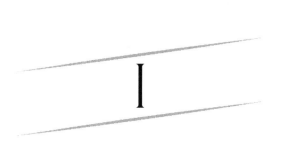

I

I WAS IN HEAVEN.

The musty scent of paper and old leather filled my nose, and my fingers tingled with the urge to touch the embossed spines surrounding me. I ambled between the tall bookshelves, my gaze caressing the tomes. Giving in, I slid my fingertips across a set of encyclopedias.

Not just any encyclopedias. The complete *Encyclopaedia Alchemia*—sixteen thick leather spines detailing every alchemic ingredient known to mythics.

Elation bubbled through me and I allowed myself one happy bounce before focusing. As much as I wanted to peek inside *One Hundred Transmutations for Everyday Life* or slip *Defensive Alchemy: An Apprentice's Compendium* off its shelf, I wasn't here to sate my endless curiosity. I was on a mission. Leaving the alchemy section, I checked the signs hanging above the entrance to each aisle.

I walked past *Arcana – Language Studies*, *Arcana – Spells & Incantations*, *Arcana – Artifacts & Artifact Engineering*, and *Arcana – History*. That last section occupied three aisles on its own.

Elementaria came next. I skipped over Psychica, then turned down a Spiritalis aisle. I couldn't help but pause to read a few titles, including *A Young Witch's Guide to Familiars*, *Power Corrupts: A Case Study of Darkfae Subversion*, and *Is Druidry an Aberration? A Dissertation by the North American Partnership of Covens*. I shook my head at the third one. The fervent loathing between witches and druids was legendary among mythics.

I emerged into another corridor, the butt ends of the shelving units marching on either side like wooden soldiers. Deeper into the library, I found the sign I was looking for: Demonica.

Was it my imagination, or did a cool shadow fall across me when I stepped into the aisle?

I squinted back the way I'd come. Ah, a privacy wall around a study area blocked the windows at the library's front end. I *had* walked into shadow. Had the librarians deliberately picked this dim corner for the section on hellish fiends and soul-binding contracts?

Nudging my glasses up my nose, I skimmed titles. The first shelf held a row of identical, and familiar, copies of *Legal Demonica: The Summoner's Handbook*. Useful, but not what I needed. I continued scanning. *Contractor Control – Advanced Demon Wielding*, *The Ultimate Weapon: Demonica Guilds in Modern Society*, *A History of Summoning*, *The Casual Contractor's Guide to Self-Defense*.

A book for casual contractors? What person would *casually* give up their soul to a demon? I slid it off the shelf and examined the glossy, modern cover with bold red typography and a cartoon demon on the front. Eyebrows climbing higher, I flipped the cover open and read the introduction. As promised, it was a how-to book for contractors who wanted to learn the bare basics and nothing more.

I turned the page. Chapter One, "Getting Started." Large, jaunty text with colorful headings in a sans serif font filled the page beside another cartoon demon, this one making a ghoulish "boo" face.

Congratulations! You're a contractor!

You now belong to the small community of mythics who command demons. Never fear for your safety again. Never take second place to a flashy mage or cocky combat sorcerer. You're a member of the most powerful class now!

But first, you need to learn the basics of controlling your demon.

Wondering where to start? Let's begin with *calling out your demon*.

All contractors have an "infernus"—the artifact that holds your demon's power. Don't lose it! Without it, you can't control your demon. Wear it around your neck on a chain, keep it in your pocket or purse, or leave it in an easy-to-access spot at home. The farther the infernus is from you, the weaker the connection to your demon.

The way this book was written, you'd think literally anyone could pick up an infernus at the local Demon Mart. I didn't know how much demon contracts cost, but I was pretty sure they *started* at six figures. Most people didn't drop that kind of cash, then learn control techniques from a gimmicky book.

> Now let's practice the first step in wielding your demon. There are two magical command words tied to your infernus, and you'll need to memorize both.
>
> **RISE** calls your demon out of the infernus
> Command: **Δαῖμον, ἀναστῆθι**
> *Daimon, anastethi!* (DHEH-mon, ah-nah-STEE-thee)
>
> **REST** returns your demon to the infernus
> Command: **Δαῖμον, ἡσύχαζε**
> *Daimon, hesychaze!* (DHEH-mon, ee-SEE-cha-zeh)
>
> Practice saying both commands. When you're ready, hold your infernus and concentrate on where you want your demon to manifest—not too close to you! Now speak the *Rise* command. Did your demon appear? Perfect!
>
> Remember, *focus is important*. Repeat the *Rise* and *Rest* commands as needed. Once you're comfortable with the process, you can transition to thinking the commands silently.
>
> (Commands not working? Turn to pg. 12 for troubleshooting help.)

I snorted at the thought of a "troubleshooting" page, imagining their suggestions. *Demon won't boot properly? Try turning your infernus off and on again.*

Under normal circumstances, a contractor controlled their demon like a puppet, manipulating its every movement through a telepathic connection. I didn't have to worry about that. In fact, I had zero control over my demon.

Which, all in all, was a terrifying problem to have.

I tapped the page. "'There are two magical command words tied to your infernus.' Hmm."

Command words tied *to the infernus*. That could mean they were built into the contract *or* built into the magic of the infernus. Since I didn't have a real contract, I suspected the commands wouldn't work, but only one way to know for sure.

Balancing the book on one hand, I tugged my infernus from under my jacket and tilted it toward the light, the chain jingling. I examined the palm-sized silver pendant. Perfectly round, flat, and thin, with a spiky emblem etched in the center. Arcane runes marked the outer edge.

Focusing on the empty aisle a yard away, I muttered dubiously, "*Daimon, anastethi.*"

Red light flared across the infernus and I almost dropped it. Arcing out of the pendant, the bright blaze hit the dusty tiles and pooled upward, as though filling an invisible mold. At almost six feet, the light solidified into the familiar shape of my demon.

My extremely displeased demon.

Crimson eyes stared down at me, their eerie glow obscuring dark pupils that had contracted to slits against the overhead fluorescent lights. Four small horns, two above each temple, hid in his tangled black hair, and a mixture of dark fabric, sturdy leather, and gleaming metal armor partially covered smooth toffee-colored skin with a burgundy undertone.

His dusky lips pulled back from his teeth, revealing pointed canines. "What did you do, *payilas?*"

Demons inspired panic in everyone and I was no exception—but my sharp alarm was for a different reason. I frantically checked if anyone had noticed that flare of light.

When no one started screaming about the demon in the library, I glanced from the book to Zylas. I had … I had called him out of the infernus?

"*Payilas*," he growled.

"Um." I hesitantly lifted the book. "I found the commands for the infernus?"

Those lava-like eyes narrowed, then swept away from me to take in our surroundings. His nostrils flared with a silent inhalation and his nose wrinkled in distaste.

"What is this place?" he asked, an alien accent swirling through his husky voice.

"It's a library … part of the Arcana Historia guild. Which, uh, means you should go back into the infernus before someone sees you."

His long, thin tail swished, the two curved barbs on the end just missing a shelf of invaluable texts. He canted his head as though listening.

"There is no one close." He waved a hand around us. "What you need, is it here?"

"I don't know. I only just started looking. Will you get back in the infernus now?"

His upper lip curled, flashing his canines again.

Nerves tightened my stomach. My demon was standing in the middle of a mythic library. If anyone saw him, at best, I would get kicked out. At worst, I would be discovered as an illegal contractor and put to death.

Time to try out the "rest" command. I concentrated on my infernus. *Daimon, hechaze!*

Nothing happened. Crap. Was I messing up the Ancient Greek? I was better at Latin. I looked down at the open book.

It vanished from my grasp. Zylas held the book up as though debating whether to burn it to ash on the spot. Turning, he stretched onto his toes, reached for the highest shelf, and shoved the book into the back.

He dropped onto his heels and faced me. Barely topping five feet, I had no chance of reaching the book without a ladder. Which he knew. Jaw clenched, I turned my back on him and glowered at the nearest shelf. What was that command? *Hecheze … hesachaze … hesychaza …*

Warm breath brushed across the top of my head.

I shot a glare over my shoulder at Zylas, who was standing obnoxiously close. "Back up. I can't concentrate."

"Concentrate on what? You are not doing anything."

I gritted my teeth. The only thing worse than a disobedient demon was a *grumpy* disobedient demon.

"You have not done anything for *weeks*," he complained. "Days and days of nothing but sleep and lounge and sleep—"

"I wasn't sleeping because I'm lazy," I snapped. "I was sick. I had the flu."

"You promised to search for a way I can return home."

"And I am. Right now. Or I would be if you'd stop bothering me." I grabbed a book at random. "The more you distract me, the longer this will take."

He finally stepped back, taking the scent of hickory and leather with him, and drifted away in moody silence. I unclenched my jaw, fighting the urge to order him back into the infernus. The harder I pushed, the more he would resist.

If I'd learned anything in the six weeks since we'd been bound together in a contract, it was that Zylas was infuriatingly stubborn. And deliberately contrary. Defiant. Ornery. Contentious to the point of—

"Should I describe *you, payilas?*"

His hiss floated back to me and I flushed. Thanks to the telepathic connection that was supposed to allow *me* to control *him*, he could hear my thoughts. Not always—it depended on how forcefully I was thinking them—but often enough to be completely unfair.

Pretending I hadn't been insulting him in my head, I opened the book I held and blinked at the title page. *Demon Psychology: Monsters Born or Made?*

Hmm. I flipped the page and scanned the introduction.

The debate of nature versus nurture has dominated discussions on psychology for centuries. Are humans inherently good or is morality a learned behavior?

In the coming pages, we will examine how this concept applies to the preternatural creatures known as demons. Though psychology is, in theory and in practice, relevant only to humans, we now apply our well-practiced diagnostic methods to the demon psyche.

The symptoms most often displayed by demonkind (aggression, violence, lack of empathy, lack of remorse, inability to form emotional bonds, narcissism, manipulativeness) would earn most humans a swift diagnosis of antisocial personality disorder, more commonly known as psychopathy.

However, the question remains: Is demonic violence a product of the demons' mysterious home environment, or, as long believed to be the case, are they born monsters?

I peeked over the top of the book. At the end of the aisle, Zylas was crouched low as he peered around the corner. His tail lashed.

Aggressive, violent, manipulative—check, check, and check. Unempathetic, remorseless, selfish—three more checkmarks. My brow wrinkled as I turned the page and skimmed the table of contents to see if there was a nice, neat "Conclusions" chapter I could read. Biting my lip, I glanced up again.

The aisle was empty.

With a horrified gasp, I shoved the book onto the nearest shelf and sprinted to the end of the aisle. It opened into a wider path with tables lined up against the wall. Halfway along, my demon, in all his horned, tailed, leather-and-armor glory, was prowling past the third table.

I dashed to him so fast I smacked into his back and bounced off, almost dislodging my glasses. Grabbing his arm, I hauled him backward—or I tried. I could've been an ant for all the notice he took of my attempt.

"What are you doing?" I whispered in a panic. "Get back in the infernus before someone sees you!"

"Be quiet," he hissed.

I yanked on his elbow. "You need to—get—back—over—*here*."

I gave his arm a final heave and my hands slipped. Lurching back, I bumped hard into a chair, which clattered loudly against the table, then tipped sideways. I caught it and shoved it upright. Its feet banged down on the floor.

"*Dahganul*," he snarled.

I had a moment to be irritated by the new insult—it was most definitely an insult, even if I didn't know what it meant—before I heard the distinct sound of high heels clacking against tiles. I lunged for Zylas as though I could forcefully mash him back into the infernus—except the bright glow of his power would be a beacon for the approaching librarian.

He shot me a withering look, then dropped into a crouch and slipped between two chairs. He disappeared under the table.

As the authoritative snap of heels grew louder, I lost my head entirely and dove after him. With the chairs jutting under the table and the wall behind it, only a narrow rectangle was free, and Zylas took up most of it. Too late to go back, I squeezed in beside him.

Not that hiding from the librarian was necessary. She was a *librarian*. I needed to work on my irrational fear of confrontation.

The librarian's steps drew closer, then hesitated a few tables away. I held my breath.

Eyes gleaming in the shadows, Zylas leaned toward me and whispered, "Move."

I shied away from the closeness of his face. "Huh?"

"Move, *payilas*."

"Why? We need to—"

"You are on my tail."

Belatedly, I realized the floor under my butt was uneven, and on my right, I spotted the rest of his tail coiled across the floor. My face heated.

"There's nowhere to move. Can you just wait?" When he glared in answer, I hissed, "This is your fault, you know. Why are you wandering around where anyone can see you?"

"I would not be seen. *You* made noise, not me."

The librarian clacked closer and I bit back my retort. A pair of black pumps and gray dress pants appeared. The woman walked past the table, and her footsteps grew muffled as she continued to the library's farthest corner.

"You are useless," Zylas added pitilessly. "You walk loud and talk loud and breathe loud—"

"I do not *breathe* loud." I sat forward, getting off his stupid tail, and crawled for the gap between chairs.

He seized the hem of my sweater and yanked. I flopped backward and landed in his lap with a muffled thump. He clamped a warm hand over my mouth.

A pair of men's leather shoes came into view, near silent on the tile floor compared to the woman's clicking heels. The man strode past our hiding spot and disappeared into an aisle.

Zylas exhaled against my cheek—then pushed his nose into the spot under my ear. I squealed into his hand and twisted away from his face. His husky laugh was more vibration than sound. He shoved me off his lap, crawled over my legs with more grace than should've been possible, and slipped between the chairs.

Muttering nasty things under my breath, I rushed out after him. As I wobbled to my feet, he was already ghosting down the aisle—not back into the Demonica corner, but toward the front of the library.

"Zylas!" I hurried to his side, quietly this time. "Where are you going?"

He paused, crimson gaze sweeping the aisles. "This way."

"Which way? What are you—"

Feet silent on the floor, he entered a short hall. A door marked with a bathroom sign waited at the end, but Zylas was interested in a door with a *Guild Members Only* plaque on it.

"We're not allowed in there," I told him.

He grasped the handle. White light sparked across it—some kind of Arcane spell. The pale sizzle ran over his knuckles and up his wrist. He narrowed his eyes, then rammed his shoulder into the door. The frame split and the door swung open, the sorcery imbued into the handle useless.

Crap, he'd broken the door. How would I explain *that?*

"Zylas, we can't—"

He ignored me and walked in. Why was I not surprised?

The interior was dark, the air heavy with dust. I felt along the wall, found a light switch, and pressed it. Fluorescent bulbs buzzed awake.

Familiarity hit me in the gut. A long table was stacked with books in various states of disassembly. Tools I'd seen my mother use daily lay across the work surface—blades and cutting tools, glue, string, leather presses, pens and ink. A large magnifying glass on an adjustable arm was positioned above the book restorer's current project.

Zylas glided toward the table, paused to inhale, then angled toward the cabinets along the wall. He homed in on the corner one, the metal doors secured with a heavy padlock.

I minced to his side. The lock had no keyhole and its face was marked with a set of runes. "What is it?"

He sniffed the air. "I smell blood."

My stomach performed an adrenaline-fueled flip. "Blood" wasn't even on the list of answers I'd expected.

"Old. Faint." His tail snapped sideways. "The scent of demon blood and magic."

He reached for the padlock but I grabbed his wrist. I didn't doubt he could break it with either pure strength or magic, but that was the problem.

"Don't," I whispered urgently.

His jaw tightened with stubbornness. I knew that look—the *"I'm about to do the opposite of what you want just to prove I can"* look.

If he broke that lock, I'd be in so much trouble.

I pulled on his arm, straining to bring up that page of commands in my mind's eye. His mouth twisted and he again reached for the padlock, dragging me across the floor.

With a shot of panic, the Ancient Greek popped into my head. *"Daimon, hesychaze!"*

Crimson power lit up his extremities. I caught a glimpse of his glowing eyes, wide and furious, just before his body dissolved into light and streaked back into my infernus. I shoved the pendant under my jacket, breathing faster than the situation warranted.

I'd forced Zylas into the infernus. It was the first time I'd ever forced him to do *anything*.

Heels clacked in the hallway outside. I spun around, my elation shriveling into dread. The footsteps snapped loudly, then the librarian stepped into the open doorway, shock and anger stamped across her face.

Damn that demon.

2

SOMETIMES, BEING A SHRIMPY WAIF of a twenty-year-old girl came in handy. My acting skills weren't great, but I hadn't needed to fake my tearful, hand-wringing apologies to the librarian. Nor had it been much of a stretch to insist that I hadn't broken the door. I'd been on my way to the bathroom when I noticed it was open. That's all.

Deciding I was too young, innocent, and wimpy to break through magically locked doors, she'd sighed, told me to leave, and started inspecting the restoration room for anything missing. Thank goodness I'd stopped Zylas from breaking the cabinet's padlock.

Thirty minutes later, I was getting off a bus in the shabby Downtown Eastside. The chill air threatened rain and I pulled my jacket tighter against the December wind. With no desire to linger, I hurried past a rundown bike repair shop and a tattoo parlor with barred windows.

Twenty yards ahead, a three-story, cube-shaped building squatted between a small parking lot and a construction site, its shadowed doorway almost lost in its blank façade. Pulling out my phone, I checked for messages—none—then sent a quick text to Amalia, reminding her not to be late.

Steeling myself—this was my guild and I shouldn't be afraid of it—I approached the door, a faded crow and mallet painted on the black wood. Above it, Old English lettering spelled out, "The Crow and Hammer." It'd been over a month since I'd first set foot inside, and I'd only been back a few times. Partly because I'd caught the worst flu of my life—probably a result of all the preceding stress—and partly because … well …

With an unsteady breath, I reminded myself I was a badass demon contractor and pushed the door open. Sound rolled out, chattering voices welcoming me into the warmth and light. I slipped inside.

The pub was both cozy and spacious. Wooden chairs surrounded the polished tables, and dark beams crossed the ceiling. Opposite the door, a bar stretched across the pub's back wall, stools lined up in front of it. A huge steel war hammer was affixed to the wall above the liquor cabinets.

I moved toward the nearest table, keeping well away from the small groups of mythics around the bar. Everyone was busy catching up, laughter peppering the exuberant conversations. Tonight was the guild's monthly meeting, and every member was gathering for a solid hour of updates, presentations, and group training.

Rubbing my hands together to warm them, I allowed myself to relax. This wasn't so bad. The atmosphere was a thousand times better than at my last guild. I even dared to unzip my coat and hang it on the back of a chair.

No one had noticed me, and I was perfectly okay with that. Being noticed was one of my least favorite things, especially when everyone here knew everyone else—and I knew no one.

The guild door swung open with the cheerful jingle of a bell. A tall, willowy woman a bit older than me and an even taller, ruggedly built man waltzed in. Her dark hair hung loose around her, and his was pulled into a shaggy topknot.

"We're here!" the guy called. "Not even late this time!"

Chuckles ran through the guild, faces turning toward them and hands waving in greeting.

"Kier, Kaveri!"

"Whoa, they're on time!"

The couple swept toward the group. The newcomers hadn't spotted me, but with their entrance, others had. I couldn't lurk in the corner any longer, not without looking like a total weirdo. Gulping, I trailed after the couple, each step carrying me closer to the terrifying prospect of social interaction.

I scanned the Crow and Hammer mythics. Ranging from eighteen to middle-aged, many of them exuded an air of toughness. Instinctively, I veered toward a group closer to my age, but when I met their eyes, hostility hit me like an icy wave.

That was the other reason I hadn't spent any time at the guild.

"Well, well," drawled a large man with brown hair and a thick beard that made his age difficult to guess. "If it isn't the little contractor."

Beside him, a guy with a rangy build and a wide smirk scanned me from head to toe as though debating whether he could pick me up with one hand.

A woman in her mid-twenties pushed between them, her pale blond hair damp as though she'd just showered. "We were wagering on whether you'd show. You haven't turned up for anything else."

Had I missed guild events while I'd been sick? No one had contacted me about anything.

Fighting not to hyperventilate, I dragged my gaze upward. "I didn't mean to miss anything, but I was—"

"I didn't hear a word of that," she interrupted loudly. "Speak up."

My face burned and I couldn't stop my hunch. Gripping the hem of my black sweater, I tried to respond but my mind had gone blank. I wanted to sink into the floor and disappear.

"You're a mysterious one," the rangy guy said. "We haven't heard a thing about you. How did you get into Demonica?"

I peered up through my bangs, squeezing my sweater tighter as I tried to determine if he was genuinely curious or about to humiliate me.

"Well?" the big guy demanded, stepping closer. "What's your training background? How long have you been contracting?"

Those questions were definitely not friendly.

"You killed the unbound demon, didn't you?" The blond woman sniffed dismissively. "How did you manage it?"

By letting my illegally contracted demon do all the work. But I couldn't say that. They were waiting expectantly so I muttered, "The unbound demon was already injured."

My response did not impress them.

The big guy sneered. "Why are you a contractor, anyway? What use does a little girl like you have for a demon?"

I flinched, wondering if I should make an excuse to leave. But where would I go? Attendance was mandatory.

"Who ordered the Moscow Mules?" The female voice rang out over the chatter. "Come get 'em before I throw them at you!"

Jolting, I peeked toward the bar, my view blocked by mingling guild members. Was that the *bartender* shouting? Was she allowed to threaten people like that?

The large man stepped closer, towering more than a foot over me. The handful of mythics looking our way wore neutral expressions, and no one was jumping to my defense. I could hear it in the undertone of conversations around me, in their aggressive questions: *Outsider.* I was an intruder in their guild.

Tears stung the corners of my eyes and I pressed my lips together before their trembling betrayed me.

"Hey, new girl!"

I started a second time. Was that voice calling to *me*? My gaze slid past unfamiliar faces and found one I actually knew. Sort of. Not really.

"Over here," the red-haired bartender ordered imperiously.

I blinked in confusion—but I wasn't about to argue. Ducking around the large man, I hurried past another group and stopped uncertainly at the bar. The woman pointed at the stool across from her, so I climbed onto the seat and braced my toes on the footrest.

She assessed me with sharp hazel eyes, her nose and cheeks dusted with freckles. Her wild curls were damp and shiny— why did half the mythics look like they'd just left a swimming pool?—and hung past her shoulders. Six weeks ago, I'd seen this woman during a demon attack. After Zylas had killed Tahēsh, she'd jumped into a car with three men and fled the scene.

As far as I was concerned, *she* was the suspicious one, but she was peering at me as though she could peel back my skin with the force of her gaze. Her eyes narrowed to amber-green slits.

Then, to my shock, she offered her hand. "I'm Tori."

She was the first person to introduce herself.

I took her hand and gingerly shook it. "Robin."

"Want something to drink?"

An actual polite question? "Um—"

"Hey!" The big, aggressive man shouldered a small guy with round sunglasses out of his way. His glower said all too clearly that I wasn't getting out of our "conversation" that easily. "Where's your infernus? Are you even a contractor or just a wannabe pretending—"

"Darren, shut your hole before you contaminate my bar with your stupidity."

My jaw fell open, and my gaze swung to Tori.

The big guy whirled on her. "I'm just asking what everyone else is think—"

"No one asked you, dipshit."

My eyes popped wider.

Tori glared at Darren, then leaned toward me. "Don't let him push you around."

Push me around? My gaze darted to him, then to the cold blond woman, the smirking guy, and the others who hadn't made a single move to defend their new member. Again, I was struck by their understated toughness, the rough edge hidden under unassuming exteriors. I'd thought this guild was far softer than the Grand Grimoire, but maybe I was wrong.

Zylas, are you paying attention? I silently asked as I cautiously reached under the neck of my sweater and closed my fingers around the cool silver pendant. Withdrawing the infernus, I settled it on my chest. Darren's gaze followed it, his expression torn between curiosity and derision.

"Would you like to see my demon?" I asked him. "Right now?"

He crossed his arms over his thick chest. "Yeah, let's see it."

I ran my thumb across the infernus. *Let's play the game, Zylas.*

The pendant blazed with crimson light. Power spilled down, hit the floor, then pooled upward into my demon's shape. The glow flared into solidity, then faded. Zylas stood still and silent, staring blankly at nothing in a flawless imitation of an enslaved demon with no autonomy.

Despite his ornery defiance, Zylas was nothing if not intelligent. He knew this moment was too crucial for disobedience. Both our lives depended on his acting skills.

At his appearance, gasps flew through the pub and I resisted the urge to shrink. We had everyone's attention now. They were staring at Zylas, measuring him, judging him, and all he could do was stand there and endure it. At least no one laughed this time.

"Seriously?"

Or maybe the laughter hadn't begun yet.

"*This* is your demon?" Darren planted his feet almost on Zylas's toes, smirking into the demon's face. "I've never seen such a small, pathetic demon in my life!"

The blond woman mock-whispered to the rangy guy, "Do you think she got it for cheap because it's a runt?"

When Darius, the Crow and Hammer's GM, had allowed me to join, I'd hoped this guild would be different from the

Grand Grimoire, but maybe all guilds were the same. Maybe Zylas and I were too small and weak for anyone to respect.

The barbed tip of his tail gave the tiniest twitch, unnoticed by the watching mythics.

"Forgetting something, dumbasses?" Tori's acidic snap cut into my thoughts. "Robin and her demon killed the unbound one on Halloween. *Obviously* they're not weak."

She was defending us?

"Not weak?" Darren scoffed. His hand rose toward Zylas. "This thing couldn't—"

Uh-oh, not good. "Don't touch him."

Darren's reach stuttered, then he boldly rammed his palm into Zylas. The demon didn't move and Darren stumbled backward, thrown off balance. He shook his head and glanced at his hand, as though confused about how his powerful muscles had failed to affect the shorter, lighter demon.

He thought we were weak. No one here respected us. Unwelcome and disregarded … but what had Tori said? *Don't let him push you around.*

I pressed my thumb against the sigil at the center of the infernus. *Zylas?*

I didn't need to finish the thought—his hand was already closing around Darren's throat. With strength the mythic could only dream of, Zylas swung him off his feet and slammed him down on the bar.

Not too rough, I warned.

He bent Darren backward over the bar. The mythic spluttered and flailed helplessly. Everyone else had withdrawn, shock and fear on their faces. I hated that we had to prove our strength, but this was much better than last time. Zylas was making the proper impression without having to pound half the guild into the floor.

I straightened my glasses, turned toward the bartender, and forced a smile. "Could I have a water, please, Tori?"

Her mouth hung open, and her gaze darted between me and Zylas. Pulling herself together, she flashed a grin that caught me off guard, then plunked a glass on the counter. Zylas held Darren against the bar, still as a statue and probably bored out of his mind. Pinning people down wasn't nearly violent enough to entertain him.

One more minute, I told him. *Then—*

His head jerked up.

Like a startled herd of deer, every nearby mythic jumped away. What was he *doing?*

Back in the infernus! I commanded urgently.

Crimson light rushed across him, softening his form, and the power swept into my infernus. As he disappeared, I tucked the pendant away and glanced around, hoping no one would question the way my demon had suddenly looked up. Darren stumbled away from the bar, rubbing his bruised throat.

I peeked in the direction Zylas had looked.

Three men stood at the end of the bar. The redhead in the middle, tallest by an inch or two, watched me with intent blue eyes, his handsome features unmarred by his frown. On his left was a dark-haired man with a leaner build and looks that had skipped handsome and jumped straight to smoldering perfection. His expression was inscrutable, his dark eyes drifting past me. The third man, falling between the heights of the other two, ran his fingers through his tousled brown hair, his bronze skin interrupted by a scar that ran from his left temple, across his eye, and into the hollow of his cheek.

I recognized them too: the three men who had fled with Tori after Tahēsh's death. And hidden among them was a demon.

I didn't know how it was possible, but Zylas was certain. A third demon had been present that night, one that wielded powerful magic. The unknown demon's scent had been all over Tori and these three men.

A water glass, rattling with ice, slid in front of me. I looked up.

Suspicion burned in Tori's eyes, her full lips pressed thin. She knew Zylas had done something strange. She'd seen him battle and slay Tahēsh with more speed and ease than a contracted demon should be capable of.

But I'd watched her and her companions flee the scene. I knew they were concealing a demonic secret of their own.

I wrapped my hand around the cold glass and gave her the smallest nod. She shifted her attention to a mythic waiting to order, and as she asked him what he wanted, I let out a shaky breath. This guild was supposed to be my haven, but it might be a viper pit in disguise.

3

AT THE FRONT OF THE ROOM, Darius called for everyone's attention. He stood near the stairs leading to the second level, his salt-and-pepper hair combed back and his beard neatly trimmed—unlike the last time I'd seen him, when he'd been sporting a Gandalf beard. His guildeds filled the tables, fifty people watching their leader with respectful focus.

Tori stood behind the bar, her elbows braced on the counter and her chin propped on one hand. Her three friends sat on stools in front of her. None of them had paid me any attention since Zylas returned to the infernus.

Several other bar stools were occupied, as were almost all the chairs … except for the three empty ones around my table. My stomach shriveled at the unspoken rejection. Amalia should have been here with me, but—I checked my phone again—she still hadn't shown up. Her last text, twenty minutes ago, said she was on her way. In Amalia-speak, that meant she'd arrive in an hour.

"For tonight's safety segment," Darius began, projecting his voice through the pub, "Felix will present a comparison of this year's job hazard assessments versus incident reports. But before we delve into that riveting topic"—a brief smile—"let's highlight last month's member accomplishments."

He pulled a paper from his pocket and unfolded it. "First, our congratulations to Katherine on the publication of her paper, "Potency Control in Alchemic Crystallization," in the prestigious *Modern Alchemy* journal."

The Crow and Hammer mythics clapped and called out to an older woman with boyishly short brunette hair and laugh lines around her eyes. She performed a playful bow from her seat.

"A special accolade for Philip," Darius continued, "who successfully identified, located, and exorcised a new shifter before last month's full moon."

As applause rang out for a middle-aged man with a kind smile, a frigid breeze hit my back. I looked over my shoulder as a petite woman slipped through the door. Bundled in a leather jacket with the hood pulled up, she closed the door quietly, trying to mute the telltale chime of the bell. Strapped to her back was a huge broadsword, the hilt jutting over her shoulder.

"Andrew led Gwen, Bryce, and Drew on a hunt for a rogue terramage, and not only did they secure the bounty, but they tagged him minutes before a team of Pandora Knights mages arrived."

The guildeds whooped. The late arrival hesitated, then slid into the nearest chair—the one beside me—and pushed her hood off.

I'd seen her before! On the night I'd helped the Grand Grimoire hunt Tahēsh, I'd spotted her with a team of three others, who were also searching the downtown streets.

Up close, I could see she was in her early thirties, with large brown eyes set in a delicate face, a blond pixie cut streaked with pale blue and pink, four piercings in one ear, and the edge of a tattoo creeping up the side of her neck, most of it hidden beneath her collar. She swiped her messy bangs away from her face and tossed me a smile.

I'd never seen anyone so cool. I wanted to be her when I grew up.

"Lastly," Darius said, "let's congratulate Aaron and Kai on capturing four wanted rogues with bounties totaling over twenty thousand dollars. And a special mention for their fifth catch of the month—with Taye's help, they tracked the notorious Sunset Beach Stalker all the way from Stanley Park to Yaletown ... only to discover they were, in fact, tracking a dog."

Laughter burst through the room. I craned my neck, trying to figure out who Darius was referring to.

"Over there," the woman beside me murmured, pointing at the three men sitting in front of Tori. "Kai, Aaron, and Ezra."

"One very friendly Labrador Retriever," Darius added over the group's boisterous amusement, "was promptly returned to his relieved owner. Aaron, what was the bounty?"

"I got two hugs and a kiss on the cheek," the red-headed guy announced proudly. "Kai got her phone number."

A chorus of wolf-whistles answered him. The dark-haired man beside Aaron casually waved off the cheers, and Tori rolled her eyes at them.

The woman beside me leaned back in her chair. "I thought the three guys were trouble enough, but then they adopted Tori as Mischief-Maker Number Four."

I blinked owlishly.

Chuckling, she offered her hand. "I'm Zora. You must be Robin, the new contractor."

I shook her hand. "Nice to meet you. That's a big sword."

Way to demonstrate my smooth conversation skills.

Zora grinned at my awkward observation. As Darius moved on to incident reports, starting with a sorcery array that had exploded—in the parking lot of all places—she unbuckled her baldric, slid the weapon off, and leaned it against the wall.

"I was on a vampire's trail," she whispered, though there was no chance her voice would carry all the way across the pub to Darius. "Almost had the bloodsucker, but he gave me the slip."

Vampires? The word alone alarmed me. "Were you out there by yourself?"

"Only at the end. My partner had just left when I caught the trail." She leaned closer. "Don't mention to the guild officers that I went after a vamp on my own. That's a guaranteed write-up."

Now *that* was what I liked to hear. A guild that took safety seriously.

"What are you smiling about?" Zora asked, amused. "Are you planning to blackmail me?"

"Oh!" I hadn't realized I was smiling. "No, not at all. It's just that my last guild wasn't very safety-oriented."

"The Grand Grimoire, right?" She nodded. "I've heard that about them. I also heard they're under MPD investigation right now. Decent chance they might get shut down."

I hadn't heard that, but considering the GM had covered up a murder and sold me to a rogue guild, I wasn't surprised.

"While we're on the topic of experimental magic," Darius said to the room at large, "it seems our local MPD precinct has added a new agent to their roster—a formidable young abjuration sorceress. Though I'm sure you would all love to meet her, if for some reason you *aren't* using our well-equipped atrium or lab, let's keep the second rule in mind, shall we?"

Laughter swept through the room and I perked up curiously. Second rule?

Zora whispered, "Where's your friend? The sorcery apprentice?"

I tapped my phone, lying on the tabletop, to wake the screen. Amalia's latest message: *I just called a cab. See you soon.* So much for being "on the way."

"She's running behind," I sighed. "At this rate, she'll miss the whole meeting."

Zora smiled conspiratorially. "Anyone who misses without a solid reason gets the minutes treatment."

"The what?"

"They have to copy the entire meeting's minutes, by hand, and present it to an officer. And they're automatically volunteered to take minutes for any and every meeting over the next four weeks."

Oh, Amalia would love that.

Zora's grin took on a wicked edge. "Once, a couple of years ago, Kai missed the monthly meeting. That month, Aaron and Ezra organized a dozen completely pointless meetings with almost every member of the guild and made him take minutes for each one."

I glanced at the three mages and the red-headed bartender. At the other end of the room, Darius was describing a near miss, where a mythic had almost backed their car over their teammate. The room was quiet, Darius's aura of authority holding every member spellbound.

I fidgeted with my phone, lining it up with the table's edge. "Can I ask … what class is Darius?"

"He's a luminamage—a light mage."

Oh, a light mage. That explained the "blindness magic" Zylas had claimed Darius had tried on him.

"He's an excellent guild master. You'll find him very different from the Grand Grimoire's GM." She cast me an amused look. "But don't be fooled. He has his soft moments, but he's a hard-ass. No one messes with Darius King."

That didn't surprise me either. "What about the other three—Aaron and … uh …"

"Aaron, Kai, and Ezra," she supplied. "Pyromage, electramage, and aeromage. A power team for sure. By the way, they're all single."

My mouth dropped open. "Huh?"

"Isn't that where you were headed with your questions?"

Actually, no. They were certainly good looking, but also big and muscly and probably loud. I'd bet they hadn't read a single book between them this year. No thanks.

Refocusing, I considered where the demon scent Zylas had picked up would have come from if all three men were Elementaria mythics. "What class is Tori?"

"Uh … Spiritalis."

Her uncertain pause caught my attention, but at that moment, the noise level in the pub rose. Darius had given the floor over to a blond man with spectacles. He was tinkering with a projector and laptop that didn't seem to be cooperating, and idle chatter was spreading through the group as they waited for the meeting to resume.

The chair across from me slid out. A plump, elderly woman lowered herself with a sweep of her daisy-patterned, floor-length skirt. Glasses with turquoise frames perched on her nose and a knitted cap topped her wispy white hair.

"Good evening, Zora," she murmured before fixing an intent stare on me. "Child, your aura is troubled."

My what was what now?

She leaned forward. "Your energy called me to you. You are in dire need of guidance, aren't you?"

I was? I glanced confusedly at Zora. The petite woman seemed to be suppressing a reaction, but I wasn't sure what sort.

"My name is Rose," the elderly lady added. "I'm the guild's *senior* diviner."

She shot a haughty look at the bar, where a young woman with a blond bob was talking animatedly to Aaron as she showed him something on her phone.

Rose reached into the floppy bag hanging from her shoulder and produced a black velvet cloth. She threw it across the table, then added a small wooden stand. Onto the stand, she placed a pale crystal ball. I watched her set everything up with a bemused frown.

"May I scry for you?" Rose asked.

Right now? Seriously? "Um … I think the meeting is going to start again soon."

"It won't take long. This isn't an ideal setup—the energies in the room may interfere—but we can begin with an exploratory séance."

I glanced between her and Zora again. "This doesn't seem like the best time."

"No sense in waiting, my dear," Rose insisted. "Your conflicted energy needs an outlet, and if you wait, you may find a lesser psychic attempting to assist you."

Her oddly accusatory gaze swung to the young woman as though the girl were about to swoop in and steal Rose's crystal ball off the table. Zora coughed in a way that sounded suspiciously like a stifled laugh.

"I have the skill and experience you need," Rose declared confidently. "Let's begin. First, clear your mind."

Unsure how to refuse, I gave in with a nod. Though I'd read about the predictive powers of psychics, I'd never seen a real diviner at work before.

"Put your hands on the ball," she said. "Just like that, yes."

I laid my palms on the cool crystal and she placed her hands over mine.

"Relax," Rose crooned. "Let your energy flow into the crystal."

I inhaled slowly, concentrating on the cold, hard quartz under my skin.

"Look into the ball. Stare deep as you empty your mind and spirit of conscious thought."

That was easier said than done. I gazed into the white crystal, wondering what I would see—then realized that was a thought and I wasn't supposed to be thinking.

The crystal ball reflected the dim lights of the pub, and the rumbling conversations around us faded into a smear of sound. The crystal seemed to draw in the light. Its depths swirled ever so faintly. The sphere filled my vision until the pub had disappeared, until all I could see was spiraling white smoke. It drifted sedately, insubstantial, empty.

As it moved, a shadow appeared in its depths. The distant shape ... a sitting figure. Dark, featureless. Male.

He drew closer as though I were sweeping into the mist's depths to join him. He sat on the fog-covered ground, legs drawn up, arms slung around them. Chin resting on one knee, black hair tangled and wild.

Zylas sat in the mist, staring into the distance.

Shadows clung to him, and in them, I tasted dark emotions. Uncertainty. Unease. A restless longing, a quiet desolation. He gazed at nothing, as still as though he were impersonating an enslaved demon, but no demon would sit like that—like a lost child waiting to be found.

A strange sorrow swirled around him, a vulnerability I'd never seen before. Here, in this endless mist, his fearless confidence had been stripped away. His aggression, his defiance, his sarcasm and insults ... all had faded to reveal what hid beneath.

His head lifted, then turned. His crimson eyes looked into me, through me. His hand drifted upward, fingers stretching toward me.

"Let's begin!"

At the loud declaration, I jerked backward with a gasp. The vision of white mist disappeared, replaced by the crystal ball, black velvet cloth, and noisy pub. The man beside the projector was talking, a laser pointer directed at the screen where a colorful line chart zigzagged.

"Robin." Zora touched my arm. "Are you okay?"

I panted in shuddering breaths. My hand was fisted around my sweater, gripping the infernus underneath. "I—I think so."

"My dear," Rose whispered keenly, "you fell instantly into the crystal's energy! What did you see?"

My gaze darted from the orb back to Rose. "What … what did you see?"

"The crystal darkened to the deepest shade of pitch—a warning of grave danger." She placed her hand on the orb. "But *you* experienced the séance—you saw the crystal's message. What vision did you experience?"

"I didn't see any black," I hedged, releasing my sweater and the infernus.

"Do not be shy!" Rose exclaimed. "Tell me! With my expert guidance, you experienced a true—"

"*And*," the presenter at the front called, staring pointedly in our direction, "if you all want to look this way, you'll see a fifty-eight percent reduction in incidents when the team spent ten minutes or more on their hazard assessment."

Zora snorted and tipped her chair back, balancing it on two legs. Flushing, I fixed my attention on the projector, ignored Rose's probing gaze, and did my best to push the crystal ball's vision out of my mind.

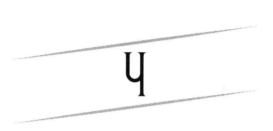

4

THE BUS'S DOORS CLANKED and hissed open. Amalia and I stepped down onto the sidewalk. My cousin tossed her blond hair over her shoulder and marched away.

As the bus accelerated, I trotted a few steps to catch up to the tall, long-legged apprentice summoner. She glowered at me and stormed onward into the afternoon gloom, the sun hidden behind a thick blanket of gray clouds.

"It isn't my fault you missed the meeting yesterday," I pointed out.

"You should've warned me they'd give me a stupid punishment. Meeting minutes? Come on!"

I shrugged as we followed the sidewalk along a curving street lined with gated properties.

"Saturday evenings aren't exactly convenient!" she added angrily. "And Christmas is, what, nine days away? Why can't they cut us some slack?" Her steps slowed, a grimace pulling at her full lips. "I guess I should get used to a guild that takes regulations seriously."

I didn't know a thing about her previous guild, but my last one—not counting the Grand Grimoire—had been a sleeper guild, meaning all its members were non-practicing mythics. My obligations had ended with paying the membership fee and attending a yearly check-in. The Crow and Hammer, on the other hand, required a monthly meeting and regular reviews by the guild officer assigned to supervise us.

Tugging my coat tighter against the icy wind, I extended my stride as much as my short legs would allow.

"It's weird being back," Amalia murmured, hitching her purse up her shoulder. "I feel like I'm going home, but …"

She trailed off as we stopped in front of a pair of wrought-iron gates, the decorative balusters crisscrossed with yellow police tape. The driveway stretched up an easy slope to what remained of the house. Where a two-story mansion had once sprawled was now a hollow, blackened skeleton. Charred studs supported the partially collapsed roof.

"Well …" Amalia said heavily. "This looks hopeless."

"We don't have any better leads," I mumbled.

Together, we approached the gates. Amalia rolled one open, tearing a few strips of police tape, and squeezed into the narrow gap. I ducked through the opening after her and we followed the paved drive to the house.

Planting her hands on her hips, Amalia surveyed the ruins of her home. The garage had crumbled to the ground, the debris heaped on scorched metal that had once been luxury cars.

"All right. Our best bet is Dad's office. After that, his bedroom."

I eyed the blackened studs framing the front door, which lay face down in the foyer. "Is it safe to go in there?"

She shrugged. "It hasn't caved in yet."

She marched up the steps and ripped the tape off the doorway. Inside, a thick layer of ash and black debris coated the floor and crunched under our shoes. Studs were all that remained of some walls, while blackened drywall clung to others, the paint peeling and streaked with burn marks and water lines from the endless December rain. The stench of smoke and wet charcoal clogged my nose.

Amalia picked her way across the foyer and into the hall, passing the formal living room where I'd once eavesdropped on Uncle Jack and his business partner Claude. The furniture had burnt to heaps of sooty fragments.

Uncle Jack's office hadn't escaped the fire. His desk was scorched black, his papers no more than crumbling cinders. His monitor, which had fallen onto the floor, had disintegrated. I could see where his computer had sat—a puddle of melted plastic was fused to the floor—but the case was gone. The MPD must have removed it, but considering the state of everything else, I doubted they'd succeeded in recovering any data.

The filing cabinet drawers hung open, their contents seemingly untouched, and I wondered why the MPD investigators had left them alone—until Amalia tried to lift out a folder. It crumbled under her fingers, a flurry of ash dusting the floor.

"Damn it," she muttered.

My heart sank. "Is it all like that?"

We checked every drawer, but Uncle Jack's records were burnt beyond salvation. Abandoning the office, we dared to creep up the crumbling staircase to the second level. Huge sections of the floor were missing, preventing us from reaching the master suite.

"What a bust," Amalia sighed as we returned to the foyer. "I knew it was a long shot, but still."

"Do you have any other ideas?" I wiped my sooty hands on my jeans. "Uncle Jack hasn't contacted you in six weeks, so chances are he doesn't plan to. We need *some* clue where to look for him."

On the afternoon the house had burned down, Uncle Jack had fled. Amalia was certain he'd reached a safe house and was in hiding, but for reasons neither of us understood, he hadn't contacted his daughter.

Personally, I couldn't care less if I ever saw my uncle again, but my mother's grimoire was most likely in his possession. The ancient journal had belonged to my ancestors, the Athanas, for countless generations, passed from mother to daughter in an unbroken line—until Uncle Jack had gotten his greedy hands on it.

So far, I'd learned only two things about the grimoire and my family roots: one, the Athanas name was world-famous in the summoning community—so famous my great-grandmother had abandoned it when she'd emigrated from Albania—and two, the grimoire contained at least one demon name worth a heart-stopping ten million dollars.

I didn't care much about its dollar value. Not only was it my last connection to my mother, but I needed it for other reasons too—reasons that had everything to do with the infernus tucked between my jacket and sweater.

"Is there anywhere else in the house he stored important documents?" I asked.

"Just his office and—oh!" She thumped the heel of her hand against her forehead. "The safe. Duh. It's in the garage."

She hurried out the front door, down the steps, and across the driveway to the remains of the garage. It had suffered the worst damage, the structure reduced to shards of wood and the twisted skeletons of the cars. Amalia bravely waded in.

Grateful for my sturdy winter boots as I clambered over a fallen beam, I joined her in the back corner.

She pointed at a collapsed wall—an eight-foot-wide section of drywall and studs. "The safe is under there."

We grabbed the wall and heaved. It shifted maybe an inch.

"No way we can move this," she declared, dusting off her hands.

Unfortunately, I had to agree. I tapped the front of my jacket, my finger striking the infernus underneath. *Zylas?*

Crimson magic blazed. In a whoosh of glowing power, the demon materialized beside me, squinting against the late afternoon light.

He wrinkled his nose. "It stinks."

"No shit, Sherlock," Amalia muttered, sidestepping away from the demon. Even after six weeks, she was still wary of him. Not that I could blame her.

His glowing eyes tracked her retreat.

"Zylas, we need to search under there." I pointed at the obstacle. "Can you move that wall?"

"It is heavy?" He gripped the edge with one hand and pulled. The thick muscles in his arm bunched and the sheet of studs and drywall rose easily. "This is not heavy."

"It is for us," I said faintly. Yes, I knew he was strong, but the demonstration was still a shock. "Can you drag it over there, please?"

Still holding the wall with one hand, he considered my request—no doubt debating how rebellious he was feeling. Lucky for us, he also wanted to find the grimoire so we could strike his House's name from its pages, making it impossible for "*hh'ainun*" to ever summon demons of his line again.

Taking hold of the toppled wall with his other hand, he hauled it out of the corner. As I assessed the burnt mess beneath, my lips turned down. The fallen wall had barely been scorched, but everything under it was blackened.

Amalia and I tossed aside scattered debris, unearthing the two-foot-tall steel safe attached to the concrete floor. She knelt in front of it and grasped the wheel combination lock.

The safe door swung open a few inches.

Amalia's startled gaze shot up to mine, then she pulled the door all the way open. The shelves inside were empty.

"No way," she moaned. "Dad must've come back to get everything."

I crouched beside her, cold with disappointment. "Or MagiPol opened it when they searched the house last month."

Zylas reached over my shoulder and ran his fingertips across the door's inner edge. Bringing his hand to his face, he inhaled through his nose. "Smells like *vīsh*."

Vīsh—his word for magic.

I scrutinized the safe's locking pins. "Amalia, do these look severed?"

She examined them too. "You're right."

Zylas leaned closer, nostrils flaring. "I can't scent the demon, only his *vīsh*. Too many other smells."

Amalia shook her head, muttering something about a bloodhound. I rubbed my forehead before remembering the soot on my hands. I'd probably just smudged up my face.

"Someone broke into the safe using *demon magic?*" I muttered. "That rules out your dad and the MPD, then."

Zylas hopped on top of the safe, startling me and Amalia. He leaned over the opening, peering into it upside down. He rapped his claws against the left side, the metal clanging, then drummed against the opposite wall. It rang dully.

"This," he said. "It is thicker?"

"It is? How can you tell?"

"It looks different."

The sides looked identical to me, but Zylas had two kinds of vision. The regular kind, plus infrared thermal vision. Could he see the difference in the heat signature of the safe walls?

I looked questioningly at Amalia. "Is that normal for safes?"

"How would I know?" With a wary look at the demon crouched above us, she poked and prodded inside the safe. "Could you shine a light in here?"

I pulled out my cell phone, turned on the flashlight function, and aimed it over her shoulder. She fiddled with the safe wall—and a side panel popped out and toppled into her head with a *thunk*.

"Ow!" She scooted backward, rubbing her forehead.

I slid a brown folder out of the hidden compartment in the safe's wall. It was blackened from heat but intact. I carefully opened it. A charred envelope lay on top, half hiding what looked like a legal document.

Zylas jumped off the safe. Landing silently on the burnt debris, he drifted away, maybe to search for more signs of the demon that had broken into the safe. Or maybe he was bored.

I barely noticed him go, my gaze frozen on the envelope.

Amalia read the blue pen looping across the envelope. "It's addressed to Dad but I don't recognize the sender's address."

My heart clenched painfully. It took me two tries to speak. "That's my address."

Her head snapped up.

"That's …" My throat tried to close as my eyes traced the loopy script, the little curl on the number three. "That's my mom's handwriting."

"Your mom sent my dad a letter?"

When I just sat there, unmoving, she pulled the folder from my lap to hers. Lifting the envelope, she held it out to me.

"Read it, Robin."

I took the thin paper with trembling hands. The top had been neatly slit; Uncle Jack had looked at it before locking it in the secret compartment in his safe. Scarcely breathing, I slid the single page out and unfolded it.

Friday, April 6

Dear Jack,

I dearly hope you will read this letter. It's been a long time since you've answered a call from me but, please, these are words you must read.

First, and this is something I have been wanting to tell you for years now: I'm sorry. From the bottom of my heart, I am so sorry for everything. I can't say that you were right about all of it, but I know now that I was wrong about many things. I'm only just beginning to realize how wrong.

I want to say more, to apologize properly, but there is something more pressing I need to share.

For twenty years, I've kept the grimoire hidden. I know you walked away from that duty. I know I refused to share either its boons or burdens with you, but I was so sure I knew how best to conceal it.

Jack, I think someone knows. I won't fill this letter with my every suspicion, but in the past few weeks, the signs have become clear. Someone is hunting us. Someone is close. I'm afraid for my family—and for yours. If they found me, they can find you too. You know what's coming for us, what will happen if they find us.

I don't know what to do. I don't know how to protect my family. I need your help. My family and I need you.

I'll be waiting by my phone. Please help me, Jack.

Sarah

My vision blurred. I gasped silently, my heart ripping itself to pieces. Amalia gently extracted the letter from my shaking grip. As she read it, I fought for composure, but I was breaking apart, the wound of my parents' deaths torn wide open.

"Someone was after the grimoire?" Amalia whispered. "And your mom knew she was in danger?"

Pain shuddered through me. I took the letter back so I could stare at my mom's name in her familiar writing.

"Robin, how did your parents die?"

"Car accident." My voice was a dry rasp. "At night in the rain. Lost control and went off an overpass. They died before paramedics arrived."

Amalia pressed her lips together, sympathy softening her face.

"April sixth," I mumbled. "She wrote this a week before she died."

I abruptly pushed to my feet. Letter clutched in one hand, I stumbled across the debris. Amalia kindly stayed put, turning her attention to the folder's other contents.

I staggered out of the wreckage and onto the driveway. The overcast sky hung low and a sharp breeze nipped at my tear-streaked face.

My mother had feared for her life—and her family's lives. A week before her death, she'd begged Uncle Jack to help her. Had he called her, or had he ignored her urgent plea? Had he left her to face whatever danger was coming, knowing her death would give him a chance to claim the grimoire for himself?

Either way, he'd gotten the grimoire—and the first thing he'd done was summon demons with its secret names and sell them to a rogue guild. My mother had spent her life hiding the grimoire, and he'd betrayed her efforts mere months after her death.

I cradled the precious letter in one hand, my other hand curled into a fist, fingernails digging into my palm.

"*Payilas?*"

I started with a frightened squeak. Zylas stood a few feet away, watching me.

"What?" I asked, rubbing the tears from my cheeks.

"Are you wounded?"

"No."

He peered at me suspiciously. Since he was asking if I was injured, he must associate crying with being hurt. He wasn't wrong, but I didn't see any point in explaining emotional wounds to a demon.

His tail snapped side to side. "I smell pain."

I jerked back a step. "You can *smell* that? How?"

His nostrils flared. "I do not smell your blood. Where are you hurt?"

"I'm not injured." Sighing, I waved the letter. "My mother wrote this. She died seven months ago. It hurts to be reminded that she's gone."

He canted his head. "That is what hurts you?"

"Yes."

A long pause. "*Zh'ūltis.*"

I didn't even flinch at him calling me stupid for grieving my mother's death. He was a demon. Sorrow, and the love that fueled it, was beyond his comprehension. "It's a human thing. You wouldn't understand."

"*Hnn.*" He scanned the property. "If you were strong, it would not hurt."

I rolled my eyes and wiped away a final tear. Another dig at how weak I was. Instead of retorting, I turned toward the garage to find Amalia.

"You were not ready to lose the one who protected you."

Almost missing his quiet words, I spun back to face him. "What did you say?"

He gazed at me. "I found the scent of fresh blood in the house."

"*What?*"

"*Ch.* Are you deaf *and* stupid, *payilas*?"

"How fresh is the scent?"

He twitched his shoulders. "I don't know. It is faint. The trail leads"—he pointed toward the backyard—"that way."

"Then let's check it out." I'd taken a few steps before realizing he wasn't following. I frowned over my shoulder. "Are you coming?"

"I am *going*," he corrected. "*You* stay here."

"What? But … didn't you come get me so we could go together?"

"No," he scoffed. "I came to tell you first so you do not make noise."

"Make noise?"

"*Zylas, Zylas, where are you? Come back!*" His accent vanished as he imitated my voice. "I cannot hunt if you are making noise."

I pressed two fingers to my temple and massaged gently, hoping to stave off the headache building behind my eyes. "I'm coming with you."

"You cannot hunt."

"I'll be quiet and follow you."

"No."

I glared at him. "What will you do? Tie me up so I can't follow?"

His eyes squinched as though he were considering whether he could pull that off. Chuffing irritably, he stalked away. No chance the impatient, contrary demon would wait while I told Amalia where we were headed.

With a frantic glance at the garage, I rushed after him, ignoring the little voice in my head warning me that, really, there was no way this wasn't a bad idea.

5

ZYLAS CIRCLED THE HOUSE'S RUINS, then paused to inhale. His steps flowing with a slow, eerie grace, he prowled toward the trees at the property's far end. Shadows closed over us, and even from a few paces away, he blended into the dimness. He circled a towering spruce with boughs drooping under the weight of their dark green needles.

"*Payilas*," he growled softly, "you are too loud."

"I'm not saying anything," I hissed.

"You walk with too much noise."

I looked down at my winter boots. I'd been stepping carefully, and the ground was so wet from the nonstop December rain that the leaf litter had turned to mush. Mush was quiet.

He slid forward again, somehow moving among the trees without even a whisper, and I tiptoed after him, aware of every tiny squelch my boots produced.

The property ended in an eight-foot privacy fence. Zylas grabbed the top edge and pulled himself up enough to peek over it. The way must've been clear, because he dropped back down, only to spring upward. He landed on top of the fence in a crouch, perfectly balanced with his tail sweeping side to side.

"The scent is stronger," he murmured—then hopped off the fence and landed silently on the other side.

"Zylas!" I hissed, rushing forward. "Zylas, get back here!"

His head reappeared above the fence, one arm hooked over the top. "Be *quiet*, *payilas*."

"Help me over."

"No. Stay there."

I glowered up at him. "If you don't help me over the fence, I'll start yelling."

He bared his teeth, pointed canines gleaming. I held my ground, waiting.

"*Mailēshta*," he grumbled.

He swung over the fence and landed beside me. Snatching me by the waist, he threw me over his armored left shoulder, sprang off the ground, and performed a smooth one-handed vault over the eight-foot barrier. He dropped to the ground, pulled me off his shoulder, and dumped me at his feet—silently.

Without a word, he was in motion again. I scrambled after him, wheezing from the recent compression of my diaphragm. The neighbor's property was heavily treed compared to Uncle Jack's and I winced with each muffled crunch underfoot. We got all of ten feet before Zylas stopped again.

"I'm *trying* to—" I began in a defensive whisper.

He turned, swept an arm around me, and clamped his other hand over my mouth. I stiffened, my nose full of his hickory-and-leather scent.

"I hear movement," he hissed almost soundlessly. "I smell blood, but not from this direction."

His arm tightened around my middle, lifting my feet off the ground, and he slid into a winter-bare thicket. He sank into a crouch, pulling me with him, and squeezed my jaw in warning before releasing me.

I knelt, his heat at my back, and strained my ears. I picked up the same faint squelching noise I'd made while walking through the soggy leaf litter. Thirty feet ahead, a shadow moved among the trees—a man picking his way through the bushes. Crouched behind me, Zylas shifted onto the balls of his feet, his chin almost on my shoulder as he watched the figure.

He sprang up.

I gasped as he whirled in the opposite direction of the man in the trees. Twisting around, I glimpsed Zylas's unsheathing claws and the flash of steel through the foliage.

"Stop!" I yelled.

Zylas froze, and so did the petite woman with her massive broadsword aimed at the demon's chest. For a long moment, no one moved, then the woman relaxed her stance and set the point of her sword on the ground.

"Zora?" I ventured, unsure whether to believe my eyes. What on earth was she doing here?

"Robin." She grinned apologetically. "Not what I was expecting out here! So this is your demon?"

She scanned him curiously. He shifted into a neutral stance, staring blankly like an obedient slave to my will. I gulped for air, hoping Zora assumed my shouted command had been directed at her and not my demon. Contractors didn't control their demons with verbal commands.

Branches snapped behind me and I jumped in fright, almost crashing into Zylas. A man pushed through the thicket to join us. He was stocky and muscular, with his hair shaved on the sides of his head and the rest combed straight back.

"What's this?" he asked in surprise. "A demon?"

"Remember Robin, our new contractor?" Zora rested her sword on her shoulder like a baseball bat. "Robin, this is Drew, my partner today."

"Hi," I mumbled. "What are you doing out here?"

"Hunting," she said brightly. "Though we probably spooked it with all that noise."

"Spooked … what?"

"The vampire."

I stared at her. Zora was hunting a vampire … and Zylas had been tracking the scent of fresh blood. That probably wasn't a coincidence.

"So," she drawled, noting my shocked expression, "I'm guessing you aren't hunting the vamp. What brings you all the way out here, then?"

"Uhh …" I cleared my throat. "I'm investigating a … rumor about Demonica. Illegal Demonica."

Her eyes lit up like I'd revealed there was buried treasure in this backyard. "Ooh, exciting. Our guild usually skips the Demonica postings, since we don't—or didn't—have any contractors. What are the details of the—"

"Zora," Drew interrupted dryly, "we should deal with the vamp first. It's close."

"Right, back to the hunt. Wanna come along, Robin?"

"Huh? Me?"

"Sure. I've never seen a demon take on a vamp before. It'll be interesting."

I gulped, unsure if I could say no without raising suspicion. "I don't know anything about vampires."

"Crash course, then! Walk and talk, my girl."

She marched past me and Zylas, who hadn't so much as blinked during our conversation. Cringing, I fell into step beside her and Zylas followed, walking woodenly. Drew cut sideways into the trees, taking a different route.

Zora glanced back. "Gotta say, that's kind of creepy. I figured you'd put the demon in front so you could see what you're doing with it."

I smiled wanly. "Direct line of sight is helpful but not necessary for a contractor."

Thank goodness I'd been studying up on how all this worked—though I wouldn't want to risk talking shop with another contractor.

"So, um, vampires?" I prompted before she could ask me anything else.

She plucked what looked like a short stick with a red marble on its end from her belt. The orb glowed faintly. "Most important tool for vampire hunting: a blood tracker. This baby is spelled to react to nearby vampires. If it's glowing, we're going the right way. The brighter it glows, the closer the vamp."

As she spoke, she swung it side to side. The glow dimmed as she pointed it east and brightened when she aimed it north.

I glanced at the overcast sky, masked by tree branches, but didn't ask if vampires could go out in the sun. I'd never studied them, but *Ancient Tales of Mythic Hunters*, one of my favorite history texts, included a story about two famous vampire hunters of the fifteenth century, a sorceress and a heliomage. Part of their technique had been to find the vampires' nests during daylight hours, when the vampires were slower and weaker.

"Vamps are, generally speaking, a bit faster than a human," Zora explained, aiming her blood-tracker artifact. "At night, or right after feeding, they're quite a bit faster. They aren't particularly strong, though."

"Okay," I agreed, not at all comforted, seeing as every adult biped on the planet was already stronger than me.

"The most important thing is don't let it bite you," she warned, lowering her voice as the blood tracker glowed brighter. "Their saliva will—"

A high-pitched yowl cut through the chill air.

Zora shoved her artifact into her belt and launched forward, sword poised for combat. I glanced back at Zylas with wide eyes, and he gave his head a slight "go already" tilt.

I raced after the swordswoman and Zylas followed on my heels. He could have outpaced all the humans easily, but he seemed to prefer a cautious approach. That or he wasn't sure how well we could keep up the farce of our contract with witnesses.

Zora cut around a manicured hedge as another shrill cry erupted. This time, I recognized it not as a human voice but an animal. I whipped after her, then slid to a halt.

A small gazebo was nestled in the trees beside a pond, and stepping stones wound away toward the sprawling mansion up the slope. Crouched in front of the gazebo, his hunched back facing us, was a man in ragged clothing—jeans, a t-shirt, no shoes.

Zora charged, swift and silent. The man sprang up and whirled around. In one hand, he held a small, furry animal. Blood smeared his mouth and jaw beneath hollow cheeks. His elbow joints were the thickest parts of his arms, his hands disturbingly large next to his emaciated wrists.

But his eyes were what horrified me—it was like someone had inverted them. His sclera were pitch black, while the irises and pupils were pearly white with the faintest red ring bordering the two colors.

He threw the limp animal aside and launched at Zora with his mouth gaping and curved fangs stained red. I thought the vampire would spear himself on her blade, but he twisted at the last moment, the point missing him as he grabbed for her face.

She ducked his grasping hand and spun, her blade sinking deep into the back of his thigh. The vampire took one staggering step, then lunged for her. She darted backward—

A small object flew out of the trees and slammed into the vampire's skull with a sickening crunch.

The vampire pitched over sideways. A man strode out of the trees—Drew, Zora's partner. He had both hands extended, his face hard with concentration. Above the vampire, a steel orb the size of a softball rose another foot, then plunged downward.

Grunting wetly, the vampire rolled clear an instant before the orb struck the ground with enough force to send up a geyser of mud. He stumbled onto his feet, wavering unsteadily. As he turned, my stomach jumped into my throat.

The steel orb's first strike had collapsed the vampire's right temple. How was the creature still standing?

He regained his bearings—somehow, despite part of his brain being mulched—and his sinister eyes swept across Zora and Drew, then found Zylas and me, standing at the edge of the trees.

The vampire's mouth fell open, fangs on full display. With a gurgling snarl, he leaped toward us, as fast as he'd moved before Zora chopped his leg and Drew bashed his skull in. I backpedaled with a terrified gasp.

Zylas stepped forward, his hand flashing up. His palm smacked into the vampire's face and he slammed the creature over backward. Bone crunched against the ground.

"Perfect!" Zora yelled. "Hold it there!"

Zylas held the writhing vampire down by his face as Zora sprinted over. She raised her sword, blade pointed downward, and rammed it into the vampire's chest. His struggles stilled.

She yanked her sword out, oblivious to the gore, while I fought to keep my stomach where it belonged. Zylas released the vampire and backed up to stand beside me like an inanimate puppet.

"If you want to stop a vampire, take off the head," she said clinically, pulling a rag from her back pocket and wiping off her blade. "If you want to kill the vampiric spirit, stab it through the heart."

"Oh," I said faintly. "That's … I see."

"I thought for a second there you'd frozen, but you got your demon moving in time. It's a fast one, eh? Nicely done."

"Yeah," Drew agreed, joining us. "Good job, Robin."

His unusual weapon hovered by his right elbow as effortlessly as a soap bubble, and I could only assume he was a telekinetic. I wondered how much that steel orb weighed.

My gaze flicked down to the vampire. "It … didn't die from … from the, uh …"

"Guess where zombie stories really come from?" Zora sheathed her weapon over her shoulder. "The vampiric spirit will keep the body moving, even if it's mortally wounded. You have to take off the head or damage the heart to kill it. Though, if you inflict lethal injuries, it'll *eventually* stop moving—after a few hours."

I shuddered violently. "By vampiric spirit, you mean fae possession, right?"

"Yep." She nudged the dead vampire with her boot. "This person was possessed and turned a long time ago. You can tell by how emaciated and sickly he looks, plus his behavior. The old vampires are the most bloodthirsty and wild. Once they can no longer impersonate a human, they deteriorate quickly. They'll attack anything."

Anything—like that small animal. Turning, I darted toward the gazebo. A dark shape lay in the grass and I knelt beside it. The vampire's victim was a young cat—a leggy, half-grown kitten with black fur and three white paws. My chest constricted as I stroked its bloody fur.

A tiny mew escaped it. It was alive?

I unzipped my coat and pulled it off. Ignoring the cold wind cutting through my sweater, I bundled up the kitten and lifted it into my arms.

"Cats can't get turned into vampires, right?" I asked Zora.

"No, but I'm not sure a cat can survive a—"

"I need to go. Come on, Z—" I caught myself, biting off Zylas's name. "I mean, are you coming, Zora? Or staying here?"

"We have to report the kill and wait for MPD cleanup," Zora replied. "If you stay, you can have a cut of the bounty. You did—"

"That's fine. It's all yours." I hurried past them, silently asking Zylas to follow me. "See you later!"

They called bemused farewells as I took off through the trees, my demon on my heels and a precious bundle in my arms.

6

"HEY, KITTY," I MURMURED. "How are you doing?"

I knelt beside a large dog crate, holding a cat treat through the bars. Inside was a fluffy cat bed, scattered mouse toys, a litter box, a water dish, and a food bowl full of drying chicken pâté. The vampire's victim crouched on the small bed, huge green eyes fixed on my face and tail fluffed to twice its size.

"It's okay, little girl," I cooed. "Want a nibble? It's a yummy treat. You need to eat to get strong again."

The frightened, half-grown kitten let out a low warning growl. Sighing, I dropped the treat through the bars, then crawled backward before rising to my feet. The vet had said the kitten should recover with food and rest, but she'd gone almost twenty hours without eating a bite.

I hadn't specifically intended to *adopt* the cat, merely get her to a vet before she died, but someone had to take care of her. The vet had assured me—after I'd invented a story about finding the injured animal in an alley—that the kitten's chances of survival would be much better with me than at a shelter, but if she wouldn't eat, what good was my care?

I turned toward my bedroom door and started in surprise. Zylas was leaning against the threshold, arms crossed and light gleaming across his left armguard.

"Why are you wasting time?" he asked in a low, biting tone.

Ignoring his question, I squeezed past him into the apartment's main living area. It wasn't much—at one end, a tiny kitchen with a short breakfast bar that fit two stools, and at the other, a living room overflowing with a single couch, a coffee table, and a small TV on a cheap stand.

The TV was secondhand. Amalia had purchased a brand new one to start, and after setting it up, she'd made me give Zylas a stern lecture about treating it with care. He'd put his barbed tail through the screen ten minutes later.

Keeping a demon entertained wasn't easy. He could survive a few days without anything to do, but then the restlessness set in. And a restless demon was destructive.

He could speak English but couldn't read it, so books weren't an option, and he hated screens. After questioning him, I discovered framerates that appeared smooth to the human eye were aggravatingly choppy to him. So all TV, movies, and video games were out. How did you keep a battle-hardened demon entertained in an 800-square-foot apartment?

A few days into the pinnacle of my flu, I'd sent Amalia to the department store with my credit card and begged her to bring back every game she could find. Zylas wouldn't touch most of them, but when Amalia dumped a 500-piece puzzle onto the floor, he'd wandered over to watch.

Amalia spent four hours on the puzzle, then broke it apart, shook up the pieces, and dumped it out for Zylas, daring him to beat her time. He laid all the pieces out face-up as she had, then, for a full ten minutes, he simply stared at the disassembled puzzle.

Just as Amalia and I wondered if he understood the game, he picked up two pieces and fit them together. Then picked another out of the 498 scattered bits and fit it in. Then the next. Then the next. One by one, he fit each piece together, only occasionally needing to test two or three to find the right one. If he got it wrong, he set the piece back in its original spot.

We watched speechlessly as he assembled the puzzle in minutes.

The next day, Amalia returned with a 1000-piece puzzle. He did the exact same thing, staring at the pieces—not even sorting them first—before assembling the puzzle as though following invisible instructions. We watched him complete four puzzles before I figured out what he was doing.

He was *memorizing* the pieces. Every one—its color, shape, and location. Then, as he started assembling, he would recall which pieces might match and where they were among the hundreds of others.

I'd known his memory was sharp, but his ability to memorize tiny details in a matter of minutes was beyond comprehension. If I dared to arm him with any new skills, I could teach him to read in a matter of hours. He could memorize letters and words faster than any human. His steel-trap memory also explained how he'd adapted so quickly to a foreign world.

I wondered if he ever forgot anything.

In the main room, Amalia sat on a kitchen stool, her blond hair twisted into a messy bun as she sifted through the documents we'd found in Uncle Jack's safe. I slid into the spot beside her, still ignoring Zylas, who was literally breathing down the back of my neck.

"What did you find?" I asked.

"Nothing about safe houses or sanctuaries." She slapped her hands down on her thighs. "The documents are all legal contracts and business agreements for everyone my dad deals with. Guilds, contractors, summoners, rogues, criminals, forgers …"

I tugged at the infernus chain resting against my neck. "Unless this was all your dad kept in his safe, whoever broke into it took everything else. What do you think they were looking for?"

"My dad's location, just like us. He—"

With an effortless jump, Zylas landed on the counter and sat on the edge, watching us with unreadable crimson eyes. He kept one heel on the counter, arm propped on his raised knee, his other leg hanging off the edge beside me.

Scowling at the demon, Amalia continued, "My dad isn't stupid—usually—but he has a weakness for money. He never should've revealed to a rogue guild like Red Rum that he had a new demon name. I'm sure rumors have leaked out by now, especially since your bloodthirsty pal there killed so many Red Rum rogues."

I shuddered at the reminder.

"I'd guess a lot of people are looking for Dad, hoping to get their hands on that demon name before he sells it too many times and the value drops."

No wonder Uncle Jack was in hiding. People like that would kill for a lot less than ten million dollars.

"It cannot be *sold*." Zylas's husky tones made Amalia and me start. His mouth had thinned angrily. "No more *hh'ainun* can know it."

"We're trying," I replied quietly. "If we can find the grimoire in time, then no other summoners will get your House name."

"What do you care if other demons of your House are summoned?" Amalia snapped irritably. "If you make it back to your world, you'll never be summoned again."

I blinked in surprise. If Zylas returned, he couldn't be re-summoned?

He gazed at her, then leaned forward and scooped me off my seat. The moment my butt was clear, he jammed his foot into my stool, which hit hers and sent it toppling. Amalia managed to jump away and landed unsteadily as her stool crashed to the floor.

"Zylas!" I exclaimed angrily, squirming against his arm around my middle. He'd swept me onto his lap, his thigh under my rear, my back against his chest. Heat radiated off him, his body several degrees warmer than a human's.

I wrenched at his wrist but couldn't budge his arm. His strength was impossible. "Let me go."

Tightening his arm, he pushed his face into my hair.

"Zylas!" I jerked my head away. "Quit that! Let me go!"

His low laugh slid under my skin. He blew on my hair, making it flutter. My jaw clenched. A couple of days ago, there would have been nothing I could do to stop him; I'd have been entirely at his mercy.

Daimon, hesychaze, I thought clearly.

With the silent "rest" command, crimson light erupted across Zylas. His body vanished from under me—*the* weirdest feeling ever—and my butt landed on the counter with a painful thump.

Zylas's power hit the infernus and bounced right back out again. He rematerialized in front of me, teeth bared and crimson eyes blazing.

"Let me go when I tell you to!" I snapped before he could speak.

"You do not command me," he snarled, stepping aggressively closer. "You do not control me."

Panic jumped in my chest. *Daimon—*

He grabbed the front of my sweater and hauled me onto my tiptoes, the sudden movement interrupting my thought. Fear thrummed along my spine as we glared at each other, our faces inches apart, his fist clenched around my sweater and my hand gripping the infernus.

Which was faster? The agile demon or the two-word command that would send him back into the infernus?

"Don't make me use the command," I said quietly, "and I won't use it."

A tearing sound as his claws pierced my sweater. His fury singed the air and the faintest hint of crimson power flickered up his forearms. If our mysterious contract wasn't enough to prevent him from hurting me, I was about to find out the hard way.

His upper lip curled. He opened his hand and I dropped back onto my heels. Tail snapping, he strode into my room.

I let out a shaky breath, my pulse thundering in my ears, and climbed back onto my stool. Amalia stood for a moment longer, then righted hers and sat down.

"That was ... intense," she muttered.

"Y-yeah. I've n-never ..." I gulped back the tremble in my voice and tried again. "I've never challenged him quite like that before."

"It was good. You did good." She lowered her voice. "He might only be doing that shit—touching you and stuff—to get a rise out of you, but what if he decides to take it further to see how you'd react?"

Icy dread rolled down my spine. I wanted to say he couldn't do that, but I had no idea what he could or couldn't do. Our contract was dangerously simple: he protected me and I baked for him. I'd made the critical oversight of failing to define "protect," which meant Zylas was obeying his own definition. I didn't think he could arbitrarily decide what the word meant to him—he was bound by his genuine interpretation of it—but I had zero clue what his interpretation was.

Fear shone in Amalia's eyes as she observed my reaction. I dealt with Zylas the most, but the contract protected me. Amalia had nothing except Zylas's promise not to kill her as long as she was helping us. How brave was she to keep coming back to this apartment day after day, never knowing what the powerful, violent demon might do to her?

She cleared her throat and turned to the papers scattered over the counter. "Okay, so, this is all legal stuff and completely useless, but I did find one valuable tidbit."

She slid a document in front of me and pointed.

I squinted at the first lines. "'This agreement is made and entered into by and between Jack Harper of 2936 Blackburn Road and Claude Mercier of 302 Theodore Way, hereafter collectively referred to as the Partners.'"

"Claude's address," she declared triumphantly.

"We aren't looking for Claude ..." I straightened on my stool. "But Claude is looking for Uncle Jack."

Claude, my uncle's enigmatic—and treacherous—business partner, had straight up told me he'd been working for years to get his hands on a demon of the Twelfth House. He wanted the grimoire for himself, and he'd nearly killed his partner's children to get it. Clearly, their relationship wasn't as buddy-buddy as we'd all thought.

"How much do you want to bet Claude is the one who broke into the safe?" Amalia asked. "He knows it's there, and you said his demon is in an illegal contract. Maybe it used demon magic to break the safe open."

I nodded. "So we're going to investigate Claude?"

"We're going to turn the bastard's place upside down and find out everything he knows about my dad—and whatever else he's got his slimy hands in."

I grinned, fighting back nerves. "Sounds good. I'll talk to Zylas. If there's a chance we'll have to go up against Claude and his demon again, he needs to decide our plan of attack."

"Go talk to him, then. Maybe a demon-on-demon fight will settle him down and he'll leave us alone for a few days." She gazed dreamily at nothing, as though remembering what her life had been like before having to share her living space with a demon. "I'm going to the grocery store. Want anything?"

"I'm good."

I hopped off my stool, feeling fired up for the first time in weeks. Our progress had been painfully slow so far. First, I'd gotten sick and lost nearly two weeks to an on-and-off fever. Then Zylas had gotten me kicked out of the Arcana Historia library and I had yet to work up the nerve to return. But finally, we were making progress.

As I walked into my bedroom, the front door banged shut behind Amalia. Mind on the coming challenge of breaking into a dangerous summoner's home, I belatedly noticed the hissing.

I stopped dead.

His back to the rest of the room, Zylas was crouched on top of the dog crate, balanced on the balls of his feet as the steel bowed under his weight. The kitten inside was plastered into the farthest corner, hissing and spitting with terror.

"Zylas!" I shouted, sprinting toward him. I grabbed his arm. "Get away from her!"

As usual, my best efforts couldn't budge him. His tail lashed in annoyance, clanging against the bars. The kitten arched her back and spat more loudly. The poor thing was scared out of her mind. Zylas peered down through the bars, head tilted as he observed the small, terrified creature.

Protective fury singed my blood and I didn't even think to use the infernus command. Releasing his immovable arm, I grabbed his tail with both hands and hauled the demon backward with all my strength.

Next thing I knew, I was on my back on the floor and a hot, heavy weight was crushing me into the musty rug. Pain throbbed through my face.

The weight vanished off me and a weird dual sound filled my ears—high-pitched hissing and low-pitched snarling. Something wet ran down my face.

"*Payilas zh'ūltis! Eshathē hh'ainun tādiyispela tūiredh'nā ūakan!*"

Zylas's face appeared above me, his eyes blazing. I pressed my fingers under my aching nose. Blood coated my fingers. I was bleeding?

"You are bleeding," Zylas accused angrily.

I pushed up onto my elbows. When I'd pulled him backward off the crate, he'd fallen on me, his miserably hard head smacking into my squishy human face. I gingerly prodded the bridge of my nose, but it felt solid. Not broken, thank goodness.

"What is wrong with you?" His snarling voice competed with the noise from the spitting kitten a few feet away. "You pulled on *my tail*."

He sounded outright *offended*. My lips twitched and I might've giggled if my face weren't hurting so much.

Since my shirt was already ruined, I balled up the hem under my nose and pushed to my feet. Taking Zylas's arm, I dragged him out of the room. He followed me to the bathroom and stood in the doorway as I grabbed a wad of tissue. His nose was wrinkled in distaste; he hated the scent of human blood.

"What is wrong with you?" he repeated in the same acid tone. "Why did you do that?"

I whirled on him, furious all over again. "You were tormenting the kitten! What's wrong with *you*?"

He bared his teeth. "I was looking at it."

"And she was terrified of you, which you knew perfectly well! You were frightening her on purpose!"

"You are wasting time." His crimson eyes glinted with impatience. "All you have done is waste time. You promised to send me home. You promised to find the grimoire and remove my House's name. You have done none of that."

"I warned you it would take a long time."

"I thought it would be slow because it is difficult, not because you are hardly trying."

"I *am* trying!" I flung the bloody tissues into the garbage and wet a cloth to clean my face, my hands shaking. "You haven't been helping! Bullying Amalia, interrupting me all the time, and now you're torturing the kitten too."

"The *kitten* is worthless. It's a distraction."

"Saving a life isn't worthless!" I swallowed hard, tasting blood in the back of my throat. "Do you have no heart at all, Zylas? Are you that incapable of empathy?"

"I do not know that word."

"Of course you don't." As I wiped the blood off my face, I decided I would deliver the kitten to the animal shelter tomorrow. She'd be better off there than exposed to Zylas's whims. "Leave the kitten alone. I'll take her away in the morning so she won't be a 'distraction.'"

He watched me from the doorway. "What is *empathy?*"

"You wouldn't understand."

"I can understand anything you can."

I shot him an icy look. "You're a demon, so no, you can't."

"Explain," he growled.

"No."

"Why not?"

"Because when it doesn't make any sense, you'll say '*zh'ūltis!*' and decide *I'm* the dumb one, even though the problem is you." I rinsed out the cloth and turned to the door. "I'm leaving the bathroom now."

He didn't move, gazing at me with an unreadable expression. "Tell me what *empathy* is."

Stubborn demon. Jaw tight, I folded my arms over my bloody shirt. "Empathy is the ability to understand and share what others feel."

His eyebrows drew down in confusion. "Share what others feel?"

"Yes." I pushed on the armor plate over his heart and he stepped back, allowing me across the threshold, but he followed right on my heels as I returned to my bedroom.

The kitten, exhausted and huddled in her bed, watched us with wary green eyes.

I opened my closet and grabbed a shirt at random. "I'm changing. Turn around."

He turned his back on me and I slid my bloody shirt off. This, at least, was a civilized compromise we'd reached early on. Sharing my room with a demon was unpleasant enough without the complete lack of privacy. He might be able to hear my thoughts half the time, but he did not get to see me undress. I'd extracted that promise from him in exchange for teaching him how to use the shower.

He loved the shower. I was pretty sure he'd save the shower before he'd save me, contract or no contract.

I tugged on the new shirt and straightened the hem. "Okay."

"Explain more," he commanded, facing me again.

I wasn't sure whether his refusal to drop it annoyed me or gave me hope that he wasn't a total lost cause. "When you scared the kitten, I could imagine how the kitten felt—how terrifying it would be, being small and weak and trapped with a huge predator so close."

As I sat on the foot of my bed, I almost missed his darting glance toward the kitten's crate.

"And," I continued, "because I can *empathize* with the kitten, her fear was almost as upsetting to me as if you'd been scaring me instead."

He looked from me to the kitten and back, his forehead crinkled under a tangled lock of black hair. "That's *zh'ul*—"

"I knew it!" I burst out, my anger surging back. "I knew you'd call *me* stupid because *you* don't understand!"

"It is stupid!" he barked. "It's *dilēran*."

Yep, he was a lost cause. A total and absolute lost cause.

"It's 'stupid' that I can care about another living thing besides myself?" My voice rose in volume and pitch. "If I was as selfish and heartless as you, you would've died in that summoning circle, because I would never have bothered to help you."

"You had reasons."

"What reasons?" I shook my head. "Helping you has only ever caused me trouble, and it almost got me killed. Now we're stuck together until I can send you home."

"I protect you."

"Yeah, but if it wasn't for you, I wouldn't need protection. No one would be trying to hurt me." I pulled a book off my nightstand. "Along with your protection, I get your bad temper, your constant insults, and your disrespect. Not a great deal."

His eyes narrowed.

"Just forget about the empathy thing," I told him tiredly. "You'll never understand. Why would you want to, anyway? Caring about others is a *waste of time*, right?"

I could feel his attention on me, but I ignored him as I opened my book to the bookmarked page. The intro to that demon psychology text was right on the mark. Zylas didn't care about anyone but himself, and he assumed everyone else was either selfish like him or a worthless animal like the kitten.

Unexpected tears welled in my eyes and I hastily wiped them away, afraid he'd notice—but when I looked up, he was already gone.

7

"IS THIS THE PLACE?" I asked.

Amalia shot me a cold look and I privately admitted my tone hadn't been particularly polite. I was still furious. Right before leaving our apartment this morning, I'd caught Zylas terrifying the kitten again. This time, he'd been crouched in front of her cage, and poor little Socks had been huddled in the back corner, shaking with fear.

I shouldn't have named her. It would just make it harder to take her to the shelter this afternoon.

"Claude's unit is the third one," Amalia said, tucking her phone in her pocket now that we were done navigating. "Do you want to find a spot to call out Zylas?"

Last night, we'd decided to tackle our infiltration of the summoner's home in two phases. First, during the day when the street was busy and loiterers would be less conspicuous, we'd scope out the area and Zylas would check for signs of

Claude and his demon. Then we'd go home, plan our attack, and return at night to sneak in.

I glanced around at the rows of neat townhouses facing each other across a narrow street, each identical front door framed by a white railing and three steps. The only differences between the houses were the drapes in the windows and the occasional blow-up Santa Claus or snowman decorating a front lawn. It wasn't as busy as I'd hoped.

"Let's walk down the street first," I decided. "We'll find a back alley and I'll call Zylas out there."

My suggestion had nothing to do with delaying the moment I had to see my demon. Nope, not at all.

Amalia fell into step beside me as we strolled along the sidewalk. I wasn't surprised to see that Claude's townhouse was devoid of Christmas decorations. His blinds were closed and no car was parked out front; he didn't seem to be home. Now that his business partner was in hiding, what was Claude doing with his time? Was he spending every minute searching for Uncle Jack?

"I can't wait for this," Amalia whispered excitedly as we turned the corner. "We're going to catch that rat bastard and find out where my dad is. I can feel it."

I wasn't so sure but I held my tongue as we cut into a back alley.

"Are you going to call Zylas now?" she asked.

Normally, she was the last person to encourage me to bring out Zylas, but as she glanced nervously across the rooftops on either side of us, I knew where her eagerness for a protector came from. In our last encounter with Claude, his demon had choked Amalia unconscious.

"Not yet," I answered as I waved at all the windows that overlooked the alley. "Anyone could be watching."

She frowned but didn't argue. We unhurriedly walked along, the alley bordered by tiny backyards with chain-link fences. The townhouses were nice enough, but any residence in this neighborhood was a far cry from Uncle Jack's oversized mansion. Yet another way in which Claude and Uncle Jack were complete opposites.

As we drew level with Claude's unit, I scanned the empty backyard. The grass behind each property was the same length, which suggested the lawns were maintained by the same company. His yard was empty—no plastic lawn chairs, no grill on the small patio beside the back door.

Was it my imagination, or was the back door cracked open an inch?

"Robin," Amalia hissed. "Do you see that?"

I started to nod.

"The window is broken."

I stopped nodding and scanned the townhouse. She was right. The window beside the door was broken, the gauzy white drapes fluttering in the icy breeze. It was easy to miss; most of the glass was gone, with only a few shards sticking out of the frame.

"The door is open too," I whispered.

"*Now* will you call Zylas out?"

I reached for my chest, the infernus hidden under my jacket, but voices rolled down the alley. Three people stood on a patio six units down, talking conversationally. No way they wouldn't notice me summon a demon.

"Shit," Amalia muttered. "What do we do now?"

I looked again at the broken window, then pulled the gate open. Projecting confidence, I walked across the grass and onto the patio. My nerves twanged as I strained my ears. No sound aside from Amalia's footsteps on the grass as she followed me.

Ready to call Zylas at the first sign of movement, I pushed on the heavy back door. It swung silently inward, revealing a living room illuminated by sunlight streaking around the blinds.

"I … don't think Claude is here," I whispered.

"Yeah," Amalia agreed faintly.

I stepped across the threshold and onto a forgettable beige rug. Amalia slipped in behind me, and we took in Claude's home.

The living room, with a leather sectional around a gas fireplace, filled one side of the space. On the other side, an oak desk sat near a chaise lounge, and its cushions and accent pillows lay on the rug beside it, their fabric slit and cotton innards scattered everywhere. The desk was empty except for the monitor, severed cords hanging off it; someone had hastily cut the computer free. The drawers hung open, and papers had been dumped all over the floor.

The flat-screen TV was on the floor too, and the drywall around the mount had been punched in. Evenly spaced holes marred every wall, as though someone had taken a sledgehammer around the room and smashed it between every stud. The sofa cushions had received the same tender treatment as the chaise.

"Shit," Amalia muttered.

"I'm thinking Claude wasn't the one who broke into your dad's safe."

"Whoever did that came here next, didn't they?" She gave her head a single sharp shake. "They searched this place from top to bottom. Damn, look, they even ripped up the carpet over there."

"Well." I gloomily unzipped my jacket before I overheated. "We should still check it out. Maybe we'll find something the other guys missed."

"But first, call out your damn demon so he can spring any nasty surprises that might be waiting for us."

Grimacing, I tapped the infernus against my chest as though knocking on a door. *Daimon, anastethi.*

At my command, glowing light spilled down to the floor and formed the demon's shape. He solidified beside me, eyes already narrowed with fury.

"Someone beat us here and searched everything," I informed him brusquely. "Check the house for danger."

A long moment passed where he didn't react.

Crimson radiance erupted. His body dissolved into light and sucked into the infernus, leaving me and Amalia alone in the townhouse.

"What are you doing?" I growled at the infernus. "Zylas!"

"Now you've done it!" Amalia threw her hands up. "Of course he won't help after that. Ugh."

"Zylas! *Daimon, anastethi!*"

Red light blazed. It spilled to the floor, reforming his shape—then blurred. The power streaked back into the infernus.

"Get out here, Zylas!"

"You're as immature as he is," Amalia snapped, stomping away. "Let's just hurry up and search this mess."

I glared at her, then shook the infernus, imagining a two-inch-tall Zylas bouncing around inside it like a pinball.

"You're horrible," I hissed at the silver pendant. "Completely *useless*. We don't need your help anyway."

Amalia's remark about my maturity echoed in my head and I scowled. Dropping the infernus against my chest, I stormed over to the wreckage of the desk. My anger faded into hopelessness as I knelt and gathered the papers. There wasn't much, mostly scraps with handwritten reminders in a masculine print. "Email so-and-so" and "pick up such-and-such."

I shuffled through a few printouts of flights and hotels, all months old. As I tossed them down, a glimpse of white caught the corner of my eye—a page that had slid under the desk. Pinching the corner, I tugged it out and flipped it over.

The MPD logo filled the top left corner, and I recognized the layout immediately—a mythic profile. All registered mythics could be looked up in the MPD archives, though the amount of information displayed depended on your clearance level. Being a nobody, I could see only a mythic's name and current guild. Someone like a GM could see everything the MPD had ever logged.

This page was the latter kind. It showed the mythic's photo, name, age, description, class, guild history, job and bounty history, even criminal charges—none, in this case. I brushed my finger across the mythic's name, utterly bewildered by the familiar face in the photo.

"'Ezra Rowe,'" I read in a whisper.

The bold white scar that cut down his face from hairline to cheek was hard to forget. He was one of Tori's mage friends who had fled the scene after Tahēsh's death. One of the mythics Zylas had said carried the scent of demon magic.

Getting on my hands and knees, I searched all around the desk. Either Claude hadn't printed out anything on the other two mages, or whoever had trashed the townhouse had already taken the additional printouts. I sat back on my heels, scanning Ezra's profile. What did Claude know about the mysterious three mages who smelled like demon magic?

A clatter sounded from the other end of the townhouse. Rising to my feet, I folded the paper and stuffed it in my back pocket. Lost in thought, I hurried past the staircase and into the eat-in kitchen.

"Amalia, I just found—"

I broke off, my mouth hanging open. That clatter hadn't been Amalia searching the kitchen. It had been the sound of the front door opening.

A strange man swung the door shut with a thump. Tall, thin, with short black hair and opaque sunglasses perched on his nose, the lenses reflecting my white face back at me from across the kitchen. His dark windbreaker was open, revealing a blue sweater underneath. I had no idea who he was.

"What's this?" the man murmured. "A little mouse wandering about?"

I inched backward, silently panicking. I'd been caught breaking and entering. Was this man a mythic? An MPD agent? A friend of Claude's? A—

He used one finger to push his sunglasses up.

—a *vampire?*

I gawked at his reverse-colored eyes, the sclera black as pitch with a blank white circle in the center. A vampire. A vampire had just walked into Claude's apartment.

"Scared, little mouse?" he breathed.

Only when he spoke did I realize he'd covered half the distance between us. My gaze was locked on his eerie stare and I couldn't look away.

He drifted closer. I needed to move. I needed to run.

"They say 'fight or flight,' little mouse, but the most common response to a predator"—his lips pulled into a smile, revealing the fangs that curved down from his upper jaw—"is to *freeze*."

He lunged for me.

"*Zylas!*" I screamed, throwing myself backward.

Red light blazed over my infernus. Zylas appeared in front of me, hand already snapping out. His open palm slammed into the vampire's chest and hurled the man backward. He landed on the kitchen table, slid across it, and fell off the other side, taking a chair out with him.

Gasping, I stumbled to Zylas. He looked down at me, his glowing eyes cold.

The vampire clambered to his feet and straightened his jacket, his sunglasses gone and creepy eyes taking in Zylas. "The little mouse is a contractor? Hmm."

A shiver ran over me. This vampire was very different from the one Zora had tracked and killed.

He studied us a moment longer, then casually picked up a chair, weighed it with one hand, and hurled it. I shrieked and dove for the floor, landing painfully. Zylas stepped aside and the chair crashed down in the hallway. As I shoved myself up, the vampire shot toward me.

He was attacking the contractor. He thought killing me would eliminate my demon too.

Screaming breathlessly, I lurched away, slipped, and sprawled onto my face. The vampire overshot me and bounced off the wall. He whirled on me again. His fingers had turned to rigid claws, the nails extending to sharp points.

Zylas stood four long steps away, leaning against the counter as he watched us.

Gawking at my demon, I almost missed the vampire's leap. I scrambled under the table, hands slapping against the tile floor, and shoved past a chair.

"Zylas!" I gasped, bursting out from under the table. "Fight him!"

"*Na?*" He folded his arms, one shoulder lifting in a shrug. "But I am useless, *payilas*. That is what you said."

My eyes bulged in disbelief.

Wood crunched behind me, and I flung myself away as the vampire vaulted across the table. I tumbled over a chair and fell to the floor, my elbow scraping painfully across the rough grout between tiles. I scrambled backward on my butt as the vampire landed on his feet and turned toward me.

His nostrils flared. He opened his mouth, exposing his fangs as a blood-red ring appeared around the white circles that had replaced his pupils and irises. A line of drool spilled down his chin.

My panicked gaze snapped to my elbow, where blood beaded from a shallow scrape.

With a feral hiss, the vampire pounced. I dove back under the table, and the vampire crawled after me. His clawed fingers caught my pant leg. A powerful hand closed around my ankle and the vampire dragged me backward.

"Zylas!" I choked, kicking with my other leg. "Help me!"

I wrenched my leg free and shot out the other side of the table, throwing a chair down behind me to block the vampire. Stumbling on shaking legs, I pressed my back to the wall. I'd come out in a corner. I was trapped.

Zylas ambled around the table, observing indifferently. The vampire shoved past the chair and rose, oblivious to the demon a few feet away. Drool dripped off the vamp's hanging jaw as he stalked closer.

"Zylas," I whispered, cowering against the wall.

A yard behind the vampire, Zylas did nothing. How could he just stand there? He'd sworn—he'd promised—

Fangs glistening, the vampire sprang.

"Zylas!" I screamed. "Please!"

The vampire's mouth flashed toward my throat—then his head slammed into the wall beside me, punching through it.

Zylas gripped the back of the vampire's neck. Tugging the man's head out of the wall, he slammed the stunned creature down on the table. Red magic spiraled over his fingers, forming six-inch talons, and he drove them into the vampire's chest.

The vampire convulsed, then his limbs flopped onto the table.

Zylas swung toward me. He caught my chin and forced my face up as he leaned down. With nowhere to retreat, I pushed deeper into the corner.

"I am no *hh'ainun*'s slave," he hissed softly. "Do not try to make me into one."

I trembled against the wall, lungs empty and head spinning as I waited for him to attack. To turn that crushing strength on me. To unleash his deadly claws. To crunch through my delicate bones.

He released my chin, stepped over the fallen chair, and walked away.

I slumped against the wall, breathing fast. My chin tingled in the absence of his touch and fear trembled through me. My every instinct told me to run, to flee, to get as far away from the dark-haired, crimson-eyed killing machine a few yards away.

I sucked in a deep breath and let it out. Then another. By the fifth breath, my head was no longer spinning. I pushed off the wall and stumbled past the table. The vampire lay across it. In death, his eyes had turned completely white.

Zylas stood at the counter again, sniffing the air and wrinkling his nose. I stopped beside him and forced my gaze up. Past his bare abdomen, banded with muscle. Past his leather-and-plate armor. Past his tight jaw.

My eyes met burning, arctic crimson. Fighting the deeply ingrained habit, I didn't look away.

"We're in this together," I said tersely, "and whether you think so or not, I'm doing my best to get us where we need to go and learn the things we need to learn. You have only one obligation in all of this—to *protect me*."

He gazed down at me without expression. My hands curled into fists, anger burning through my fear of confrontation.

"You're bigger than me!" I yelled. "You're stronger and you're faster! I can't *make* you do anything—except get in or out of the infernus for *two seconds*! Is that really so offensive to your pride? Is it reason enough to go back on your word? You bully me and disrespect me and torment my only friend and destroy my belongings *every day*, but I'm still keeping up *my* end of our agreement!"

"I did not go back on my word."

"You let that vampire attack me!"

"You were not in danger."

Enraged, betrayed tears stung my eyes. "So the bare minimum is all you're willing to do? You'll keep me alive and nothing more?" I paused. "But you expect far more than *my* minimum effort."

He said nothing, unmoving. Not even his tail snapped back and forth to betray his anger. We stared at each other and I struggled to hold eye contact, unwilling to concede.

His arm swept out, nearly knocking me off my feet—and suddenly, I was behind him. He backed into me, pushing me into the wall. I was too short to see over his shoulder so I squeezed sideways to peer around his arm.

Two new arrivals stood just inside the front door, one propping a sledgehammer on his shoulder. Two pairs of ravenous black eyes, red rings glowing eerily around the white irises, were fixed on us, and the newcomers' fingers were already extending into long, sharp claws.

Two more vampires had just crashed our party.

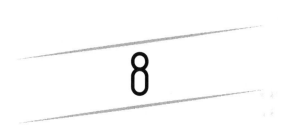

8

I PRESSED MY HANDS against Zylas's sides as though holding on to him would steady the swirl of confusion and fear in my head. What were *more* vampires doing in Claude's destroyed townhome?

The taller vampire cocked his head. "Recognize the girl?"

His comrade nodded. "The niece, right?"

"Seems so. We should take her alive. Might be useful."

"Fine with me." The shorter vampire ran his tongue across his teeth, the pink tip resting against one curved fang. "Don't want that demon vanishing on us before we get a taste."

Zylas stiffened.

The short vampire swung the sledgehammer off his shoulder like it weighed nothing. "This is going to be good."

Zylas stepped sideways, pulling me with him, then pushed me toward the hall with one hand. I understood. He wanted me to get clear.

The short vampire gave the sledgehammer one more swing, then launched across the kitchen. Zylas sprang to meet the charge, sliding past the sledgehammer's heavy metal head. His claws caught the vampire's chest, tearing through clothes and flesh. The man twisted frantically away.

Zylas spun on the tile floor, slashing at the stumbling vampire. Halfway through the motion, the demon ducked and the other vamp's talon-like fingers just missed his head.

The three combatants whirled through the tiny kitchen in a confusing blur of limbs. Zora had warned that vampires were faster than humans, but these two were almost as fast as Zylas.

He dove away from another sledgehammer swing. Landing on his hands, he kicked backward, catching the vampire in the jaw and nearly snapping his neck. Zylas pivoted in a handstand and his spinning kick smashed into the second vampire. With a flip, he was on his feet again, claws shredding the tall vampire's arm.

But flesh wounds had no effect on vampires.

Zylas leaped sideways to evade the sledgehammer—and hit the kitchen table. Thrusting his arm up, he caught a vampire's fangs on his metal armguard, then rammed his fist into the vamp's ribs, bones snapping loudly.

The sledgehammer swung again. Zylas darted away, and the sledgehammer split the table in half.

The other vampire tackled Zylas to the floor. Straddling the demon's chest, the vamp grabbed Zylas's wrists and pushed. The demon's muscles bunched with power as he pushed back—and neither creature moved. Zylas's eyes widened with shock that the vampire could match his strength.

Grinning, the shorter vamp pulled his sledgehammer out of the floor and prepared to swing it down onto Zylas.

I ran out of the hallway. As the vampire raised the sledgehammer over his head, I grabbed the end with both hands. The sudden addition of my weight tore the tool out of the vampire's grasp. I dropped to the floor, the sledgehammer smashing the tiles between my feet.

The vampire whirled on me. I stumbled backward. My heel caught on the trim where the tile floor transitioned to the hallway carpet and I fell on my butt. The vampire stood over me, smirking hungrily.

Zylas!

He was across the room, pinned under a vampire. He'd never reach me in time—not without teleporting to my side. The vampire reached down, grabbed my jaw, and wrenched me toward its fangs.

Daimon, hesychaze! I screamed in my head.

Zylas's body turned to crimson light and shot out from under the other vampire. The blaze flashed across the kitchen, hit the infernus on my chest, and rebounded.

Zylas reformed from the light, claws flashing as he lunged. Glowing talons sprouted off his fingers and he rammed them deep into the vampire's chest. As the vamp fell back, Zylas tore his claws free. The other vampire was still scrambling to his feet as Zylas slashed his hand sideways. Crimson runes blazed up his arm and a blade of power flashed out. It whipped across the kitchen and hit the cabinets, shearing through the wood.

The second vampire's severed head tumbled off its body and both fell to the floor with sickening thuds.

I panted for air, still sprawled on my butt, a dead vampire lying just beyond my toes.

Zylas's crimson eyes swept over me. "So helpless, *drādah*."

Great. A new insult. I wondered what this one meant.

"I helped," I said stiffly. "Or didn't you notice while that vampire was holding you down?"

His tail snapped side to side. "The female *hh'ainun* said vampires are not strong."

"She did." I winced as I pushed to my feet, fighting my squirming stomach as blood pooled across the broken tiles. "These vampires looked pretty strong."

The stairs creaked and I whirled around, stepping sharply backward and bumping into Zylas. Amalia peered around the corner, her face white.

"Is it over?" she asked.

"Yeah. Thanks for your help."

"Like I would've been of any use." She sniffed, descending the last few steps. "Robin, did you hear what they said? They recognized you as 'the niece.'"

"Wait, as in *Uncle Jack's* niece? How do they know Uncle Jack? Unless—"

"Unless they're also looking for my dad. There was a vampire at our house too. They're searching for him. They beat us here and—"

I glanced at the sledgehammer. "They searched this house for clues about Uncle Jack's location, just like we wanted to. But what would vampires want with a demon summoner?"

"I don't know," she said quietly. "But there's a real good chance they might find my dad before we do."

PERCHED ON A STOOL at the Crow and Hammer's bar, I sipped my glass of water. Why did it feel like we were further from finding Uncle Jack and the grimoire than when we'd started?

Uncle Jack's disappearance. My mother's letter and the unknown danger she'd feared. Claude, who was missing as well, and his illegal demon. And now vampires.

Vampires. It didn't make any sense.

Zylas was, in my biased opinion, nearly unstoppable. With his speed, the only opponents who presented a real threat were unbound demons like him, and even if an enemy could neutralize that advantage, Zylas had demonic strength that far outstripped any human's.

But what happened if Zylas's adversaries were almost as fast *and* almost as strong as he was?

That was a big problem, especially if they outnumbered him. As he'd shown at the townhouse, his magic could tip the scales, but he had to be very careful about using it. If anyone witnessed his magic, it would mean a death sentence for us both.

I pulled my glasses off and rubbed my face.

"Want to talk about it?"

Lowering my hands, I peeked at the bartender. I'd seen him before—a tall, thin man in his late twenties with dyed black hair that hung over one side of his face, hiding one dark-lined eye. He smiled in a friendly way as he set a bowl of limes beside his station.

"I'm Ramsey," he added.

I blushed as I slid my glasses back on. "Sorry. I couldn't remember."

"I figured," he replied good-naturedly. He picked up a knife and sliced a lime in half. "Don't worry about it. You have lots of new names to learn."

"Are you the bartender?" I asked hesitantly. "Or is Tori …?"

"Tori is the all-mighty overlord of the bar. I'm just the cook."

"Overlady," I corrected with a shy smile.

"That too." He chopped a few more limes. "She's off for Christmas. Went to Vancouver Island with the guys, so Cooper, Clara, and I are taking turns covering the bar for the next two weeks."

Tori was gone? Well, that was one less thing to worry about, though I couldn't help but feel a prickle of disappointment too. She might be alarmingly suspicious of me, but she'd also defended me from other guild members.

My mind turned to the paper folded in my pocket. I wanted to ask about Ezra Rowe, the mage from Claude's printout, but I needed to be careful. "How long has Tori been a member here?"

"Six months—wait, no, seven. She's the next newest member besides you and Amalia."

"What about the three mages? How long have they been members?"

"Aaron and Kai, almost seven years now, I think. Ezra, not as long. He—"

A bell jingled as the pub door opened and closed. Outside, rain fell in fitful sheets, whipped sideways by the wind.

"Hey!" Ramsey greeted the new arrival. "How's it going?"

Zora swung onto the stool beside me and unzipped her rain-splattered coat. "The weather is a nightmare today."

"It's December, so that's nothing new."

She scrubbed her short hair, making the damp locks stand on end. "Hey Robin."

"Hi Zora," I murmured, nervousness lightening my stomach.

"Want anything, Zora?" When she shook her head, Ramsey scooped his halved limes into the bowl. "I need to juice these suckers. Holler if you change your mind."

He pushed through the saloon doors behind the bar, leaving Zora and me alone. The pub was empty, too late for lunch and too early for dinner. I swirled my straw through the ice in my glass, wishing Amalia were here to do the talking.

"So." Zora planted her elbow on the bar and faced me, her brown eyes bright with curiosity. "What can I help you with?"

I forced a smile, trying not to look terrified. After my vampire encounter this morning, I'd looked up her number in the guild directory and asked her to meet me. Now that she was here, I didn't know how to broach the topic.

"I, uh, well … I have questions about … vampires."

She blinked, then laughed. "I was expecting something more urgent."

I cringed. "Sorry, but—I mean—yes, it kind of is. I think vampires are involved in the Demonica rumor I'm … investigating."

It felt weird to describe my fumbling search as an *investigation*.

"Oh, hmm. Now that's interesting. What makes you suspect vampires?"

"Well, the, um …" I pulled myself together, shrugging off my nervousness. Amalia and I had gone over what we would reveal. I knew what to say. "The house I was searching on Sunday is the location where the unbound demon on Halloween was summoned. You uncovered a vampire on the neighboring property."

She nodded slowly.

"A clue Amalia and I found there led us to another address, where three more vampires attacked us."

"*Three?* You handled them all right with your demon?"

"Yes, but they were much faster and stronger than we expected. And more … human."

"Their mental competency depends on what stage of the transformation they're in. Over time, their humanity erodes until you get beasts like the one we tagged. Until then, they can pass as human, though the scent or sight of blood can send them into a frenzy."

I described how the vampires had searched the house and stolen Claude's computer and documents. "Do you know why vampires would be interested in a demon summoner?"

"Hmm." She crossed her legs at the knee. "How familiar are you with the process of vampirization?"

"Uh … all I know is vampires are created by parasitic fae spirits that infect people."

I'd never seen a fae, but I'd read about them. Any story about the elusive creatures, who existed somewhere between our world and their own demesne, was an automatic favorite for me; they were so fascinating and mysterious, as were the Spiritalis mythics who dealt with them.

The fae we were talking about right now, however, were an unpleasant subset. They were spirits that preferred human hosts—which wasn't a good thing for the human.

"A newly infected person," Zora explained, "what we call a new vamp, usually has no idea what happened to them. The spirit will drive them to start biting victims, but they can control the blood cravings and continue on with their lives for a while—months or sometimes years, depending on the person.

"Eventually, the new vamp can't keep up the act anymore and they have to ditch their regular life. They usually join a nest. Safety in numbers, right? Nested vampires hunt nightly and hide during the day. They can blend in with the masses, usually to make hunting easier, and they'll live like that for a long time. Old vamps are easy to find and exterminate because they've lost all ability to reason, but nested vamps are problematic. Hard to identify, difficult to catch."

"Do you think the ones I fought this morning were nested vampires?"

"I guarantee it. Thing is … their behavior is weird. Going out during the day, for starters. They're weaker in daylight. Why take that risk? But what really bothers me is their methodical search of the house. Nested vamps care about three things: survival, comfort, and their next blood fix. They aren't long-term thinkers."

I shifted in my chair. "So you don't know why they'd be involved in Demonica?"

She braced her elbows on the bar, hands fisted under her chin. "This is the weirdest occurrence yet in a string of weird vampire occurrences over the last four or five weeks. I've never been as busy with exterminations as I have this past month. Increased vampire activity throughout downtown, and way more new vamps than I've ever seen before." Her expression closed. "I really hate exterminating new vamps."

"Do vampires have any interest in … money?"

"Money?"

"Like, acquiring something very valuable to sell."

She gave me an odd look. "Nested vampires are still human enough to see a profitable opportunity and take it, but like I said, I've never known them to plan more than a few days in advance."

Searching for Uncle Jack in order to claim the Athanas Grimoire and sell it was a lot of steps to take for creatures that didn't plan ahead.

"Clearly, there's *something* interesting happening." Zora's eyes flashed with excitement. "I think it might be time to go scouting."

Interesting was not the word I'd choose. "What do you mean, scouting?"

"There are only so many places where a large vampire nest can settle in for an extended stay. The guilds around here routinely flush them out, but I think we might be overdue for the next round. You in?"

"In? In for what?"

"In for some vampire hunting!" She grinned like she'd just offered me a basket of delicious goodies. "You and your demon are more than a match for a few bloodsuckers."

"Uh …"

She laughed. "Don't worry, I'll get a good team together. Do you have a champion?"

I'd told the Grand Grimoire that Amalia was my champion, but we'd abandoned that farce when we joined the Crow and Hammer. "No …"

"I've never championed for a contractor before. We can partner up."

"But—" My shoulders drooped at her eager expression. "Sure. That'd be great."

"Awesome. I'll schedule a team and send you a message with the details." She hopped to her feet. "A contractor on a vamp hunt! I can't wait to see you in action."

I grabbed her wrist as she stepped away. "Zora, I'm not—"

With a flash of chagrin, I cut myself off. How could I tell her I wasn't combat experienced? She'd never believe it, especially since Zylas and I were semi-famous now for killing the unbound demon on Halloween.

My hand slipped off her arm and I smiled weakly. "Keep me posted."

"You bet." She strolled across the bar, calling a loud farewell to Ramsey on her way out.

I slumped in despair. Vampires like that first one? Sure, no problem. Or even like the second one. We could handle that.

But what if we found an entire nest of super-strong, super-fast vampires like the last two?

I puffed out a breath. Did I really have a choice? If I didn't go, I'd have no chance of finding out why the vampires were searching for Uncle Jack—and no chance to stop them from reaching my uncle, and my grimoire, before I did.

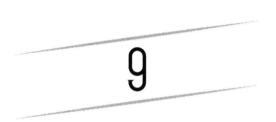

9

"THERE'S A GOOD KITTY," I cooed. "This is a yummy treat."

The black kitten cautiously stretched her neck out, whiskers twitching as she sniffed intently. She inched toward the morsel of deli chicken I held between the bars and her pink tongue poked out, licking it.

"Good girl, Socks."

She licked more enthusiastically, then pulled the chicken from my fingers and gobbled it down. Smiling, I ripped off another strip and stuck it through the bars. Bite by bite, I coaxed her to eat the entire slice. I breathed a happy sigh as she licked her chops and looked up with eager green eyes.

"That's all for now," I told her. "You don't want a tummy ache."

Her stare grew reproachful, and she mewed sadly as I swung a light blanket over the crate, enclosing her for the night. Between the vampire attack and my meeting with Zora, I hadn't had a chance to take her to the shelter. I'd do it first thing tomorrow.

Stifling a yawn, I tugged my tank top down, cotton shorts hugging my hips. The mattress creaked as I crawled into the middle, flipped the blankets over myself, and leaned back into my pillow.

My bedroom door opened. Crimson eyes glowed in the darkness as Zylas crossed to my bed and stopped beside it, towering over me.

He'd been quiet this evening. No bullying Amalia, tormenting Socks, or antagonizing me. I wasn't sure what to make of his mood, but I was too tired to worry about it.

"Going out tonight?" I asked drowsily.

"*Var.*"

We'd arranged this compromise only a couple of weeks ago. Prior to being summoned to Earth and imprisoned in a ten-foot circle, Zylas had enjoyed a life of comparative freedom. Spending every day trapped inside an apartment or contained inside the infernus had been driving him mad—and he, in turn, had been driving me and Amalia mad.

After a full day of debate, we'd decided he would remain with me at all times, either in the apartment if I was home or in the infernus if I wasn't home, except when I slept. At night, he could explore the neighborhood—on the condition that he was never seen, entered no buildings, and interacted with no one.

Letting a demon loose in the city caused me daily indigestion, but I wasn't *that* worried about what he got up to on his own. He understood the consequences of causing trouble.

"Zora texted me," I murmured, eyes drifting closed. "She's organizing a vampire hunt for tomorrow evening."

"These vampires, don't they prefer night?"

"Yeah, but she's the expert. I'm sure she has a reason." I forced my tired eyes open. "Should we back out?"

His face was a shadow in the darkness, his silhouette broken only by his softly glowing eyes.

"I'm worried," I confessed. "The vampires this morning gave you a lot of trouble. If we hunt them at night, when they're even stronger, and you can't use magic …"

The mattress dipped as he sat on it. "I am not helpless like you, *drādah*. I know how they fight now."

"*Dray-da?* What does that mean?"

The faint light from my window caught on his teeth as he smirked. Damn it. He wasn't going to tell me. I scowled at him.

He thumped a hand against my thigh under the blanket, making me jump. "You are weak."

My scowl deepened and I rolled onto my side, putting my back to the demon.

"You are slow and easy to scare. When you see hunters, you scream and fall down."

"Yes, thank you," I ground out through clenched teeth, burrowing my head into my pillow. "And I'm helpless and stupid, too. You don't need to keep reminding me."

The mattress bounced as he shifted his weight. I expected him to get up and head for my window, but the bed dipped again. Glowing eyes appeared as he leaned over me, his face six inches from mine.

"Zylas!" I exclaimed, lurching onto my back. "Would y—"

I broke off. By rolling onto my back, I'd put myself directly under him as he braced himself on one elbow.

"You are bad prey," he said decisively, his quiet voice too close for comfort.

"Can you lay off the insults for two minutes?"

He leaned down even more, his warm breath tickling my cheek. "Listen, *drādah*. I am telling you an important thing."

"Get off my bed."

A moment of silence—then he pushed up. Instead of sliding off the bed, he swung a leg over me and sat on my hips, pinning me with only the blanket between our bodies. My eyes bulged.

"Zylas, get off—"

His hand closed over my mouth. I went rigid, adrenaline stinging my nerves. Trapped under his weight, desperately aware of his strength, I sucked in air through my nose.

Don't make me use the infernus command, I warned.

"You are not listening, *drādah*."

I made an angry noise against his hand. *This is not making me want to listen!*

"You must listen anyway."

Hesitating in the midst of wrenching my arms free from the blankets, I peered up at his shadowed face, wishing I could see his expression. He sounded … unusually serious.

"When you are scared, you scream and fall. I watched you. You do not evade your hunter. You do all the wrong things."

My temper flared again. Why did he keep pointing that out? I knew I was useless in a fight.

Either he saw the anger on my face or heard it in my thoughts, but his hand tightened over my mouth, his warm fingers pressing into my cheeks. It didn't hurt, his touch firm but careful. I grabbed his wrist and tried to pry his hand off anyway.

"Against many enemies, I cannot be beside you every moment. You will be in danger."

My defensive anger faltered. *What are you saying?*

He lifted his hand from my face, my fingers wrapped around his wrist. "You must learn differently before we hunt the vampires."

"Learn differently? I don't understand."

He stared down at me, silence stretching through the room—then he heaved a long-suffering sigh. "I will teach you."

My hand reflexively squeezed his wrist. He was going to teach me, the stupid human, something from that mysterious demonic brain of his?

I angled my head, face scrunched with suspicion. "Teach me what, exactly?"

His weight pressed into my hips and then his face was inches from mine. His glowing eyes filled my vision, blocking out everything else.

"I will teach you how to be *drādah ahktallis*."

My breath locked inside my chest as I pressed back into my pillow. "How to be *what?*"

He laughed, the sound low and husky. "Smart prey."

ONCE ZYLAS GOT AN IDEA into his demony head, he wouldn't let it go. Nothing short of the apocalypse would distract him.

Which explained why I was currently walking along a gravel path as rain poured down on my umbrella, the icy December wind stinging my cheeks. Bare-limbed maple and alder trees, mixed with dense stands of towering fir and spruce, bordered the path. The weak morning sun offered no warmth.

Zylas had bossily insisted on "wilderness" where we wouldn't be disturbed, and Stanley Park was the only stretch of greenery in the downtown area large enough to hide a demon from any passersby. Not that I expected *anyone* to be out in this weather. Even hardcore fitness junkies had stayed inside today.

Half a mile from the parking lot where the cab had dropped me off, I left the path and wandered into the woods. Long grass and ferns swished against my legs, leaving wet streaks across my jeans. I stepped over a moss-coated log, my lower lip caught between my teeth. This was a bad idea, but changing Zylas's mind wasn't happening.

I meandered until I found a decent-sized clearing surrounded by thick Douglas fir trees, their trunks shooting thirty or forty yards into the stormy sky before sprouting dense branches of green needles. Umbrella balanced over my head, I tugged the infernus out of my jacket.

"Okay, Zylas."

Light flared over the silver pendant, then spilled onto the forest floor. Zylas materialized beside me and peered up at the treetops high above. A long moment passed as he surveyed his surroundings.

"So, um." I cleared my throat. "We're here."

He crouched and prodded the wet moss.

"Are you going to teach me how to defend myself?"

"No." He rose to his full height. "Prey does not *defend* against the hunter."

I pursed my lips. "How is learning to be 'smart prey' helpful? I don't want to be hunted. I want to—"

"What prey wants to be hunted?" he interrupted. "The prey does not get to choose."

"But—"

His hand closed around the front of my jacket and he lifted me onto my toes. My umbrella tumbled from my grasp as I clutched his wrist.

"You are small and weak, *drādah*," he informed me, lifting me a little higher to prove how helpless I was. "Hunters will come for you, and you cannot fight them. You must learn how not to die."

He opened his fingers and dropped me back onto my feet.

Huffing a breath, I stepped out of his easy reach. "How do I not die, then?"

"By being smart prey." He circled me, and I stiffened as he disappeared behind my back. "You react to fear in the wrong ways. You make it easy for the hunter."

As he reappeared, I gave him my meanest glare. "I'm not going to—"

He lunged at me. I gasped and lurched back. My heel caught on a tree root and I landed on my butt, the impact jarring my teeth. Then Zylas was on top of me, a knee on either side of my hips, his claws resting on my throat.

"And now you are dead." He tapped a finger against the racing pulse in my neck. "See? This is what I am telling you, *drādah*."

"You scared me," I protested breathlessly, resisting the urge to shove at him. "I didn't mean to fall."

"That is why you must learn a different way."

As swiftly as he'd pounced, he was on his feet again. He held out his hand.

I blinked, scarcely believing the offer. Half expecting a trick, I placed my hand in his. He pulled me onto my feet with easy strength. I blinked again.

Pushing his hair, already drenched from the cold downpour, away from his eyes, he studied me. "Do not go backward. That is why you fall so much. You cannot see where to step. Go sideways. Keep your sight on the hunter. If you turn your back, you will die."

"Sideways," I repeated dubiously.

"Sideways." He gestured at himself. "I will show you. Attack me."

My cheeks flushed. "How …"

"Do not think, just attack."

I swallowed my embarrassment, then took a half-hearted step toward him.

"*Gh'vrish?*" he complained in the exact same tone I would've said, "Seriously?" He snapped his tail. "Try harder, *drādah.*"

He was teaching me something he thought would improve my chances of survival. He was trying to help, and the least I could do was give it my best effort.

I coiled my body, then jumped at him like I was going to tackle him to the ground. He stepped backward and I jumped forward again. He kept stepping backward and I kept going for him.

His heel snagged on the uneven ground. He stumbled, tail snapping, and I crashed into his chest and bounced off. He caught my elbows, pulling me upright.

"You see, *drādah?*"

I nodded, a bit breathless. "I could just keep charging you. It made it easy to keep attacking."

He pushed me two steps back. "Now attack again."

I sprang. He stepped sideways and I flew past him, sliding on the wet moss. When I whirled around, he was four steps away and still moving in a steady sidestep that allowed him to retreat while watching me and his trajectory at the same time.

"Oh," I muttered.

His lips curved in a pleased smile. "You understand, *na?*"

"Yes." I definitely understood that stumbling backward and falling was the most useless reaction to an attack I could possibly have. It was so obvious that I didn't understand why I hadn't figured it out myself.

"Now you will practice."

"Wait." My eyes widened in alarm. "I'm not ready. What are y—"

He flashed toward me. I lurched backward—and, of course, tripped and fell. I winced as I hit the ground. Peeking up, I expected him to be scowling angrily.

He was holding his hand out again. Confused, I let him pull me up.

"Try again," he said.

I braced myself, chanting "step sideways" over and over in my head. He backed up two steps, then vaulted at me. As before, my body automatically lurched in the opposite direction of the incoming attack. I stumbled back while also trying to step sideways. Instead of falling, I just didn't move and he bowled me over.

As I pitched backward, he scooped me out of the air and set me on my feet.

Embarrassed by my failure, I raked my wet hair off my face. "Again."

He waited a moment, then charged. I darted sideways and he flashed past. Tail swinging out, he pivoted on one foot and leaped at me again—and I backpedaled in a panic, tripped on the rough terrain, and slammed down on my butt.

"*Argh!*" I burst out. "Why can't I do this? It's simple. It should be easy!"

"Your instincts tell you to go backward." He crouched beside me. "That is hard to change."

An odd flutter of confusion disturbed my center. I wouldn't call his tone *kind*, but it wasn't angry, impatient, or insulting.

"*Hh'ainun* instincts are stupid," he added. "It is why you are all so easy to kill."

Ah, there was the insult. Somehow, I felt better. Zylas being patient and considerate was just weird.

We reset our positions, and Zylas mock-charged me again and again while I struggled to override my panicked instinct to retreat backward. It was a slow process. I managed to dart sideways half the time, but as soon as he changed direction and sprang again, my instinctive backpedal took over.

After thirty minutes, I was panting for air and aching all over from falling down so many times. Instead of taking his "pounce" stance, Zylas assessed my fatigued state. He, of course, showed zero signs of weariness.

"You must practice when you cannot see the hunter coming," he decided.

I warily raised my head.

"You will walk in the trees, and I will hunt you."

Apprehension zinged through me. "That doesn't seem like a good idea."

"*Na?* Why not?"

I opened my mouth, but admitting his proposal sounded terrifying wouldn't get me anywhere. "I'm tired."

"So weak, *drādah.*" He pointed. "Walk."

Scowling, I stomped into the trees. I managed five steps before peeking over my shoulder. The clearing was empty. Zylas had already vanished into the rainy gloom.

Pulling my jacket collar tighter around my neck, I walked faster. My heart pounded and the back of my neck prickled. I shivered from cold, and a fresh rush of adrenaline couldn't quite compensate for my tired muscles. The patter of rain and whoosh of the wintry wind covered all other sounds.

Somewhere nearby, a demon was stalking me.

I scanned the trees, stopping every few steps to check for any sign of him. My nerves wound tighter, jitters quivering through my fingers. He was watching me. I could feel it. I hastened past a stand of fir trees, angling away from a short but steep drop into a water-logged gully. Puffing out a shaky breath, I reached up to unstick my wet bangs from my face.

A flash plunged down from a nearby tree. Zylas hit the ground and pounced, claws unsheathing. A scream burst from my throat as I sprang backward in unthinking panic. I stumbled but he was still coming and I stepped back again.

The ground wasn't there.

I pitched over with another shriek. As Zylas came to a stop, I splatted on my back and slid down the wet side of the gully. I squelched all the way to the bottom, my mouth open in horror.

Zylas stood at the top, gazing at me without expression.

My shoulders made a sucking noise as I sat up. I lifted my hand out of the soupy brown muck and stared in revulsion. Rain pattered on my head.

I looked up at the demon. "Why didn't you catch me?"

He could have. I had no doubt about that.

His tail lashed. "You should have gone sideways."

"You—" Fury boiled through me. "Did you make me fall down here *on purpose?*"

Another snap of his tail. "Next time, go sideways."

My teeth crunched. I fought the outrage burning through my innards, but it burst free. I shoved myself up, my entire back coated in reeking mud, and shouted every insult I knew.

And that's how my first lesson in being "smart prey" ended.

I **GLARED THROUGH** the apartment lobby's door, the glass reinforced with security bars. This morning's downpour had let up a few hours ago and the pavement shone wetly.

Despite having an entire afternoon to cool off, I was still furious with Zylas for deliberately ambushing me so I'd fall into a mud-filled gully. He was angry too. During our shouting match—which had resumed the moment I'd gotten home and he could leave the infernus again—he'd declared I was too "*zh'ūltis*" to learn anything and he'd completely wasted his time.

Needless to say, I hadn't taken that well.

Headlights blazed through the door and a boxy van pulled up outside the apartment. Someone in the passenger seat waved at me.

I stepped out into the cold wind. The van's side door slid open, the interior light illuminating the mythics sitting on the bench seats. I climbed inside, surprised to find Zora on the middle bench, patting the empty seat beside her, instead of driving.

"Ready for this?" she asked as I fumbled for the seatbelt.

Her previous partner, the telekinetic Drew, rolled the door shut and settled back into his seat on the rear bench. The van rumbled into motion.

"I think so," I answered, hoping I didn't sound terrified. "What's the plan, exactly?"

"First, let's make sure we all know names here." Zora gestured to the backseat. "You met Drew already. This is Laetitia, a hydromage."

The tall woman smiled, teeth flashing against her dark complexion, her thin braids pulled into a high ponytail.

"And at the front are Darren and Cameron, offensive sorcerer and defensive apprentice sorcerer, respectively."

Darren? My heart sank at the sight of the hulking bully from a few days ago—the one Zylas had slammed down on the guild's bar—in the driver's seat. In the passenger seat, his rangy buddy gave me a friendly-ish smile.

"I'm partnering with Robin," Zora announced to the group. "Laetitia and Drew, and Darren and Cameron will make up the other pairs. Partners are responsible for each other, but we'll all be sticking close together anyway."

She leaned forward, elbows braced on her knees as Darren navigated the dark streets. "Now, this is a scouting mission. We're here to confirm a vampire nest and where it is, not to engage or attempt an extermination."

"Not even a little bit of exterminating?" Cameron asked plaintively.

"Not even a little. We'll save the fun for the next round, which will be during the day."

"Um," I began uncertainly. "Can I ask … why are we doing this at night?"

"It's easier to find vampires while they're active," Zora explained. "Keep in mind, guys, that we've seen increased vampiric activity over the last four weeks, so we're using extra caution. No messing around, Darren and Cameron."

The van rolled to a stop and Darren shifted into park. We exited the vehicle into an unremarkable back alley, the narrow stretch of pavement surrounded by skyscrapers. We were in the heart of downtown.

As the others followed Zora to the van's rear, I eyed their dark leather clothing, assorted weapons, and magical artifacts. In comparison, I felt ridiculously out of place in my regular winter coat, blue jeans, and sneakers.

Zora opened the van's rear doors and handed out armfuls of shiny fabric. She tossed me a bundle. "Smallest size we have."

I unfolded it. The waterproof overalls were smudged with dirt and the legs ended in attached rubber boots. The rest of the team were stepping into theirs, so I gulped down my pounding heart and donned my pair. My shoes fit inside the rubber boots with room left over, and even tightening the straps as short as possible, the overalls sagged down to my waist.

Zora helped me crisscross the straps to use up a bit more length, then passed out yellow hard hats with built-in lights. When I set mine on my head, it rocked around loosely and I nervously tightened the chin strap.

Pulling a rectangular device out of the van, Zora switched it on. The front lit up with a loud beep. "Who wants to carry the gas meter?"

"I'll do it," Cameron volunteered. He clipped it onto the shoulder of his overalls.

"Gas meter?" I whispered fearfully, but no one heard me.

Zora passed a pair of metal hooks to Darren. I watched in confusion as he stepped over to a weathered grate embedded in the center of the alley and used the hooks to heave it up. He dragged it aside, then tossed the hooks back to Zora. She returned them to the van and started to shut the doors.

"Wait." She reached inside again. "Almost forgot. Phone, keys, and wallets over here, guys."

As she held out a plastic tote, everyone dug their valuables out of their pockets and set them in the plastic bin. With no choice, I added mine to the collection, wondering what madness I'd volunteered for.

As Zora put the tote in the van and locked the vehicle, Cameron descended feet first into the black hole. Rushing water echoed beneath the pavement. Darren started after him, his shoulders almost too wide to fit.

"We …" I cleared my throat. "We're going into a sewer?"

"It's a storm drain," Zora corrected. "It won't smell great, but there's no raw waste down there, just rainwater." She glanced at my face, and I imagined I was paler than usual. "Um. I should've asked—you're not claustrophobic, are you?"

Not normally, but I was seriously reconsidering my stance on confined spaces.

"We'll be following large tunnels," she assured me. "It's dark and wet, but it'll be fine, you'll see."

"There are vampires down there?"

"We'll find out. I once helped exterminate a nest of thirteen in these tunnels. Biggest one I've ever seen."

As Laetitia followed Drew into the hole, I struggled to calm down. I could do this. We were scouting. Just scouting. We wouldn't be fighting any vampires down in the wet darkness.

Zora nudged me forward. My heels dug in, my gaze darting from the hole to the grate and back.

"What if someone puts that cover back on?" My voice sharpened in a panicky way. "Will we be trapped?"

"We can push the grate off from the inside, and there's an exit like this every block. Trust me, Robin. I've been down here dozens of times." She peered into my face and her expression softened with sympathy. "You don't have to come. The tunnels aren't for everyone."

Crap. I was ruining my reputation as a badass, demon-slaying, vampire-exterminating contractor.

I forced myself to laugh. "No, I'm good. I just wasn't expecting this, that's all."

"If you'd rather—"

"I'm fine," I said brightly, striding toward the square hole. I groped at the light on my hard hat and clicked it on, shining its beam into the narrow chute. Steel rungs stuck out of the concrete, leading downward, and a steady trickle of water spilled off the asphalt and splashed into the drainage system below.

I crouched at the hole's edge, turned, and felt for the first rung with my oversized rubber boot. The chute's sides scraped at my elbows as I fumbled my way down the ladder. The cramped confines opened into a wider tunnel, and I felt around with my foot, searching for the next rung.

"You're on the last step." Drew appeared beside me, his headlamp glaring. "Here."

The telekinetic lifted me down the final four feet. My boots splashed into knee-deep water. It rushed past, pressing coldly against my waterproof overalls. The air was disgustingly humid and reeked of rot. Zora's boots appeared on the ladder rungs above my head and I waded out of the way.

The team stood a few yards down, waiting calmly. The tunnel was six feet high and almost as wide, and only Darren and Cameron had to duck their heads.

"Okay!" Zora called above the black water's deafening echo. "We're heading northwest from here. Blood trackers out!"

Each mythic pulled out a wand with a red stone on the end. They spoke the incantation, their words lost in the splashing clamor, and the end of each artifact lit with a faint glow. Was I supposed to have one of those?

Zora answered my unspoken question by holding out a spare, the end already lit with magic. "Gotcha covered, Robin. Cameron, you have the gas meter, so take the lead."

Cameron grinned at his team and splashed away from the chute. My chest constricted as I fell into step beside Zora, last in line.

What on earth was I, a bookworm who didn't practice magic, doing down here?

We followed the tunnel, water pushing on the backs of our legs. I was here because Amalia and I needed to find out why vampires were searching for Uncle Jack. While I tackled the "bloodsucking monsters" angle, she was searching for her father the old-fashioned way—by asking everyone who knew him for information. I wished we could switch jobs.

"So," Darren began, raising his voice above the water's clamor. He glanced back at me. "How many vampires have you tagged, Robin?"

"Three."

He hesitated. He'd probably expected me to say none. "I suppose it isn't difficult for a contractor. All you have to do is stand there while your demon does all the work."

Darren had no idea how right he was.

"Vampire hunting is a bit different when you have to get your hands dirty. Ever been bitten, Robin?"

"No." I glanced at Zora. "Wouldn't I turn into a vampire?"

"A bite increases the risk of infection," she said. "As long as you get to a healer fast enough, the infection rate is less than one percent."

"Assuming you survive long enough to reach a healer," Darren called back. "A bite will put you down like a shot of horse tranquilizer. Once a vamp starts sucking on you, you can't do a damn thing to stop it."

I cringed fearfully.

"Oh," he added, "and unlike shifters, there's no spell, potion, or exorcism that can save you if you *do* get infected."

"Thanks, Darren." Zora adjusted her sword hilt. "I love when teammates bolster each other's confidence. I'll remember it next time I put together a job."

He shot an alarmed look over his shoulder.

"Let's stay focused," she called to the group. "Echoes carry far in here and we don't want to tip off the nest—if there is one."

I looked down at my blood tracker, but the faint red glow hadn't brightened. No sign of trouble yet.

Our headlamps flickered and flashed across the tunnel in dizzying patterns as we sloshed downstream. Small pipes connected with the main tunnel at regular intervals, disgorging frothing spouts riddled with leaves, mud, and bits of garbage. The water level crept over my knees.

"Heads up," Laetitia called back.

I looked up and my light beam hit the tunnel's slimy ceiling. A swarm of two- and three-inch-long cockroaches scuttled away from the light. Shuddering, I sloshed faster.

The tunnel gradually widened as more pipes connected to it, dumping runoff into the system. My breath puffed from exertion and foul air coated my mouth. Was it my imagination, or was the current picking up?

"Okay!" Zora called just loud enough to grab everyone's attention. We clustered around her. "A hundred yards farther along, this tunnel empties into the main channel, and that's where we've found nests in the past. Laetitia, you have our safety line?"

The tall hydromage pulled a coil of climbing rope from under her overalls, the end clinking with a dozen heavy carabiner clips.

"Good. We'll approach the end of this tunnel with caution. If our blood trackers light, that's it, we're done. We know they're here. If they don't light, we'll have to descend into the main channel. It has a walkway along one side that should be above the water. We'll start by—"

A foaming wave splashed into our group, almost throwing Zora and me off our feet. Drew grabbed my arm and Cameron supported Zora, the taller mythics bracing against the increased current. The water broke across my thighs.

"Zora!" Laetitia's voice was sharp with warning. "The water is rising too fast. It must be raining upstream."

"Get the safety line ready. There's a drain access just ahead. Move!"

Laetitia and Darren rushed forward while Cameron and Drew held on to me and Zora, helping us stay grounded as the water rose up to my hips. I stuffed my blood tracker down the front of my shirt as we waded after them.

Metal ladder rungs protruded from the cement wall, and Laetitia clipped carabiners onto the lowest rung. She snapped one onto a sturdy loop built into her fitted combat vest, then tossed the rope to Darren. He clipped himself in, then slung the rope to Cameron.

A deep roar was growing louder, the cacophony rolling down the tunnel from somewhere upstream.

Cameron snapped a carabiner onto his vest, then clipped Zora in as the water broke over my waist. Drew caught another loop of rope, one arm hooked around me, and snapped himself in. He held a carabiner out to me.

I stared at it in terror.

His eyes widened as he realized what no one had noticed before: I wasn't in combat gear like they were. I wasn't wearing a fitted, secure, heavy-duty vest with loops that could be clipped onto the line.

The deafening roar boomed in warning.

Drew snapped the clip over the strap of my overalls, then grabbed me by the waist and heaved me toward the wall. Cameron and Darren gripped my arms, fingers biting down hard. Our headlamps flashed as we all looked up the tunnel.

A frothing wall of water charged toward us.

Laetitia thrust her hands out. The wave bent as though diverted by an invisible barrier, but the water level kept climbing.

"Get out!" Laetitia gasped, arms trembling.

Drew threw Zora up into the chute. He must've added a boost of telekinesis, because she flew upward and grabbed the ladder rungs. She climbed for the hatch, boots slipping on the rungs, and Drew caught me next. As Darren and Cameron released my arms, he heaved me out of the waist-deep water.

Laetitia's sharp cry rang out as water smashed into her. Her invisible diversion vanished and the full force of the torrent hit us.

The impact slammed me into the concrete wall, my hard hat bouncing off a ladder rung. As the water struck them, Cameron and Darren made wild grabs for me, but the raging current swept us all off our feet.

The safety line snapped taut. The men jerked to a halt, water breaking over them. Hanging by my overalls' strap, I flailed desperately as icy liquid hammered my head. I couldn't see, could scarcely breathe.

"Robin!" a voice shouted urgently.

Water pounded over me, pulling hard on my overalls. They'd become an underwater parachute, the current dragging at them with inexorable force. I stretched my arm up, blindly searching for the rope. My fingers brushed the braided cord.

The plastic buckle on my overalls snapped.

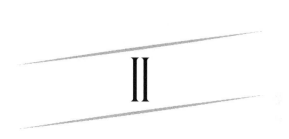

II

THE VIOLENT TORRENT whipped me down the tunnel on a foaming wave, gaining speed by the second. My headlamp flashed across the concrete walls and illuminated a square opening ahead. The water echoed even louder.

The end of the tunnel. I sucked in a breath and clamped my hand over my nose.

I shot out of the tunnel like it was the world's most terrifying waterslide and plunged into deeper water. My hard hat tore off my head, the light spinning away. I caught a glimpse of the cavernous new tunnel I'd fallen into. Water poured in on both sides from huge pipes, and a platform ran along the right side, with drains gushing down onto it.

My tumbling headlamp blinked out and darkness swept in.

As I spun in the deluge, I shoved the remaining strap of my overalls off. The water tore the garment away and I kicked, hands flailing in search of a solid surface. My bulky coat dragged me under.

I yanked the zipper down and my head dunked beneath the freezing water. As I was sucked into the spiraling turbulence where a pipe dumped into the main channel, I ripped my jacket off and let the water take it too. Freed of its weight, I kicked back to the surface.

When my head broke free, I gasped. Light! Dim light illuminated the channel and the platform speeding past me. I flung my hands out, reaching frantically for a handhold as the water carried me along. My fingers scraped across the rough concrete, then caught on a lip.

I jarred to a painful halt. The current pulled at me, splashing over my face and filling my mouth. I spat, coughed, and shook the water from my eyes. My handhold was a one-foot-diameter pipe. Hooking my arm into it, I felt upward with the other and found the edge of the platform.

Gasping for air, I dragged one leg up and stuck my foot into the hole. A terrified voice in the back of my head screamed I couldn't do it, that I'd slip and fall and drown. I grabbed the ledge and launched myself upward as hard as I could. Arms grasping at the slick concrete, I heaved myself onto the solid platform. The water rushed by, dark as ink in the dim light.

Lying on my back, I panted harshly, my throat aching and limbs trembling. I was alive. Somehow.

The infernus under my drenched sweater pulsed, a brief flash of heat and vibration. With unsteady arms, I pushed myself into a sitting position and reached into my shirt. My numb fingers found a smooth stick. I tugged the blood tracker out and dropped it beside me, then slid the infernus out of my sweater.

"Zylas," I rasped.

Red light flared across it. The power ballooned into his shape and he solidified beside me in a final blaze.

"*Drādah.*" He crouched, swiftly assessing my condition. "Are you hurt?"

I coughed up water. "Don't think so."

"I could feel your fear. You did not call me!"

Startled by his angry exclamation, I waved vaguely at the water. "I couldn't. You might've drowned. Do you know how to swim?"

"*Var!* Why would I not swim?"

He wrapped his hands around my arms and pulled me up. I wobbled, my knees trembling and teeth chattering. Water dripped off my clothes and pooled around my feet.

"Where is this place?" he asked sharply.

"Under the c-c-city," I chattered. "Need to f-f-find a way t-to the s-s-surface."

He stared around, hands tightening on my arms, then pushed me backward until I bumped into the side of the channel, as far from the water as possible.

"Wait here," he ordered. "I will find a way out."

"I'll c-come too. We should s-stay t—"

"You are slow. I will be faster."

As he stepped away, I grabbed his wrist. My breath rasped with a hysterical edge. "Don't leave me alone."

His eyes moved across my face, his dark, dilated pupils more pronounced than usual in the red glow. A wolfish smile pulled at his lips, flashing one pointed canine. "*Na, drādah,* did you forget?"

"Forget w-what?"

He tapped a claw against the infernus. "I am never far from you. Now be *drādah ahktallis* and wait here. Quietly."

Pulling away from my hand, he prowled swiftly down the platform and ducked through the spray falling from a four-foot-diameter pipe high on the channel wall. With a snap of his barbed tail, he disappeared.

Drādah ahktallis. "Smart prey." If Zylas wanted me to wait quietly, then I would wait quietly.

I sucked in air, my whole body trembling. My coat would've drowned me if I hadn't discarded it, but I regretted its loss anyway. The damp chill permeated my skin and my sweater stuck to my body. I slid down the wall and curled into a tight ball, my arms tucked between my stomach and my thighs.

Seconds dragged into minutes. I lost all sense of time as I shivered in the dim light. My gaze darted across the pipes and tunnels that vomited frothing water into the main channel. Had I fallen from one of those, or was that tunnel farther upstream, out of sight?

Would the others search for me? Had the rising water forced them back to the surface? I squinted nervously at the underground river, but it would take way more water to flood this massive channel. Hard to believe all this existed beneath the downtown streets, unseen by the hundreds of thousands of people who walked above it every day.

At least it wasn't a sewer. It stank like rotting things, but it wasn't *that* bad. Though my shivering continued, I didn't feel as cold anymore. And it wasn't pitch dark either. I glanced toward a small bulb, leaking a faint orange glow, that dangled from a black wire looped around a fat, rusty nail. The wire trailed along the wall to another nail and matching bulb twenty feet away. Crude, but better than darkness.

Nerves prickled through me but I had no idea why.

I wished Zylas would hurry. My muscles were tired from shivering and my body ached. Plus, I was tired. So tired I could scarcely keep my head up. How long had he been gone? Shouldn't he be back by now?

Blinking drowsily, I wondered why everything had a reddish haze. Was there something wrong with my vision? The friendly little light bulb glowed orange. It wasn't red, so what …

The marble-like end of the blood-tracker artifact, lying in the middle of the platform where I'd dropped it, was blazing with scarlet light.

Lips quirking, I pushed my cold, weary body up. My numb feet stumbled across the floor, and it took my clumsy fingers three tries to pick up the narrow stick. Straightening, I watched the tracker's red light glint off the wet walls. The jewel glowed even brighter. My dull thoughts prodded at the realization, trying to remember what it meant. Shivers racked my exhausted body.

Warm air brushed across the back of my neck as an unfamiliar voice said, "What's a pretty little thing like you doing down here?"

Strong arms pulled me back into a solid body. A hand closed over my jaw and forced my head to one side. Terror burst through me, clearing the drowsy haze from my mind.

A wet mouth closed over the side of my neck and teeth sank into my skin. Pain shot into my collarbone, spreading from the sharp fangs buried in my flesh. Numbness swept outward in the wake of the pain, bringing intense dizziness with it.

My legs buckled. The vampire held me against his chest, mouth clamped on my neck. Numbness deadened my limbs. I twitched helplessly, the concrete platform swimming in my vision.

Then I remembered.

Daimon, hesychaze! The command screamed through my head, laced with terror. For an agonizing heartbeat, nothing happened. The vampire gulped another mouthful of my blood.

The infernus jumped against my chest. Heat burned through my wet sweater.

A streak of crimson light burst out of the channel's ceiling like it was an illusion instead of solid concrete. The power leaped downward, hit the infernus, and shot right back out. Zylas materialized in front of me, his eyes blazing as brightly as his power.

The vampire's head jerked up—and Zylas's glowing talons shot past my face. Bone crunched. The vampire's arms fell away and I crumpled. Zylas caught me, sweeping me against him.

"*Kasht!*" he hissed. "*Drādah*, can you hear me?"

I couldn't close my sagging mouth, let alone form words. My limbs spasmed as I fought to stand under my own power.

I can't move. Panic screeched in my head. *I can't move!*

"The vampire bite. The *hh'ainun* warned of it." He pressed a hand to my cheek, his palm blazing hot. "You are too cold. Your heart has slowed."

Considering my level of terror, my heart should've been racing. A stinging sensation built in my neck and the alarming numbness slowly morphed into cold and pain.

Crimson power flickered, followed by a strange buzz of magic that slid into my body from beneath his hand. "I do not know the *vīsh* to fix you."

Just get us out of here!

"We will leave," he agreed, scooping me up into his arms. "I found a way—"

He broke off, looking down. With a huge effort, I forced my head to turn.

The blood-tracker artifact lay on the concrete, dropped yet again. It had dimmed when the vampire died, but it was brightening fast. And this time, my thoughts were clear enough that I knew what it meant.

Vampires are coming!

12

ZYLAS HEARD MY TELEPATHIC WARNING. Holding my limp form, he kicked the artifact off the platform, then jammed his foot against the dead vampire and shoved. The body rolled limply. With a second kick, it tumbled over the edge and hit the black water with a splash.

He took two quick steps, then froze, head cocked as he listened. Hissing under his breath, he threw me over his shoulder, the air whooshing from my lungs. With a powerful leap, he grabbed the lip of a pipe high on the wall and hauled us up with one arm, then pushed me into the confined space.

Water drenched my front. Zylas shoved me in deeper, then crawled in after me. As I spluttered helplessly, he tugged on the back of my sweater to get my head out of the water.

"Quiet," he whispered.

Somewhere in the main channel, voices echoed beneath the ever-present noise.

Zylas scooted deeper into the pipe's confines, pushing me ahead of him. Icy water washed over me, stealing the last of my body heat. I shivered violently as more sensation returned to my body.

With half his attention on the opening into the main channel, Zylas reached for his shoulder. His dexterous fingers snapped across the leather straps of his chest plate and they came apart. He shoved the armor off so it hung behind his left arm, then lifted the fabric underlayer over his head.

Beneath the numbing cold and fear, confusion buzzed through my head.

He unbuckled his armguard and set it just above the line of flowing water, then stripped the fabric from his arms.

"What ..." I slurred in a whisper, "are ... you ..."

Turning to me, he grasped the bottom of my sweater and pulled it up.

I squeaked in disbelief, feebly twisting away. He dragged the soaked material over my head and tossed it aside. I forced my shaking arms up to cover my bra.

Zylas! I cried furiously in my head. *Stop—*

His hands closed around my waist. Vertigo swept over me as he pulled me up—and the next thing I knew, I was sprawled on top of him as he leaned back into the curved pipe, his knees bent and feet pressed against the opposite side.

He held me down, forcing our bodies together. My bare front pressed against his naked torso—and heat blazed from his skin into mine. Gasping, I instinctively pressed into his warmth. His hot arms banded across my icy back.

Holy crap, he was *warm*.

My chilled skin burned from his body heat. He was hotter than any human—or, at least, any human without a dangerous fever. I burrowed my frozen face into the side of his neck, only then realizing that my glasses were missing, lost in the turbulent water.

Somewhere outside our hiding spot, voices sounded louder than before.

"... smell blood ..."

"... missing ... do you see ..."

"... who killed ..."

"... keep searching!"

The words bounced off the walls, half lost in the water's din. Vampires. More than one, and they were close. Would they find us hiding in this pipe? If they did, we had no escape. We were trapped.

Fear prickled over my skin and adrenaline sharpened my fuzzy brain. As my head cleared, my attention diverted from the voices to something far more immediate: Zylas's warm hands running up and down my bare arms.

I was on top of Zylas.

No, not just on top. I was *straddling* him, my thighs pressed against his hips, my knees squeezing his sides. Our naked torsos were pressed tight together, skin against skin. My arms were tucked in close, hands gripping his bare shoulders as he rubbed more warmth into me.

With a mortified gasp, I shoved backward. Icy air hit my bare front, and as his gaze snapped from the pipe's opening to me, I clamped my arms over my chest.

His mouth thinned in annoyance, then he grabbed my shoulders and pulled me back down.

"Zylas!" I hissed frantically, struggling to free myself. "Let me go!"

"You lost too much heat," he growled. "Share mine, stubborn *drādah*."

I gave one more desperate shove against his immovable arms, then slumped in defeat. The hottest blush in the history of blushes burned my cheeks as I rested my face against his shoulder.

Zylas stared at the pipe's opening, his jaw tight—though whether with worry over the vampires' proximity or annoyance with the stupid human, I didn't know. As voices bounced through the cavernous channel, he tilted his head to catch the words with his sensitive hearing.

Something banged in the distance and Zylas gave the slightest start. I tensed in response, my blush reigniting and uncomfortable butterflies swirling through my gut. He stretched his neck, an ear tilted toward the sounds—and his hand slid up the length of my spine.

I shuddered from head to toe.

His eyes returned to me, fixing on my face. I peered up at him, frozen and unmoving, and he stared back, his expression a mystery in the near darkness.

Seizing my arms, he pushed me back against his thighs, his knees bent to keep his body—and mine—out of the water. As I blinked dumbly, he pulled his gear back into place and buckled the leather straps over his shoulder.

He found my shirt and wrung it out, then offered it to me. I snatched it from his hands, shook out the sleeves, and pulled it over my head. Gasping as the cold, damp fabric settled against my newly warmed skin, I suppressed another shiver.

"They have left this spot," Zylas whispered. "We will go now."

I nodded, distracted by the fact I was still straddling his waist.

"I will carry you," he said. "You must hold on."

"What—"

He nudged me off him. My knees splashed into the water and the cold burned. I'd forgotten how frigid it was. How hypothermic had I been before Zylas warmed me up? He'd probably saved my life with that alone.

Crouched in the flowing water, he caught my wrist and pulled me against his back. I gripped his shoulders, gulped hard, then wrapped my legs tightly around his waist. Scooting forward, he ducked low under the pipe's curved ceiling and cautiously approached the opening.

I squinted in the dim light. Without my glasses, the main channel was unpleasantly blurry, but I could tell the water had risen. The frothing current splashed onto the concrete platform and violent streams poured from the connecting pipelines.

Zylas squeezed my thigh in warning and I tightened my legs around him, sliding one hand under his leather shoulder strap for a better grip.

He sprang out of the pipe and landed on the platform in a crouch. I clamped myself around him as he sped down the platform and cut through an icy torrent from another pipe. Water drenched my clothes all over again.

We came out the other side. The platform stretched on and Zylas broke into a smooth trot past small light bulbs hanging from rusted nails. Now that I wasn't hypothermic, I knew why the sight had unnerved me. The lighting was a rudimentary addition to the channel's original construction. I should've realized the lights meant people—or rather, vampires—had taken up residence down here.

Zylas zoomed past pipes and tunnels, large and small, each one disgorging runoff into the main channel. At a seemingly random point, he slowed, turned, and sprang into a tunnel as large as the one Zora had led us down earlier.

"How do you know which way to go?" I muttered.

"This one smells like blood."

He sloshed through the thigh-deep water, fighting the current. His foot slipped and he lurched, grabbing the wall for balance. I gripped him more tightly. If I fell, I'd be swept right back into the main channel.

He waded upstream, the tunnel growing darker and darker as we left the lights behind. Ahead was an opening—another offshoot. Zylas hopped into it and ducked so neither of us hit our heads. Only the smallest trickle of water ran out and the walls were dry. More small bulbs hung from a long wire, casting a soft glow across the grimy walls.

Voices echoed down the tunnel.

Zylas prowled closer. The tunnel ran at a slight curve, hindering our view, and he drew to a stop. He sniffed at the air, then tapped my leg. Unclamping my limbs, I slid off his back. He started forward and I followed two steps behind.

Around the curve, I glimpsed moving shadows. People with dark clothing, thin builds, and no sign of gear or weapons. Vampires.

Gaze locked on the enemy, Zylas reached back and nudged my hip. I stopped. He took three more stalking steps, then coiled his body. His fingers curled, claws unsheathing.

"—can't get a signal." The vampire's gravelly voice reached us. His silhouette held up a small object. "If we don't report the—"

Zylas launched into a charge. The vampires didn't see him until he was almost on top of them, and only then did crimson magic rush up his arms in glowing veins. Six-inch scarlet talons formed at the ends of his fingers.

I knew he wanted me to wait, but I bolted after him. As he slammed into the vampire trio, claws tearing and the creatures shouting, I homed in on the one who'd spoken. Zylas rammed his talons into the vampire's heart, killing the fae spirit inside him, and the small object the man was holding spun through the air.

I ran forward, hands outstretched. The object bounced off my fingertips and flipped end over end. I snatched it out of the air.

Wow, I'd caught it? And without my glasses too.

The last vampire crumpled under Zylas's claws, and he turned to me with a questioning look. I uncurled my fingers. A small flip phone rested on my palm.

The vampires' other belongings were scattered around us—heaps of tattered fabric, garbage bags of who knew what, a disgusting amount of trash, and for some bizarre reason, a rusty shopping cart. Farther into the tunnel, a tarp formed a tent-like shelter, and sleeping bags were bundled in the corner. This section of tunnel was dry, suggesting a blockage somewhere along the line, and it stank.

Really stank.

Zylas's magic faded from his arms and the darkness around us deepened—but not so much that I didn't notice the metal rungs on the wall beside him. Shoving the phone in my wet pocket, I rushed toward the ladder and grabbed the bottom rung—so high above my head I could barely reach it.

Hands closing over my waist, Zylas lifted me. I scrambled onto the rungs and rushed upward. A grate waited at the top of the chute and a streetlamp's orange glow leaked through it. I pushed on the metal, but it didn't shift.

"I can't …" I looked down. Zylas stood at the bottom, head tipped back as he watched me. "I can't open it."

"Weak *drādah*. Try harder."

Bracing my forearm against the grate, I shoved with all my strength. The grate tilted up, then tipped over and hit the pavement with an ear-splitting clang.

I heaved myself out of the chute and collapsed beside it, panting with relief. An anonymous back alley surrounded me— towering buildings and concrete walls interrupted by blank metal doors and loading bays.

The infernus flared with light and heat. A streak of crimson power leaped from the chute, hit the silver pendant, and vanished inside it. My fingers closed around the warm disc, the center carved with the sigil of Zylas's House.

"We did it," I whispered, scarcely able to believe I was alive.

13

I STARED GLUMLY AT THE TALL GLASS in front of me. In it, liquid the color and texture of mashed corn bubbled. I had no idea what was making it bubble like that. Cautiously, I touched the side of the glass. Wasn't hot.

I didn't want to know why it was bubbling.

Slumping in my chair, I tugged my blanket closer, the soft fabric wrapped around my shoulders and over my knees. My drenched clothes had gone straight into the garbage, and I wore a loose sweatshirt and black sweatpants, borrowed from Zora.

The Crow and Hammer pub was quiet—unsurprising for a weekday night. I was the only person sitting at a table, though half an hour ago, the rest of my "team" had been here too. All of them, even the bully Darren, had waited while a guild healer repaired the wound to my neck and performed the additional anti-vampire magic to stave off infection. With a final blood test, she'd confirmed I was safe. No contamination.

The team had cheered the good news. Maybe guilt, more than concern for my wellbeing, had fueled their celebration, but it had still been nice.

Footsteps pattered down the stairs from the guild's upper level. Zora strode to my table, unclipping her baldric. She leaned her broadsword against the table and dropped into a chair.

"Drink your potion," she ordered, nudging my glass closer to me.

"Sanjana didn't say what it was," I mumbled. A yellow bubble bulged from the lumpy surface, then popped with a tiny *pff*.

"It's for the hypothermia. It'll keep you from getting sick." She gave a short laugh at my expression. "It looks worse than it tastes."

Grimacing, I lifted the glass but couldn't bring myself to drink it.

"Try closing your eyes."

I squeezed my eyes shut and took a sip. Thick liquid hit my tongue and its rich flavor pinged across my taste buds.

"Popcorn?" I said disbelievingly, eyes opening.

"Told you it wasn't that bad. Drink up!" She leaned back in her chair, her humor fading. "You're lucky to be alive."

I took a few uneager gulps of the liquid popcorn. "I need a proper vest like the rest of you have."

"I thought you were wearing combat gear under your jacket." Her face contorted with emotion before she rubbed her hands over her cheeks. "Robin, I'm so sorry. I should have confirmed you were prepared for the job. I just assumed ... but I should have checked!"

Her final word came out harsh and fuming, but her anger was directed at herself, not me.

"Zora …" I cleared my throat, wondering if I was about to make a huge mistake. "It isn't your fault. I don't have any combat training, but I let you and the others think I did so I wouldn't be left out."

Brow furrowing, she studied me. "*No* combat training? How is that possible? Your demon …"

"I'm … gifted at controlling my demon," I lied. "But me, on my own, I don't have any training. I've been a contractor for less than a year"—correction: for six weeks—"and aside from defeating the escaped demon on Halloween, I haven't done any combat jobs."

She frowned, deep lines framing her lips.

"I'm sorry I misled you," I mumbled, my gaze dropping to my half-empty glass of potion. I took another gulp.

"I see," she said after a long pause. "The responsibility is still mine, but … thank you for telling me." Another uncomfortable pause. "Now I'm even more shocked that you survived tonight."

Suppressing a wince, I downed the rest of my potion and set the glass aside. Popcorn. So wrong. "I got lucky."

"How did you find your way out?"

I silently panicked, casting around for a plausible explanation. "The vampires had lights set up. I followed the lights to an exit."

"You said you killed four. Do you think there are others?"

"Yes." I wasn't sure where my conviction came from, but it was strong. "I think there are a lot more."

"Hmm." She gazed thoughtfully at the ceiling. "If you're right … We sweep the drains every couple of months for new nests. How could a large nest have formed in a few weeks?" She drummed her fingers on the table. "Too many vampires too quickly … and their behavior … I don't get it."

"Oh! I forgot." I slid a hand into my sweatpants pocket and pulled out the flip phone. "I took this from a vampire. It got a bit damp, but I think it's okay."

She picked it off my palm. "Okay, now I'm freaked out."

"Huh? Why?"

The display lit up as she flipped the phone open. "Vampires steal things they need—clothes, food if they haven't transitioned to an all-blood diet yet, and other essentials—but a phone? I've only seen new vamps who haven't broken away from society using phones."

She pressed a few keys. I leaned over to see what she was doing, wishing I hadn't lost my glasses. Maybe I should get one of those straps old ladies used to hang their eyeglasses around their necks.

Zora pulled up the phone's call history. One number repeated over and over, with only a few others scattered throughout the list. We exchanged a look, then she selected the predominant number and pressed the call button. The speaker began to ring. One … two … three …

The line clicked.

"Report," a male voice barked.

Zora snapped the phone shut, ending the call.

"Well," she said slowly, "that's ominous."

I nodded. "I'm guessing vampires' lack of organization means they don't normally report to each other."

"Nests appear to have a loose pecking order, but you're correct. They don't normally answer to anyone." Her hand tightened around the phone. "I'll take this home so Felix can start working on it immediately."

My brow crinkled. Felix was the guild's third officer, but the rest of her sentence wasn't making much sense.

She noticed my confusion and laughed. "I guess no one's mentioned that Felix is my husband."

"He … oh." Her husband. Huh.

"He's our tech expert. He can find out more about that phone number." She slid the phone into her pocket. "Whatever's going on with the vamps, it's got me worried. They don't normally act like this, and I want to get to the bottom of it before anyone else is bitten." She pushed back from the table. "Do you need a ride?"

"Yes, please."

Zora led me behind the bar and through the empty kitchen to the back door. Outside, rain poured down in sheets—the water that had nearly drowned us in the storm drains.

As I settled into the passenger seat of her black coupe, exhaustion permeated my bones. I felt hollowed out and wrung dry, and hopeless frustration kindled deep in my gut. I'd nearly died tonight, and what had I accomplished? All I had were more questions.

Were the vampires from the storm drains connected to the ones at Claude's townhouse? What was their interest in Uncle Jack? How close to finding him were they? Where was Claude? Did he know vampires had searched his house, destroyed his belongings, and stolen his computer? Was he searching for Uncle Jack, or had he gone into hiding too?

As the wipers swept back and forth across the windshield, my mind whirred to the same beat. An image rose to the top of my churning thoughts: the letter my mother had written to

Uncle Jack, every word in her loopy script emblazoned in my memory.

I know now that I was wrong about many things. I'm only just beginning to realize how wrong.

What had she been wrong about?

You know what's coming for us, what will happen if they find us.

What had been coming for them? Who had she been afraid of?

I don't know what to do. I don't know how to protect my family.

In every memory I had of her, my mother was a woman of light, laughter, and confidence. I could scarcely imagine her as uncertain or fearful. She'd always known what to do, no matter what had happened or what trouble I'd gotten myself into.

Please help me, Jack.

My parents had died in a car accident, I reminded myself. A regular accident. Thousands of people died in collisions every year. It had been raining and dark. The road had been slippery.

Was it too much of a coincidence that they'd died a week after my mother had realized her family was being hunted?

The Athanas Grimoire was worth ten million dollars just for the demon names it could reveal, but was it only those names my mother had dedicated her life to concealing? What else did the grimoire's ancient pages contain?

Zora dropped me off at my apartment building and promised to keep me posted on any leads the vampire's cell phone might produce. I let myself in and trudged up the stairs to the third floor. Though I tried to be quiet, Amalia's bedroom door opened as I was toeing off my wet shoes.

She leaned against the jamb, wearing a fuzzy housecoat. "How did it go?"

"We found vampires," I answered evasively. "I'll tell you all about it in the morning."

"Sure." Her nose wrinkled. "By the way, you stink."

I was sure I did. "The shower is my next stop."

Not waiting for her reply, I hurried into my bedroom, but I wasn't ready to shower and collapse into bed yet. My plain desk was stacked with books about Demonica, and I shifted the piles to uncover a title that predated my obsession with the darkest magic of the mythic world.

The Complete Compilation of Arcane Cantrips, the book that had sparked my fascination with magic. I searched through the pages, and when I couldn't find what I wanted, I shook it by the spine. The pages flapped and a single white sheet, folded in half, fell out.

Grabbing the paper, I dropped into my chair and unfolded it. The grainy photocopy displayed a single page of the Athanas grimoire, the paper dark with age, the handwritten ink faded. Greek letters scrawled across most of it, but in the bottom corner was an illustration.

It was a drawing of Zylas, or a demon that looked very similar to him.

I ran my finger across the Ancient Greek writing, then pulled out a scrap of paper and a pencil. Lower lip caught between my teeth, I studied the first line of the page—a title. I scribbled across my scrap page before firing up my laptop to check a suffix.

The final word stumped me until I realized it wasn't a word. It was a name.

The Twelfth House - Vh'alyir

I gulped against the cold shiver creeping up my spine. My attention shifted to the short paragraph below the title. I copied the lines onto my scrap paper, identifying the clauses, cases, pronouns, conjunctions, root words, and anything else I could pick out. My pencil scribbled urgently, then my fingers zipped across my keyboard, looking up the words I didn't know. I scrawled a new line, honing the translation.

A few minutes later, I sat back in my chair and lowered my pencil. I couldn't tear my eyes off my careful printing, staring at the result, wondering if I'd messed up the translation.

But I'd made no mistake.

Never summon from the Twelfth House.
For the trespass of this sacred covenant,
the sons of Vh'alyir will destroy you.

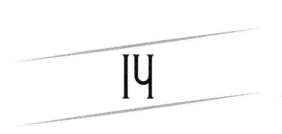

14

WAS I BLUSHING AGAIN? I pressed my inner wrist to my warm cheek. Yep, I was blushing again.

What was *wrong* with me?

Grimacing, I sank my hands into the soapy water and resumed scrubbing a mixing bowl. The counter was piled with dirty dishes—bowls, measuring cups, spoons, baking sheets—and the heavenly smell of apple cinnamon pie hung in the air like a delicious cloud.

My gaze trailed to my left and I commanded myself not to look. I looked anyway.

Zylas was sprawled across the living room sofa. On the plate beside him, what had been a stack of a dozen mini apple pies, their tops sprinkled with a cinnamon and sugar crumble, was almost gone—only two left. He'd shed his armor, which he only did when he was feeling particularly relaxed, and the overcast light streaking through the windows bathed the reddish-toffee skin of his bare torso. His head was reclined on the armrest, face pointed toward the light, eyes closed.

Embarrassment twinged through my center and I pointed my hot face at the sink again. I was so lame. *He* wasn't stammering and blushing every time he looked my way. I'd been hypothermic, and he'd warmed me up. Big deal. I couldn't have been more awkward about this if I'd grown up in the Antarctic with penguins for company.

But I really wished Zylas hadn't picked today to lounge around the living room with half his garments missing—and he didn't even wear much clothing to begin with. Then again, I supposed it was my own doing. I'd baked for him.

Movement out of the corner of my eye had me snatching my hands from the dishwater. I dove out of the kitchen and scooped Socks up by her furry tummy.

"No, little kitty," I cooed. "Stay out of the living room. There's a scary demon in there."

She mewled in complaint as I set her down in the kitchen by my feet. She was finally eating well, so I'd let her out of her crate to explore the apartment. For most of the morning, she'd lurked in my bedroom, but her confidence was growing.

Eyes half-lidded, Zylas watched me rescue the kitten. Yawning—and flashing his pointed canines—he reached for another mini pie. Crumbs scattered across the rug as he broke it in half and shoved a piece in his mouth. He crunched it once, then swallowed it down in a single gulp.

I shook my head. *Chew your food.*

He didn't acknowledge my loud thought, but I felt his annoyed stare on my back. Smirking only because he couldn't see it, I resumed washing dishes, stopping every few minutes to scoop Socks off the floor and move her out of the living room before she got too close to Zylas. Whenever she crept into his line of sight, his crimson eyes turned toward her.

As I worked, my thoughts drifted to last night's translation of the grimoire page. *The sons of Vh'alyir will destroy you.*

"Zylas," I said impulsively. "What's your House name?"

He cracked his eyes open. "*Hnn?*"

"Your House name. Is it Vh'alyir?"

"Not *valyeeer*," he grumbled. "*Vuh*-al-yer."

I carefully repeated the sounds. "So your full name is Zylas Vh'alyir?"

"*Zylas et Vh'alyir.*" He indulged in another languid yawn, seemingly unbothered by my new knowledge or where it had come from. "But I am usually called *Dīnen et Vh'alyir.*"

An odd shiver whispered over me. *King of Vh'alyir.* Before being summoned out of his world, he'd ruled his House and all demons who belonged to it—or that's what I was guessing, based on his vague comments.

"What are the other House names?"

"*Na*, so many," he complained lazily. "Lūsh'vēr, Dh'irath, Gh'reshēr, Ash'amadē ..."

I choked in disbelief. Demon names were worth millions of dollars and he was casually listing them off. Though, come to think of it, summoning required the name's proper spelling. I could barely pronounce the names, let alone spell them.

"They are the first ..." He frowned. "I do not know the word. First rank? They are close in strength. Next four Houses are second rank. Last four are third rank."

And Vh'alyir, as the Twelfth House, was at the very bottom in both rank and power.

"How did you become the Vh'alyir king?" I asked.

"I am oldest." He gazed thoughtfully at the last mini pie, then tipped his face toward the light again. "Oldest survivor is *Dīnen*."

Did that mean all the demons of his House were younger than him? Setting the last bowl in the drain tray, I grabbed a towel and dried my hands. "For a demon, are you young or old?"

"I am …" He scrunched his nose. "I have less years than the other *Dīnen*. Why so many questions, *drādah*?"

I lifted my hand to adjust my glasses, only to remember I'd lost them. I was wearing contacts instead. "How long have you been *Dīnen*?"

"Some time."

Not helpful. I gave up on that line of questioning. "What does being a *Dīnen* involve? What do you have to do?"

He rolled onto his back, resting one leg on the sofa's back cushions. "Too much to explain. Go away."

I rolled my eyes. "I live here. I'm not going away."

"Then be quiet."

Such a friendly, polite demon. I caught Socks as she tried to sneak past me and carried her into my room. I set her beside the window, hoping the view outside would distract her, then returned to the sofa and peered down at Zylas with my hands on my hips—working hard to ignore his bare, muscular torso.

He squinted one eye open. I parted my lips, ready to fire off another question about demon kings.

"Your face is changing color," he noted.

My hands flew to my cheeks and my gaze darted to his bare chest. I stumbled back a step, bumping the coffee table. He observed my reaction with a calculating gleam in his eyes that I didn't like.

I hastily pointed at the last mini pie. "Hurry up and eat that. I want to wash the plate."

He plucked the pie off the dish, but before he could take a bite, his jaw popped open in yet another wide, sleepy yawn— giving me a fantastically unwanted view of the inside of his mouth. No manners at all, but he was a demon, so I couldn't really expect him to—

I blinked down at his face as he finished his yawn. Then I pounced.

He yipped in surprise when I grabbed his jaw.

"Hold up," I said breathlessly as I tried to open his mouth. "Let me see."

"What?" He twisted away. "No—"

As he spoke, his mouth opened enough for me to hook my fingers over his sharp teeth. "I want to look. It'll only take—"

"Geh awh!" he slurred around my fingers, holding his mini pie clear as he pushed me away with his other hand.

I put a knee on his chest to hold him down and pried his jaw open. Leaning over his face, I peered into his mouth.

He shoved me off the sofa.

I landed on the floor with a thud but barely noticed the jarring impact. "You don't have molars!"

He clamped his mouth shut and glowered at me.

"Well, okay, you have molars," I corrected excitedly. "But they're pointed like a cat's, not flat like a human's. You can't actually grind up food. *That's* why you never chew anything properly!"

"*Dilēran,*" he muttered under his breath. "*Adairedh'nā id sūd, ait eshathē kartismā dilēran.*"

I beamed, too delighted that I finally had an explanation for one of his strange quirks to let his insults annoy me.

Amalia's bedroom door swung open. She stuck her head out and scowled at us. "What are you two freaks doing out here?"

"He doesn't chew food properly because his molars are the wrong shape."

She pulled a disgusted face. "Were you looking into his mouth? That's gross."

I shrugged. "It was for science."

Zylas looked between us, eyes narrowed. Then, as though to make a point, he folded his mini pie in half, shoved the entire thing in his mouth, and swallowed it whole.

"Any progress?" I asked her.

"Define progress," she replied drily, leaning against the doorframe and flipping her long blond ponytail off her shoulder. "I heard back from three of my stepmom's relatives and they all claimed to have no clue where she is. Then I threatened to blackmail them. They still denied it, but I got four more numbers to call, including her former lawyer. I left a message with the lawyer's office and I'm waiting to hear back from the others."

"So … nothing," I concluded.

"Nothing at all. Oh, but I've started asking around about Claude. No one seems to know him, but I'll keep trying."

She retreated into her room. Deciding to leave Zylas alone, I scooped up Socks before she could sneak under the coffee table and returned to the kitchen. Zylas tracked my withdrawal, then leaned back into the sofa. As I dried and put away dishes, his eyes slid closed again. Even annoyed with me, he was too lazy today to do anything about it.

Smiling to myself, I dried the baking sheet. How did you take a demon's edge off? Why, simply feed him a dozen small apple pies.

It wasn't that my home-baked offerings softened his mood. I suspected it was physiological. By my best guess, sugar wasn't a significant part of a demon's diet, and large quantities of sweet desserts made him sleepy. I'd used that knowledge to my advantage several times over the past few weeks.

Finishing in the kitchen, I collected my photocopy of the grimoire, scrap paper, and my laptop. Since Zylas was hogging the sofa, I sat on the floor, set up my stuff on the coffee table, and started translating the next paragraph of the grimoire page. Zylas dozed, his tail hanging off the cushions and the barbed end flicking in a relaxed way. I scribbled on my page, working through several sentences, all of them describing the generalities of a Vh'alyir demon's appearance. Nothing shocking like the warning to never summon a Twelfth House demon.

Zylas didn't know why, before him, no demon of his House had ever been summoned, or I would've asked if he knew what that warning meant. I pondered it again, then resumed translating the rest of the page. From Amalia's room, the muffled hum of her sewing machine started up. She hadn't cracked a single Demonica text since leaving her father's house; instead, she devoted her free time to sewing projects—her custom-designed "hex clothes"—though I hadn't seen a finished garment yet.

The afternoon slid by, the dull monotony of Ancient Greek translation a nice change after yesterday's near-death adventure. The heavy overcast broke, allowing a rare return of December's elusive sun. I shifted around the coffee table so the golden light could warm my face, my back to the sofa. Zylas's hickory-and-leather scent teased my nose as I worked. Socks wandered into the middle of the room and sprawled in a sunny spot, her black fur gleaming.

As I puzzled over an unfamiliar word with my pencil poised above my notes, an unexpected realization slid through me: I felt content.

I lowered my pencil, my brow wrinkling. Behind me, Zylas's slow breathing was a quiet rhythm. Every few minutes, Amalia's sewing machine would whir energetically, then stop. Sprawled in the sun, Socks rolled onto her back, furry tail swishing.

This was the most peaceful I'd felt since my parents' deaths.

Tears clung to my eyelashes. Sniffing back a sob, I rose quietly and hurried into the bathroom. I blew my nose, dried my eyes, and smiled weakly at my reflection. It was okay to feel content. I could miss them and find my way toward a new happiness at the same time.

Opening the door, I paused.

Socks had left her sunny spot on the carpet. She now stood on the back of the sofa, her huge green eyes on the napping demon. Her tail flicked back and forth. Crouching, she cautiously stretched out a paw.

The kitten booped the demon on the nose.

His eyes snapped open. Socks cocked her head, ears perked forward, and lightly batted at his hair. He observed the kitten with that predatory stillness that always unnerved me. Socks hopped onto the armrest and stretched out her neck, whiskers twitching forward.

He finally moved—lifting his arm, reaching for the kitten. I tensed, certain he was about to shove poor little Socks right off the sofa.

He brushed his fingers across the top of her head. She inched closer, eagerly smelling the strange creature sharing her new domain, and he stroked her delicate ear like he'd never seen such a thing before.

A visceral memory hit me: Zylas gripping my wrist in one hand while he carefully traced my fingers. The first time he had touched me—first time he had touched any human. Curiosity had motivated his gentle touch—right up until he'd dragged me into the summoning circle and asked what my blood looked like.

Before I could decide if I should rescue Socks, the muffled trill of a ringing phone broke the quiet. Socks hopped off the sofa and Zylas looked toward Amalia's room.

"Hello? Oh, yeah … Okay … Sure, I'll let her know."

Her door opened. Amalia scanned the living room and spotted me. She waved her cell.

"Is your phone dead? That was Zora. She's been trying to reach you."

My phone was in my room … on silent. Oops. "What did she say?"

"She wants you to meet her at the guild. She's got an update on the vampires."

An update? Maybe, finally, we could get somewhere with all this. "Then I'd better get going."

15

I PUSHED OPEN THE GUILD DOOR and a wave of conversation rolled out, followed by the aroma of hot French fries and spicy chicken wings. A dozen people were scattered throughout the pub, sitting at the tables in twos and threes, eating food or chatting casually.

A few faces were familiar: the assistant guild master, her brown hair sticking to her face as she rushed behind the bar; Girard, the first officer, poring over papers with a middle-aged man I didn't know; a short, skinny young man with round sunglasses, looking at something on his phone; and the elderly diviner Rose, easy to spot with her turquoise eyeglasses and pink knitted cap.

The diviner gestured me toward her table, beaming eagerly, but I pretended to misunderstand and merely waved. As intriguing as my first crystal ball séance had been, I wasn't in the mood for another one.

The door behind me swung open, chiming loudly. Zora grinned as she entered the pub. "Good timing! Let's sit."

I followed her to a table in the corner and she shrugged off her coat, revealing a black corset-style top that laced up at the front. I instantly wanted one, even though I'd never be brave enough to wear something like that.

"No glasses yet?" she asked, sounding guilty.

"I put in an order but it takes a few days." I blinked against the uncomfortable dryness in my eyes. "I'm wearing contacts."

"Oh, good. I was worried you'd have to go around half blind until you got new glasses." She dug into her jacket and pulled out a folded map. "Let's get to it."

She spread the map across the table. Vancouver's downtown was unmistakable, and red and purple marker highlighted two dozen locations, most of them clustered around the downtown core, with a few outliers in Gastown, Chinatown, and Yaletown.

"Felix did his magic with the vamp's phone," Zora said, smiling at her pun. "The vampires called the same number three or four times a night for the past two weeks. Felix narrowed down an address—we think it's this building right here."

She poked at a blue circle only a few blocks from the big downtown library.

"Is it an office building?" I asked. "That seems like a strange place for vampires."

"I thought so too, but it turns out the building has been closed for renovations for almost a year now." She arched an eyebrow. "Prime vamp real estate."

I nodded.

"These other marks are the locations of all the exterminations performed over the past six weeks by local guilds. Thirty-six vamps in total. In comparison, the total vampires exterminated in the six *months* prior to this was thirty-two."

"That's a big increase."

"A *huge* increase. The red marks are nests of mature vampires. The purple marks are new vampires."

I counted fourteen purple blotches. "Is that a lot?"

"I've exterminated more new vampires in the past month than I have in the last five years." Her eyes clouded. "No one likes hunting new vamps. We usually don't get the chance because they tend to fly under the radar. We don't catch wind of them until …"

"Until what?" I asked, unnerved by the tightness in her expression.

"The amount of blood a vampire craves increases over time. A new vamp might bite a person once or twice a week, and doesn't consume enough blood to do any real harm. Nested vampires, on the other hand, tend to leave unconscious victims lying around in alleys every night, so we can home in on their locations that way."

She stared down at the map for a long moment. "New vamps often don't understand what's happening. They deny it, resist the urges … Even if they figure out they're a vampire, they'll fight the changes in their mind and body for as long as they can. But there's no cure. There's no way to stop the transformation. They'll eventually need blood every night, and ultimately, they'll degenerate into a crazed monster like the old vamp we took out.

"You can't explain all that to a new vamp. You can't convince them it's better to die now, with their mind intact, than waste away and hurt a lot of innocent people in the process. No one wants to believe they're doomed, especially not a desperate, confused person who doesn't know what's wrong with them."

She gazed unseeingly at the map. "So you just kill them, as quickly and cleanly as possible."

Silence settled over us, and my heart ached, not only for the innocent people who lost their lives to vampiric infection, but for the mythics like Zora who had to kill them to prevent its spread.

"I'm sorry," I whispered.

"It's a mercy. Sometimes, it can be hard to remember that, but it's truly a mercy to give them a swift end." She pulled herself upright in her chair. "So, yes, we've had more vampires in general, and more new vamps as well. The reason we've found all these new ones is they were involved with the nested vampires."

My brow furrowed. "What do you mean?"

"Infection usually occurs from a feeding, but it seems now like these vampires are deliberately creating and almost … rearing new vamps."

"They're building up their numbers?" I realized.

"If they are, that's a level of foresight and planning I've never seen from them." She pointed at the markings. "The reason I wanted to meet was to see if you could spot any patterns connected to your Demonica investigation."

I leaned over the map. After a moment, I found the Crow and Hammer's location, then the Grand Grimoire about fifteen blocks southwest. Uncle Jack's house was across the harbor in West Vancouver, and Claude's townhouse was south of False Creek—outside the downtown peninsula entirely.

"No," I said slowly. "I don't see any connections or patterns, but that address—the office building—is right in the middle of all the vampire activity."

"I noticed that as well." She thumped back against her chair, almost tipping it over. "Next step is investigating the building—and probably an extermination. If there's someone masterminding all this, I'd bet my next bounty check they're in there."

That's what I was thinking too, and it made me very nervous.

"Based on this activity, we could be facing a large nest. I'm already assembling a team." She grimaced. "I wish Aaron, Kai, and Ezra were in town. They're our strongest combat team outside of guild leadership. We could use their help."

My mind jumped to the profile of Ezra I'd found in Claude's apartment, but Zora continued before I could bring it up.

"I want to put a rush on this in case the vampires decide to switch locations. Who knows if they'll realize we're on to them. I'm aiming to hit them tomorrow morning."

"That's fast," I stammered.

"No time to waste, right?"

An awkward moment pulsed between us. Even though I suspected I knew her answer, I asked anyway. "Can I come for the … mission?"

"I'm sorry, Robin," she said kindly. "I'm sure you could contribute, but I need experienced combat mythics who know the drill. It'll be too dangerous for a newbie."

Hiding my wince, I mumbled, "I understand."

"I'll keep you posted on what we find."

"Okay."

Another uncomfortable silence. Words bubbled in my throat and I fought them back, not wanting to further embarrass myself, but they built and built until they burst from my lips.

"How can I be strong too?"

Zora blinked.

Ugh. Wow. I couldn't have phrased that in a cringier way if I'd tried. "I mean … I feel so useless. I'm the smallest and weakest person of anyone I know, but you're so tough and capable, even though you're … you're … petite," I finished lamely.

"Robin, you killed an unbound demon."

"No, my *demon* killed it. I didn't do anything but stand there—and control him," I added hastily. "But without him, I'm just pathetic."

Planting her hands on the table, Zora sat forward, a stern gleam in her stare. "You survived the storm drains, which were crawling with vampires. That's freakin' badass, girl. You're tougher than you think."

My mouth opened but I didn't know what to say.

Zora relaxed into her chair. "If you want combat training, tell a guild officer and they'll arrange it. The harder you train, the faster you'll learn." She scanned me up and down. "To start, you could use some basic tools."

"Like what?"

"Proper gear, for starters. A weapon requires training, but self-defense artifacts wouldn't be a bad idea."

I liked the sound of that. "What sort of self-defense artifacts?"

"Personally, I prefer something from the *impello* set for newbies. Simple but effective."

"A push spell? I've used the cantrip, but …" But it wasn't very powerful.

"I was thinking something with more *oomph* than that. An advanced artifact."

My nose wrinkled. Thanks to the bounty from killing Tahēsh, my bank account looked pretty good right now, but seeing as I didn't have a job, I needed to make the money last. "I'm not sure I can afford an artifact like that."

"Ramsey could get you a good deal. Or one of our sorcerers could make one for you. Lim, Jia, and Weldon are all skilled artifact engineers."

Make one? Why had it never occurred to me that I could *make* an artifact—something better than a simple cantrip—to protect myself?

"Does the guild have any resources for Arcana engineering?" I asked eagerly.

Zora laughed. "Someone skipped giving you a tour." She folded up her map and pushed away from the table. "Come on, I'll show you."

I hurried after her toward the stairs that led to the upper floors. Waving at Rose, who tried again to summon me over, I trotted to the second floor—a room as large as the pub below but filled with worktables, computer kiosks, whiteboards, and an intriguing row of bookshelves at the back.

Zora kept going to the third level—the domain of the guild officers. Instead of entering the three-desk office, she turned down a short hall. A sign hung on the door at the end, white with no text, and a container holding several fat markers was attached to the wall beside the jamb.

When Zora plucked a marker from the container, I expected her to write on the sign. Instead, she pressed the thick felt tip right to the door and drew a swift rune across it in vivid pink.

"*Recludo*," she declared.

A shimmer rippled over the wood, followed by the loud clack of a lock. A spell unlocked by a rune? That was clever—and meant only Arcana mythics could enter.

"Get a good look at that," she told me as she capped the marker. "It'll fade in about ten seconds."

The pink lines were already losing their vibrancy. I squinted, memorizing the shape—a variation of a common cantrip—then nodded. Zora threw the door open.

I followed her inside, my jaw dropping.

The first thing I noticed was the three-foot-diameter circle drawn in the middle of the room. The smooth, polished black floor looked like poured glass, without a single seam, crack, or blemish. Next, I spotted the huge skylight built into the flat ceiling above the circle, the glass speckled with raindrops. A worktable and a stool occupied one side of the room. On the other side was a long counter with tiny, neatly labeled drawers underneath it and cupboards above. The back of the room contained a massive bookshelf overflowing with leather-bound texts.

"The Arcana Atrium!" Zora pointed at the ceiling. "Skylight for spells that need sunlight, moonlight, starlight, all that jazz. The cupboards have basic ingredients and components, and if anything is missing, they probably have it downstairs in the alchemy lab. There's a testing room down there too, for more experimental spellwork."

She opened a cupboard. A tangle of rulers and giant protractors tried to fall on her head and she slammed it shut. "See? Everything you need. And ..."

Striding to the bookshelves, she gestured dramatically. "And all the spell compilations, grimoires, and instructional texts you could want. Unless you plan to jump right into abjuration or something. We're not *that* advanced."

Grinning at my stunned expression, she perused the shelves. "Let's see … this one? No … aha! This one."

She slid a book off the shelf and flipped it open. Stepping around the circle on the floor, I joined her.

"This book has a whole bunch of *impello* variations. Some of these—wow, look at *this* beast of a spell!—yeah, some are pretty demanding. How far into your apprenticeship are you?"

"Yeah," I said vaguely, avoiding her question about my apprenticeship. Admitting I'd been a sleeper—a non-practicing mythic—up until a few weeks ago would be excessively dumb. Though I'd never officially apprenticed, I'd studied enough Arcana to sort of count as a sorceress. Maybe.

Zora handed me the book. "See what looks doable. You could make a few simple artifacts and try them out before investing in a high-quality one."

"Good idea," I breathed, drinking in the diagrams and instructions that filled the open pages of the book.

Chuckling at my obvious distraction, Zora headed for the door. "If you want to start something, check the schedule clipboard to make sure no one else has reserved the room. And don't forget to turn the sign over!"

By the time I dragged my stare off the book, she'd disappeared through the door.

"Turn the sign?" I muttered.

Balancing the book on one palm, I crossed to the door and flipped the sign over. On its opposite side, bold black text read,

"Arcana In Progress." Under that, in red marker, someone had scrawled, "So keep out, losers!"

I settled the sign in place, text showing, and closed the door. Sliding onto the stool at the worktable, I began paging through the book, skipping past the easy spells to the more difficult ones. The room was quiet, the smell of books, leather, herbs, and a hint of something burnt tickling my nose. Part of me instantly relaxed, while another coiled with building tension.

I was going to make an artifact. I was about to do *real magic*.

Cantrips were the most basic form of sorcery—building blocks more than usable tools. The next level up was a hex—a reusable cantrip. But a sorcerer's true power lay in artifacts. Spells of immense power and complexity, some of which took hours, days, or even weeks to construct, could be sealed into portable objects and triggered by a simple incantation.

Zora's blood trackers were a type of artifact. For myself, I wanted something more impressive, something that would make an adversary think twice about attacking me—assuming I could pull it off. Considering I'd never made an artifact before in my life, that might be a stretch.

At least if I screwed it up, no one would see. This room was comfortingly private.

The infernus tucked inside my shirt buzzed with heat. Red light sprang off it and Zylas took form beside the table.

I sighed. "What have I told you about popping out whenever you think I'm alone?"

"But you are alone."

"What if I wasn't?"

"Then you would not have thought about it, *na?*"

Rolling my eyes, I returned my attention to the book. Each spell had a short description of what the resultant artifact would do, and I skimmed through them, searching for something good. Zylas wandered to the room's other end. Sniffing at the air, he opened a drawer, peered inside, then shut it. Opened the next one, checked its contents, closed it. Opened the next.

Exploring the drawers and cabinets kept him busy for almost ten minutes. I flipped back through the pages and reread a spell description. Defensive, reasonably powerful, and not too difficult to engineer. This was the artifact I was going to make.

The back of my neck prickled and I looked up.

Zylas stood beside me, studying the page. "What is this?"

"This," I replied, sliding off the stool, "is a set of instructions for creating magic. I'm going to make a spell."

"You are going to cast *vīsh*?"

"Well … more like build magic than cast it." I opened the cabinets in search of the tools I needed. "Mages and psychics can use their magic instantly, like you do, but that's not how sorcery works. Aside from cantrips, my magic involves putting spells into an object. We call those artifacts. Some can be used over and over, while others can only be used once."

Zylas followed, watching curiously. "We have *vīsh* like that too. That we put into objects."

"You do?" I turned excitedly toward him, my arms full of rulers of different shapes and angles. "Like what?"

He tapped the armor plate over his heart. "This is magic so it does not break."

"Did you make it yourself?" I asked as I piled the rulers beside the circle on the floor.

"Who else would make it?"

"I don't know." Returning to the cabinets, I searched around until I found drawing utensils—odd markers that smelled like candy canes, and a spray bottle I assumed was for cleanup. "Do demons trade or barter for things they can't make?"

"Sometimes. Or we kill and take what we want."

"How are there any demons left?" I muttered, placing the textbook beside the circle for easy reference. "I'm surprised you haven't wiped your whole species out of existence."

"We used to be many more." He crouched beside me as I flipped to a step-by-step diagram that illustrated how to draw the spell array. "The oldest demons say we did not always kill so much."

As I laid a ruler across the circle, I looked up. "You didn't?"

"They say that long ago, *Dīnen* were powerful and wise. They commanded my kind to be more ..." He canted his head. "To hunt each other less."

"What changed?"

"The powerful *Dīnen* were summoned and never returned. The next *Dīnen* were summoned away, and the next. The new *Dīnen* were younger and more *zh'ūltis*."

An uncomfortable chill ran through me. "Zylas ..." Bits and pieces of comments he'd made spun through my head. "How often are *Dīnen* summoned?"

He gazed at me, somber, almost sad, as though pitying my lack of understanding. "Only *Dīnen* are summoned, *drādah*."

The chill in my blood deepened with disbelief. "What do you mean? How can *only* demon kings be summoned? That would mean *all* the demons here in my world are *Dīnen*."

"Yes. We are all oldest of our Houses, given the power of *Dīnen* when the one before us dies or disappears."

"But ... but there are only twelve Houses." Shaking my head, I tried to make the math work. "And—and—how many demons are summoned each year? I don't even know—"

"Hundreds and hundreds," he answered. "Most from the third rank. Their *Dīnen* do not rule. They disappear before any of their House know who was next."

Horror muted my voice.

"*Dīnen* were wise in the old times, but now they only think about the short future, because they will not live to see the long future. There is no one to tell us to stop killing."

Demon summoning was, more often than not, a death sentence for the demons called into our world, but I'd never considered that summoning might have a larger effect on demonkind—that we were destabilizing their society. That we were stealing their leaders, the oldest and wisest males of their species, and making them our slaves.

Did summoners know they were calling the demons' kings away, one after another, so swiftly that some Houses had lost all structure? But how could they know? What demon, trapped in a circle and forced to give up his autonomy for a slim chance to return home, would reveal that?

No wonder demons hated humans.

Too disturbed by this new knowledge to ask more, I returned my attention to my spell and began the painstaking process of drawing the array—the longest and most tedious part of artifact construction. Over fifty lines and curves would fill the circle by the time I was done, but despite having to measure each angle about six times to ensure I wasn't screwing anything up, excitement buzzed through me. My very first spell!

"What is all this?" Zylas picked up a monster-sized protractor and turned it over in his hands. "This is magic?"

"No, these are tools for making spells. I have to draw it all out very carefully. See this here?" I pointed to the hexagon I'd drawn inside the circle, its corners touching the white ring.

"This contains the spell and directs the magic inward. And this"—I indicated a triangle with one line missing, positioned like a downward-pointing arrow with its tip outside the circle—"will direct the power into whatever object I place here." I touched the small circle I'd drawn under the triangle's point. "It all has to be exactly perfect to work."

Turning to the book, I flipped three pages ahead and showed him the finished array. "I have to add more lines to direct the different elements, and runes to dictate how I want the magical forces to behave."

I expected a scoffing "*zh'ūltis*" but he was frowning at my book.

"You will draw this on the floor? And that will make the *vīsh*?"

"Yes. When I'm done, the magic will be imbued into an artifact."

Another frowning appraisal. I waited. His tail swished, then he sat beside me, legs sprawled out, and propped himself up on one arm.

My eyes narrowed. "Aren't you going to comment? Tell me how dumb and useless and pointlessly complicated this magic is?"

He smirked, which only increased my defensiveness. "I already knew *vīsh hh'ainun* was weak and slow."

Ah, the insult. Finally. I felt better now. "Well, we can't *all* wave our hands and make magic appear out of thin air like you."

Smirk widening to show a hint of teeth, Zylas pulled the book away from me.

"Hey!"

I reached for the text but hesitated, confused by his intense focus. He analyzed the detailed arrangement of lines, angles, shapes, and runes, the seconds ticking past.

At three minutes and fifty seconds—I counted—he handed the book back to me. Answering my unspoken question with the return of his wolfish smile, he raised his arm. Crimson light sparked across his hand and veined his wrist. He spread his fingers as concentration tightened his face.

A glowing red circle flashed into existence, hovering an inch above the floor, perfectly aligned with the white one permanently marked on the smooth surface. But his spell was … was …

I looked down at the diagram in the book. Back up at his glowing red spell. Pure demonic power … in the shape of an Arcana array. *The* Arcana array I'd barely begun to create, except his was complete, showing every line and rune. Based on how perfectly his spell aligned with my work in progress, I didn't doubt that every angle was flawless.

"How …" I whispered.

He relaxed his hand and the glow died away. "My *vīsh* is not so different, but I do not *draw* it. So slow. *Gh'idrūlis.*"

"Then how do you …" I recalled his careful study of the diagram. "You *memorized* it?"

"My *vīsh* must be perfect too. I learn and learn it, practice it until I can never forget."

His insane memory—the way he could memorize a thousand puzzle pieces in a few minutes—suddenly made a whole lot of sense. All those complex, tangled demonic spells I'd seen him cast … they didn't appear from some mysterious spell cache in the ether; he'd memorized them all in perfect detail, down to the exact angles and tiniest runes.

"Wow," I whispered.

His lips curved, but I wasn't sure if he was gloating or flattered by my awe.

"Are there limits?" I asked. "How many spells have you memorized?"

"I do not know the number. Hundreds and hundreds." He leaned back again, braced on one hand. "Sometimes it is hard to think of the one I want."

"But if you know it, you can cast it instantly?"

"*Hnn.* I need … some seconds? I must see it perfect and clear in my mind before I cast. Bigger spells are more difficult. If it is wrong, it is …" He tipped his head back, gazing at the skylight. "It is dangerous."

I absently ran my finger down the page of the book. "That sounds like it requires a lot of concentration."

"*Var.* If I am fighting, I do not always have time to cast."

"Still, your magic is really powerful and faster than mine. But," I added brightly, "mine will still be pretty fast once it's ready, assuming I can make it right."

He waited, with only the occasional impatient scoff, as I resumed building out the array. Though he'd memorized it in a few minutes, his reproduction of the spell was powerless. Anyone, mythic or human, could speak an artifact's trigger incantation to activate it, but only Arcana mythics like me could *create* them. I was a conduit, and through the process of creating the array, my passive magic would infuse it.

It took me two hours of careful, intensive work to finish, every line and angle measured and remeasured. Then I spent another hour adding the runes in painstaking detail.

When I went to the cupboards, Zylas stirred out of his bored stupor. I collected bags of iron powder, salt crystals, copper calcinate, and black sulfur, as well as a jar of oil. Using the scales on the counter, I measured out exact amounts and added them to the small, circular nodes I'd drawn into the array.

Finally, I selected a thin rectangle of pure iron the size of a domino. With a small silver marker, I drew three runes down the front as shown in the text, and placed it in the node at the point of the open triangle—the spot where all the magic would be directed.

"There," I declared proudly, standing over my work. "It's ready."

Zylas wandered to my side. He stared down at the array, dotted with piles of colored powder and three drops of oil.

He waited a beat. "Now what?"

"Now"—I consulted the book—"the array needs to charge for at least sixteen hours."

"Charge?"

"Arcana is powered by the natural magical energies that flow across the earth. Spells like this absorb that energy, then expend it when they're triggered."

He scrunched his nose. "You spent *hours* making this, now you must wait even longer? So slow, *drādah*."

I shrugged. "Making the spells *is* slow. Some of these"—I patted the book—"have to charge for *months* before the sorcerer can complete them."

"What will you do while you wait?"

"Well …" I drew in a deep breath. "Zora thinks she found the vampires' hideout—where the ones controlling all of this might be. She's taking a team in tomorrow morning."

His bored lassitude vanished as he focused his full attention on me.

"I'm not invited on their mission. And even if I were, I couldn't search for answers with a bunch of witnesses. If we're going to learn what's really going on, and why the vampires are so interested in Uncle Jack, I think we need to go see this place for ourselves … before she and her team get there."

Zylas glanced at the skylight, the dark glass reflecting the room and my Arcana array back at us. "Then we have until the sun returns."

Which meant we needed to go now—when the vampires were at their strongest.

16

THIS VAMPIRE "LAIR" was several steps up from the last one. Not that the last one had qualified as a lair, really. I didn't know what to call them. Hideouts? Dens? … Habitats?

I lurked in a shadowy doorway across the street from the building Zora had marked on her map. Tucked deeper in the shadows behind me was Zylas. His heat radiated into my back as he studied the building over the top of my head. Traffic zoomed past, headlights glaring in the misty rain.

We were in the heart of downtown. In fact, we weren't far from the storm drain I'd escaped through last night.

Neither the tallest nor the nicest building on the block, the tower was anonymous among its neighbors. It could be full of offices or condos, and stood out from the rest only in that the front doors were blocked off by construction barricades and the second through fifth floors had plywood in place of windows.

"What do you think?" I whispered to Zylas.

"Too many *hh'ainun* here. They will see me."

Though darkness had fallen, it was still early evening and the remnants of rush-hour traffic was whizzing by. Zylas, with his horns, tail, red eyes, and armor, was a tad noticeable.

"I'll go around to the back," I told him, "and let you know when it's safe to come out again."

Crimson light rushed over him and his power returned to the infernus. I hugged my arms to my chest—having lost my coat, I was wearing three sweaters instead—and ventured into the light rain.

A few minutes of nonchalant ambling later, I entered the back alley and whispered, "Okay, Zylas."

He materialized beside me, and together we studied the new view—a blank wall with a loading bay and a single, featureless steel door. Red light flared up Zylas's arm, forming a pattern of runes, and he pressed two fingers to the thin gap between the door and frame. Crimson power blazed out of the gap, then he pushed on the steel.

The door swung open.

I squinted suspiciously. "Where did you learn to do that?"

"It is how the metal box in the summoner's house was opened."

Uncle Jack's safe, broken open with demonic magic. Zylas learned too fast for comfort.

A dark hallway waited for us. The dusty smell of drywall hung in the air, and a layer of white grit covered the concrete floor, yet to be finished with carpet or tile. I followed Zylas, my heart thudding so loudly I wouldn't have been surprised if it was making more noise than my shoes.

The corridor led us to an unfinished lobby, lit only by the streetlamps outside. The ceiling was full of missing tiles, and bundles of wire and unattached ductwork hung from the dark space above. Steel studs were piled beside a stack of drywall, buckets were scattered around, and extension cords snaked across the floor. An industrial fan pointed toward the closed and blockaded front doors.

I nudged my toe through the dust. The half-completed construction appeared abandoned.

Zylas angled toward the opposite end of the lobby, his steps silent. He paused at a door, then pushed it open. The soft clack of the latch echoed through the dark concrete stairwell on the other side as he started up the steps.

"Up?" I whispered, hesitating with one hand on the door. The basement seemed more bloodsucking-monster-friendly. "Are you sure?"

He glanced back, eyes glowing. "I smell fresh blood."

Gulping, I eased the door closed. The instant it snicked shut, utter darkness plunged over the stairwell. There were no windows and no lights.

"Zylas?" I whispered faintly. "I can't see anything."

His softly glowing eyes reappeared as he turned. Judging by their location, he was already halfway up the first flight of stairs. His eyes drew closer as he returned, then warm hands touched my wrists. He drew my arms around his neck, then hooked his fingers under my knee and tugged. I pulled myself onto his back and locked my legs around his waist.

As he trotted up the stairs, I sighed glumly. "I really am useless, aren't I?"

"Yes."

I lightly smacked his right shoulder—the unarmored one. "Don't agree with me. You should say something encouraging."

He glided up the next flight. "Why?"

"To make me feel better."

A pause. "Why?"

"Do you ever do anything that doesn't benefit you somehow?"

"Like what?"

His gait leveled out as he turned away from the next flight. His shoulders shifted, then I heard a door open. The faintest light, leaking around the plywood blocking the windows, scarcely penetrated the darkness of what looked like a hallway.

Seeming to realize it wasn't enough light for a human to navigate by, Zylas didn't try to put me down. He continued onward with cautious steps.

I wiggled against his back, getting more comfortable, and he hooked his arms under my knees to better support my weight. "Okay, here's a hypothetical situation."

"I do not know that word."

"Hypothetical? In this case, it means imagining an event as if it's real, so you can decide how you would react. So, imagine you're walking through the woods and you hear someone calling for help."

He paused, inhaled through his nose, then turned down a corridor that led away from the boarded windows and their weak light. "This sounds *zh'ūltis*."

"Just play along, okay?" I put my mouth closer to his ear so I could whisper more quietly. "You hear a call for help in the woods. What do you do?"

"I would see who is calling."

Surprised, I allowed a spark of hope. "What if you found … a woman? She's trapped under a fallen tree. What would you do next?"

He paused again and released one of my knees. The clack of a door. He leaned forward, sniffing at the air, then withdrew and walked on. Away from the windows, the darkness was eerily complete, and I doubted Zylas could've navigated it without his infrared vision.

"Who is the woman?" he asked.

"What do you mean?"

"The trapped female. Do I know her?"

"No, you don't. She's a stranger."

"Is she a demon or *hh'ainun*?"

"Uh … a demon."

"Then I would flee before she saw me." He dropped into a crouch and I squeaked, clutching his back. I felt his arm move. "There is old blood here."

"Are there vampires close by?"

"They have walked here, but not in many days." Rising, he hitched me higher on his back and continued on. "I can hear voices. They are close but I do not know how to get to them."

We must have come in the wrong door. I was betting there was a closer stairwell to wherever the owners of the voices were stationed.

"We'll find a way eventually," I assured him. "We don't need to rush."

"The longer it takes, the longer I have to carry you."

"Oh, come on. I'm not that heavy."

His shoulders twitched in annoyance. "You are not heavy at all, but you keep talking in my ear. *Mailēshta*."

I smiled into the darkness and leaned close to his ear again. "So why would you run away from a trapped female demon?"

"Because she might kill me."

Oh, right. He'd told me that female demons had magic more powerful than males. "Maybe she would be grateful to you for saving her."

"Or she would kill me."

I rolled my eyes. "Okay, fine. Let's say it's a female human. What would you do?"

"*Hnn.*" He walked a few steps in silence. "How is she trapped?"

"Under a tree. You could lift it no problem," I added to make this easy for him.

Another thoughtful silence. "Why is she there? In the woods under a tree?"

"Does it matter?"

"It is suspicious."

I huffed with impatience. "Pretend there's nothing suspicious about her. She isn't armed or dangerous. She's just a trapped human who needs help or she'll die."

He rounded an invisible corner and prowled onward.

"Well?" I persisted. "Would you save her?"

"You want me to say yes."

"Of course I do!" My heart was sinking, leaving an unpleasant burn in my chest. "Why wouldn't you? You could save her life with almost no effort. It would cost you nothing."

He crouched again, inhaling through his nose. "Your *hypothetical* does not make sense, *drādah*. I cannot be seen by any *hh'ainun* or you would be in danger. You told me this."

"What if you could save her without being seen?" I asked desperately.

He held himself still, either thinking or listening. "Why are you upset?"

"I'm not upset."

A soft scuff behind us, and I imagined his tail swishing across the floor.

"You are lying."

Damn it. I'd forgotten he could tell when I lied. "I want you to say you would save the woman, because if you wouldn't save her, then you're …"

"I am what?"

"Evil," I whispered.

He said nothing, and in his silence was the answer I feared. He wouldn't save a helpless person from certain death. His questions revealed his thought process. Did he know the person? Were they dangerous? Why were they there? In other words, he wanted to know the risks or rewards for *him*.

Selfish. A selfish demon who only cared about himself.

"Why?" I whispered miserably. "Why wouldn't you help someone who was hurt or trapped?"

Another scuff of his tail. "I hear voices behind this door."

I gripped his shoulders. "What door? Where?"

"The one right here. If I open it, they will probably see."

Pushing the hypothetical scenario out of my head—he was right, it had been stupid—I focused on our mission. How would we get into the room without being seen? Squeezing my eyes shut since I couldn't see anyway, I tried to think of a different way in. The unfinished lobby materialized in my mind's eye.

"Zylas," I whispered. "What does the ceiling in here look like?"

He looked up, his head so close that his hair brushed across my cheek. His muscles tensed, then he stood.

"*Var*," he whispered. "Good idea, *drādah*."

FINALLY, THERE WAS LIGHT. It streaked up from the room below through rectangular openings where the ceiling's plastic panels were missing. Thick wiring and shiny gray ducts wound among steel crossbeams, and a metal grid stretched into the farthest corners of the building, unbroken by the rooms and halls underneath.

The crawlspace, hidden between the ceiling of the room below and the floor of the level above, was barely two and a half feet high, forcing me to lay face down with my arms and legs braced on metal supports. The steel bruised my skin as I held my torso off the flimsy white panel under me. Zylas had disappeared into the darkness, crawling noiselessly across the beams. The ceiling was too low for a piggyback ride.

As I waited, voices drifted to my ears, their words inaudible. One male voice, one female. Conversational tones.

Crimson eyes appeared as Zylas crawled under a silver duct. He moved cautiously, navigating over and around heavy crossbeams and bundles of wiring. The muscles in his arms and thighs flexed with strength I didn't have as he shifted across the awkward, fragile obstacle course.

He braced himself on the grid beside me. "Vampires in three rooms."

"How many?"

"I cannot see into the third room. In the others, there are *rēsh*. Ten," he corrected, translating for me.

Ten vampires plus an unknown number in another room? Well, this would probably break Zora's record for the largest nest she'd ever encountered.

"In one room," he whispered, shifting so close his warm breath teased my ear, "there are … papers. Do you want to see this?"

"Yes," I breathed. "Which way?"

He started cautiously across the ceiling. I crawled after him, trying to keep up but not rushing. The slightest noise could betray our presence. My muscles burned from the effort of holding my body rigid above the panels as I ducked under hanging wires and cables. The murmuring of voices from below grew louder.

Zylas crept up to a missing panel, the rectangular opening lit from below. I wobbled over to him, arms trembling. Talk about a workout. It was like nonstop planking and pushups.

As I puffed out a pained breath, I realized I couldn't hold myself above the panels. My muscles were too tired—which left me only one option. Brow scrunching and cheeks already heating, I put an arm across Zylas. His head tilted in my direction as I pulled myself on top of him and lay across his back, letting him support us both.

He *had* said I wasn't heavy. I refused to feel guilty.

Holding his shoulders, I peered into the spacious room below. Surrounded by closed doors and scattered with abandoned construction supplies, it would probably be filled with cubicles once the reno was finished. The farthest end was set up like a slumber party—rows of sleeping bags, pillows, yoga mats for mattresses, and a few extra blankets.

In a different corner, someone had laid a sheet of drywall across a double stack of twenty-gallon buckets, and loose papers and folders were arranged on top in three tidy piles.

A few feet from the makeshift table, a man and woman sat on the floor. They'd propped an old lamp, its lone bulb glowing half-heartedly, on top of a dusty piece of equipment with a yellow tank on the bottom. An air compressor? Three red jerry cans were lined up nearby, as though the tool's owner had expected to return the next day to resume work.

The woman was peering at a monitor, set up on the floor beside a black computer with severed cords hanging off it. Claude's computer, stolen from his townhouse.

The man threw a handful of papers into an empty bucket. "Found anything yet?"

His companion glanced up from the monitor, her brown ponytail bobbing. "Everything important is encrypted. This isn't my area of expertise."

"You're a computer science major."

"That doesn't make me a hacker. I didn't even get to graduate," she added, bitter accusation layering the statement.

The other man shrugged as he skimmed another paper. "We can't change what happened to us. Just be glad you were turned around the time Lord Vasilii arrived."

Lord Vasilii? What kind of name was that? It sounded like a cartoon villain.

"You're too new to know," the man continued in a low voice, "but we used to hide in sewers all day hoping the hunters wouldn't find us. All we could think about was blood. But in the last two months, Lord Vasilii changed all of that."

"How?" she asked uncertainly.

"When he's nearby … can't you feel it? Maybe you can't yet, but it's like being new again. It's like my head is clear for the first time in years. I can think about more than blood." He tossed another page into his discard bucket. "He makes this life almost bearable."

The woman's shoulders drooped as though she were discomforted rather than reassured by his words.

He tilted a few papers toward her. "This looks promising."

She hunched more. "Add it to the pile."

Pushing to his feet, the man placed the new pages on the makeshift table. He returned to his spot and read the next document. Were those papers also from Claude's townhouse? Or could they be from Uncle Jack's safe?

Zylas, I thought clearly, not wanting to speak aloud with the vampires so close. *I need those papers.*

Shifting back from the opening, he canted his head in a silent command. I slid off him and onto the nearby crossbeam. He drew his legs up, positioning himself in a compact crouch at the edge. Faint red magic veined across his hands.

He hopped through the gap and landed on the concrete with barely a thump, but both vampires turned at the sound. He was already flashing toward them. His hands closed around their throats, crushing their windpipes so they couldn't cry out, then crimson talons sprouted from his fingers and he rammed them into the vampires' chests. Catching both his victims as they collapsed, he eased them silently to the floor.

My heart twisted as the young computer science major slumped lifelessly, and I reminded myself about Zora's hard-earned wisdom: Killing them was a mercy.

I clambered off the beam, scooted closer, and dangled my feet through the hole. Returning to the opening, Zylas reached up. I pushed off the edge. He caught me and set me down.

Too many blank doors—probably leading to future executive offices—looked into this large room and it made me nervous. I turned to the papers. The sheet the male vampire had added contained a handwritten list of names and phone numbers titled "Emergency Contacts." I recognized Uncle Jack's messy scrawl.

I scooped the papers up and clamped them to my chest. For good measure, I snatched the other piles too.

"This is what I need," I whispered. "Let's—"

"Do you smell that?"

The sharp question, muffled by a wall, echoed from somewhere nearby, but I didn't know which room the sound had come from.

Zylas snatched me by the waist and boosted me toward the ceiling. I grabbed the lip and scrambled into the gap, and he jumped up after me. He rolled away from the opening, tail sweeping up into the darkness.

Footsteps thudded across the concrete.

"What?" a shocked voice barked. "They're dead?"

Not daring to move, I peeked sideways through the gap. All I could see were the slain vampires' legs. At least three new figures had gathered around the bodies.

"Stabbed through the heart," another vampire gasped, crouching to examine the body. "I've never seen wounds like this."

"What could have …" Stiffening, the third vampire faced something I couldn't see.

The crouching vamp shot to his full height, going equally rigid as footsteps much quieter than the others drew closer. A long pause.

"Find the intruders."

The low, dry voice issued the command without inflection, and the vampires leaped to obey. I held my breath as they spread throughout the room, opening office doors and searching amongst the construction supplies. They didn't react to my and Zylas's scents, so I was guessing they were only sensitive to the smell of blood. Good thing neither of us was bleeding.

Zylas, I thought, *we need to get out of here.*

He scanned the darkness, tense and focused. Holding the bundle of papers against my chest, I looked around for the quickest way out of the crawlspace. Not far to my left, two large, round duct lines descended from a square hole in the floor above us. I crawled closer, mentally calling Zylas to follow me. Beside the ducting, I peered up. Was that an unfinished opening above?

As vampire voices and the clatters of their search filled the room below, I cautiously pulled myself up. Ducting and wires ran through the spacious gap—large enough for Zylas to fit easily. I reached up and found the open edge above.

"*Drādah,*" he hissed.

"I can fit," I breathed, feet braced on a beam as I pulled myself up one-handed, holding the folders tightly with my other arm. "The wall up here isn't finished. I can get onto the next floor."

"*Drādah—*"

Adrenaline flowing hot in my veins, I clambered onto the edge and squinted into the room of the floor above. A small office, perhaps? The empty doorway across from me was a black rectangle, too dark to make out anything beyond it.

Zylas, hurry up and …

My thoughts fizzled. My mind went blank.

In the doorway, a shape darker than the shadows had appeared. Larger than any human, armor glinting faintly—and crimson eyes burning like seething magma.

The demon entered the room in a silent prowl. I recognized his powerful build, his sharp face, his curving horns and dark hair, his long tail and huge bat-like wings. The last time I'd seen the demon, he'd choked Amalia and Travis unconscious at Claude's command.

Moving with deadly silence, he crossed the small room. Perched on the edge with the opening behind me, I couldn't even recoil.

The demon stopped in front of me and a cold, cruel smile curved his dusky lips. He reached out and my lungs locked with terror. His huge hand closed around the bundle of papers I clutched.

He dragged the papers from my grasp with no effort at all. Satisfaction tinged his smile—then his open palm struck my chest.

I pitched over backward, plunged into the gap, and smashed headfirst through a plastic panel in the ceiling below.

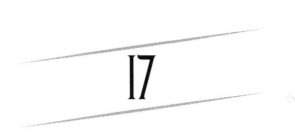

17

THE CONCRETE FLOOR rushed up to meet my face—and I jarred to a painful stop, the crown of my head inches from cracking open like a dropped melon. As pieces of the broken panel rained down, my infernus hit the floor and bounced away.

Zylas clutched my ankles. He hung upside down out of the ceiling, his knees hooked over the steel grid.

A surprised exclamation. Three vampires, spread throughout the room, had frozen in the midst of their search. Dread cut through me and I slapped my palms against the floor so Zylas could release my legs. I toppled over. He dropped headfirst out of the ceiling, landed on his hands, and flipped onto his feet. I clambered up with far less grace, head throbbing from my impact with the ceiling panel, and scoured the area for my infernus.

Hungry grins spread across the vampires' faces as they closed in on us.

Zylas grabbed my sleeve, swung me behind him, and curled his fingers. Crimson power swept across his arms and solidified into six-inch talons. The vampires didn't so much as blink at the sight of his forbidden magic. If anything, their ravenous expressions intensified.

Their dark eyes—black sclera, white pupils, and thin red rings—ran over him. I backed away, pulse drumming in my throat. The vampires prowled closer, surrounding Zylas, and his tail lashed as he sized up his enemies.

He had to kill them quickly. I didn't know how far the other vampires had wandered in their search for intruders, but considering the noise I'd made falling through the ceiling, they would return soon. Zylas sank lower into his defensive stance.

The first vampire sprang—and his movements were a rushing blur.

Zylas darted aside, scarcely evading the man's grasping hands. Another vampire jumped onto his back. The demon whirled, his powerful motion throwing the vampire off. He cut open the vamp's shoulder, but the creature didn't even stumble. Zylas dove away, and his three opponents moved with him, attacking from every side.

And they were fast. Faster than the pair of vampires Zylas had fought in Claude's townhouse. So fast they matched the demon's speed.

He broke free of their ensnaring circle, only to be surrounded again an instant later. Crimson light burst off his hand. A female vampire flew backward and he thrust his talons toward the chest of another one. The vampire grabbed his wrist, halting the attack with the demon's talons scraping his sternum. Blood drenched his shirt.

Zylas pushed into the vampire, and the vampire pushed back. Zylas slid across the concrete, overpowered, then slashed his other hand out, talons ripping across the vampire's throat and snapping his neck. The vamp collapsed, but the other two charged him.

A door slammed open. A new vampire sprinted across the room and tackled Zylas from behind. His greaves hit the concrete with an earsplitting bang.

With their numbers returned to three, the vampires piled on him. Red power flared, then exploded off Zylas, throwing the vampires back. He sprang up, hands extended, crimson runes flashing over his arms as he prepared a spell.

A vampire kneeling on the floor caught Zylas's outstretched wrist. Mouth gaping, the vamp wrenched the demon's arm down and sank curved fangs into his hand.

Zylas's magic sputtered out. He whipped around, fist swinging, and smashed his knuckles into the vamp's face. The vampire lurched back, fangs tearing free. Zylas sprang away— and landed with an unsteady stagger.

Darren's words from last night flashed through my head: *A bite will put you down like a shot of horse tranquilizer.*

But Zylas was a demon. Surely he wasn't susceptible to— His knees buckled.

The vampires were on him before he could fall. One grabbed his arm and bit down on his bicep. Another caught his hand, tore his sleeve out of the way, and latched onto his wrist. The third stepped behind him, a hand gripping his jaw, and pulled Zylas's head back.

Crazed thirst burning on his face, the vampire licked Zylas's throat, savoring the moment, then bit into the demon's smooth skin. Zylas hung in their hold, his legs twitching weakly as he fought to move. His wide eyes stared, breath rushing from his lungs.

Horror rooted me to the spot, then I tore free of my paralysis. *Daimon, hesychaze!*

Nothing happened. The vampires clung to Zylas, mouths fixed on him, throats working as they swallowed with frenetic intensity. The red rings in their white-and-black eyes glowed brightly.

The infernus—I needed the infernus! It was too far from me for the command to work! I spun in an unsteady circle, but I couldn't see it among the litter of construction supplies. Finding a small pendant in this mess would be impossible.

I snatched a piece of rebar from an untidy pile of scrap metal. Turning on the vampires, I swung it into the female clamped onto Zylas's wrist. It smacked her skull with a dull thud and bounced off. Her gaze, clouded with greed and ecstasy, focused on me.

As I lifted the bar again, she flung her arm out. The blow hit my chest and hurled me off my feet. A whoosh of air, then I slammed into a wall. Pain burst through my ribs and spine. I slid limply to the floor, unable to breathe.

Vaguely, I remembered these vampires were monstrously strong … and I was a feeble, breakable human.

Slumped against the wall, my vision blurring, I tried to bring the room into focus. Zylas hung limply, spasms no longer moving his limbs. His unseeing stare had gone dark, the crimson dimmed to flat, lifeless black. The vampires continued to feed with frenzied gluttony. They were killing him.

"Control yourselves, children." The dry voice was quiet but its commanding power seared the air. "Even a demon will succumb to death if you drain it."

The vampire drinking from Zylas's throat lifted his head, a trickle of dark blood running down his chin. The other two reluctantly pulled their mouths away.

"My lord," the female breathed, licking her lips clean. "Does the demon *need* to live?"

The newly arrived vampire glided across the room and stopped, unhurriedly assessing Zylas. Tall, pale, dark hair. Wearing a charcoal sweater and black jeans, he could've walked in off the street, but despite the dim light, a pair of curved sunglasses hid his eyes, the lenses reflecting the room. Four more vampires were arranged behind him, all staring hungrily at Zylas.

"Our own source of demon blood," the man, who could only be *Lord Vasilii*, said in that emotionless voice, "will benefit us far more than a single indulgent meal."

The female vampire pouted as she dropped Zylas's wrist. The other male let go of his arm, and the final vampire pulled the limp demon against his chest, holding him possessively close.

Vasilii stepped closer. With a pale hand, he lifted Zylas's arm. Inhaling over the bite wound on the demon's wrist, the man ran his tongue across a trickle of blood.

"Exquisite," he whispered.

The other vampires stirred restlessly, fixated on Zylas like starving hounds on a slab of meat.

"My lord." The woman rotated on the spot until she faced me. "If we can't have the demon, can we drink from the girl?"

"No, Bethany. If the girl perishes, her demon will be released from this world." Vasilii frowned slightly. "She seems familiar."

"She's Jack Harper's niece," another vampire supplied. "I recognize her from the photos."

Photos? What photos?

"Ah." Vasilii looked across the room, then back to me. "Why are you here, niece of Jack Harper?"

I stared up at him, too terrified to make a sound.

"Is she injured?" His mouth shifted with irritation. "Did you wound her, Bethany?"

"I only struck her once."

"Hmm. Bring them."

As he walked away, the vampire holding Zylas followed. The woman leered at me, then grabbed a handful of my hair. Pain tore through my scalp, and I whimpered, clutching her wrist as she dragged me across the floor.

The vampire lord stopped at the makeshift table. Bethany flung me down, and a moment later, Zylas landed beside me, his head striking the concrete with a horrific thud.

After studying the empty table, Vasilii ordered one of his minions, "Watch over them. I will return shortly to question the female. If the demon stirs, bite him again—but do not feed on him."

My panicked breath whistled through my clenched teeth. I dragged my aching body to Zylas's side. He was sprawled on his back, blood streaking his neck, and his half-open eyes were black as pitch and empty. How much of his blood had the vampires drained—and how much tranquilizing saliva had they pumped into his body?

I wrapped my fingers around his upper arm. His skin was cool. *Zylas? Can you hear me?*

He didn't react. Not even a flicker of awareness in his dark eyes.

"Can you smell it?" Bethany breathed. "His blood ... the *power* in it."

Another vampire licked his lips. "We will all get to drink."

"Why can't we have him now?" another whispered.

"The demon could die. We have to be careful. Lord Vasilii will make sure the demon keeps feeding us."

My stomach turned over. They intended to keep Zylas as their personal blood bank? My hands tightened around his arm. *Zylas, return to the infernus.*

I waited for crimson light to overtake his body. Was the infernus too far away for him as well, or had the tranquilizing vampire saliva and blood loss anesthetized him? His comatose state, so much worse than when I'd been bitten, terrified me.

"Zylas," I whispered, pressing against his side, my lips against his ear. "Go back to the infernus. Quickly."

A shadow moved across me. Bethany grabbed my hair and hauled me away from Zylas. She threw me down and I hit a bucket, knocking it over. Discarded papers spilled across the floor and fluttered toward the abandoned air compressor and red jerry cans.

"Stay there and be quiet, girl," she ordered.

I lay on my stomach, pain burrowing deep in my muscles from my earlier impact with the wall. A foot from my nose, a glossy photo lay amidst the scattered papers: my face, smiling back at me. A square graduate cap sat on my head and matching robes draped my small frame, while my parents beamed with pride on either side of me.

My throat closed. My high school graduation two years ago. How had the vampires gotten that photo?

"The demon smells so good," a man groaned longingly.

Half under the photo was a lined sheet torn from a notebook, the cream paper filled with handwritten blue ink.

"Control yourself. Lord Vasilii doesn't allow disobedience."

My fingers closed around the paper, and as I squinted at that familiar loopy handwriting, I slid the page closer. Something small clattered softly against the concrete—a ballpoint pen. *A pen.* Sucking in a wild breath, I stuffed the paper down the front of my sweater and took hold of the pen.

"Lord Vasilii has promised we'll get all the demon blood we want," Bethany crooned delightedly. "Can you imagine?"

I flipped the photo over and drew across the back in a single, swift stroke.

"Mythics won't dare hunt us then. We'll be as powerful as they are."

"Even more powerful! Only we can bring demons down with a single bite."

Pressing the pen into another scrap, I drew a different rune across the paper's full span.

"Demons are even more susceptible to our bites than humans. We're the ultimate demon hunters, and mythics have no idea."

The vampires laughed, voices coated in eager hunger. I crawled forward, belly sliding across the rejected papers they'd stolen from Claude, from Uncle Jack … from my parents.

"Do you think Lord Vasilii would notice if we took one more sip from the demon?"

Eyes fixed on the air compressor and the row of jerry cans beside it, I pushed myself across the floor.

"He ordered us not to feed again …"

"Just a little taste?"

I glanced back and my lungs constricted. The three vampires were crouched around Zylas's prone form. Bethany held his wrist, staring at the punctures in his hand from the bite that had brought him down.

"I need more." Drool spilled out of the corner of her mouth. "I *need* it."

"Bethany …" another vampire began sternly.

Her mouth opened wide, fangs gleaming, and she pulled his hand to her mouth.

I shoved off the floor and jumped toward the air compressor and its collection of jerry cans. A vampire shouted in warning. I flung my arm into the air, clutching the photo with a rune scrawled over the back. "*Luce!*"

Light as bright as the sun flared, and the vampires cried out in pain. I grabbed the nearest jerry can and stuffed my second paper into the nozzle.

"*Ig—*"

An arm clamped around my neck, cutting off my air. The vampire dragged me backward and the can slipped from my grasp, landing on its side. Gasoline spilled out. With beastly strength, my captor hauled me over to the other vampires. They surrounded me, black-and-white eyes glaring down, the red rings brighter than I'd ever seen before.

The arm around my neck loosened enough that I could breathe. Focusing as hard as I could on the slip of paper I'd shoved into the jerry can, I gasped, "*Igniaris!*"

The paper burst into flames—and the gasoline fumes exploded. A fireball ruptured the can and whooshed out in a blaze of light and heat. It caught the other cans and they burst, flinging flaming liquid across the room. Fire roared, engulfing the exposed drywall. The papers all over the floor caught and the flames leaped higher, smoke boiling toward the ceiling and heat scorching the air.

Yelling in alarm, the vampires jerked back from the spreading inferno. I tore free from their restraining arms and leaped toward the dark shape on the floor.

Zylas!

Chill air tingled across my skin, then arctic cold swept over the room, sucking away the fire's heat. The flames shrank. Frost webbed across the floor in spreading fractals as the temperature plunged past freezing and kept dropping.

Darkness swept through the room, drowning out the firelight—but within the darkness, crimson eyes glowed.

I tripped over something and crashed down, half on top of Zylas. A warm hand pressed against my cheek. Power buzzed against my skin, then the heat rushed out of my body and flowed into the demon. As suffocating cold plunged over me, his eyes blazed.

Power erupted over his hands in twisting veins. It raced up his arms, his shoulders, his neck, and leaked across his cheeks like creeping scarlet vines. Light bled around his eyes, which burned even brighter.

His hand was still pressed to my face as he raised the other, muscles trembling with weakness but spread fingers steady.

Inside my head, a ruby-colored array appeared: a radiant tangle of lines and jagged runes that crisscrossed and overlapped with wild complexity. Like sorcery but different. Not human magic but demon magic.

It seared deep in my mind like a laser etching the pattern inside my skull.

Power flared over Zylas's hand. Magic erupted all around us, shapes and runes forming in the air. The magic I could see in my head took form in front of my eyes, the tangled shape arching over us. Power built in the runes, pulsing through every line. The air went colder, the fires snuffing out, the darkness pressing in.

Evashvā vīsh.

The spell blasted outward like a detonating bomb, ripping through steel and concrete. A cacophony of shrieking, banging, and crashing shattered my eardrums. The explosion tore the ceiling away, obliterating everything in its path.

Zylas pulled my face into his shoulder and wrapped his arms over my head. Debris plummeted down on us, painful thuds and stinging cuts. The clamor died away, my ears ringing in the new quiet, broken only by the patter and crunch of falling rubble. Darkness lay over everything.

A flicker of light. Somewhere among the wreckage, flames had reignited among the burst jerry cans and smoldering paper. I lifted my head, pulling free of Zylas's arms.

The room was … not really there anymore. A massive hole gaped above us, the ceiling little more than twisted steel.

Zylas's hand tightened around my wrist. His skin was chill, almost icy, and his eyes were dark again, his power expended.

"Run, *drādah.*"

Crimson power flared over him. His body dissolved and the light streaked toward a tangle of debris. I leaped after it and shoved aside smoldering drywall. The infernus lay on the floor, glowing with Zylas's returning spirit. I snatched it up, and then I was running toward a dark threshold, the door torn off its hinges by the detonation.

As I flew through the doorway, a voice shouted. The vampires weren't dead. Some had survived that demonic unleashing. They were coming for me.

I sprinted down the hallway, the dancing firelight fading the farther I ran. Dropping the infernus chain over my head, I wheeled around a corner and darkness engulfed me. My fingers tightened on the photo I still clutched. "*Luce!*"

The cantrip flared, lighting my way, but it wouldn't last long before the rune had to recharge. I raced down the corridor, trying vainly to remember the route Zylas had followed on our way in.

As the cantrip's light faded, I glimpsed an unlit exit sign above the next door. I shoved through it and into the inky stairwell. Reaching out with fumbling hands, I found the railing. I flew down the steps, rounded a bend in the staircase, and descended farther. When the stairway curved again, I stretched my hands out, blindly searching. A concrete wall … a door! I slid my hands down, found the handle, and shoved it open.

Light bloomed, the lobby bathed in the orange glow of streetlamps.

A bang echoed through the stairwell behind me. I flung the door shut, sprinted across the lobby, and slammed full force into the front door. It didn't budge. Locked. I grabbed a heavy bucket of joint compound and threw it into the nearest window. The glass shattered.

I was outside an instant later and clambering over a barricade. Then I ran as fast as my exhausted legs would carry me, one panicked thought in my head: get away from the vampires.

Lights flashed and a horn blared. I stumbled to a halt as a car swerved around me, its brakes squealing. Another horn went off and a pickup truck roared past.

I was in the middle of a road.

The first car, stopped in its lane, gave another beep. The window rolled down and a middle-aged woman leaned out. "I almost ran you over! Are you all right?"

My gaze darted to the building. Shadowy figures appeared in the dark interior, gathering around the window I'd broken.

"Will you drive me home?" I blurted. "Please? I don't live far from here."

As another car beeped angrily and pulled around us, the woman scanned me worriedly. "Maybe I should take you to the police station. Or a hospital?"

"No, just—please. Please take me home."

She grimaced, then jerked her head toward the passenger side of the vehicle. "Okay. Get in."

I rushed around the car and yanked the door open. The moment I closed it, she accelerated, more beeping from the inconvenienced traffic accompanying us.

"Where to?" the woman asked. "Hon? ... Hon, you okay?"

Tears streamed down my face. I slumped back in my seat, the infernus safely tucked under my sweater. The tower and its vampire nest disappeared behind us.

"Thank you," I whispered, pressing a hand over my eyes. "Thank you for helping me."

The woman patted my leg. "You're safe, sweetie. Just tell me where to take you."

I mumbled my address, then belatedly buckled my seatbelt. As the woman changed lanes to head east, I looked down. Crumpled in my fist was the photo. I stared at my parents' smiles, and for a moment, just a moment, I allowed myself to pretend that the helpful stranger in the seat beside me was my mom ... and we were going home.

18

THE MOMENT I WAS THROUGH the apartment's front door, I kicked my shoes off and rushed past the kitchen.

"Robin?" Amalia appeared from her bedroom. "Holy shit!"

I had no idea what I looked like. Every bit of me hurt, especially my back, but I wasn't worried about *my* health. I dashed into the bathroom, pulling the infernus out of my sweater with my other hand.

"Zylas," I said breathlessly. "Come out."

The silver pendant glowed. Red light spilled down, then expanded into Zylas's shape. As his body solidified in front of me, his dark eyes gazed into mine—then he crumpled.

I grabbed him, gasping at his weight, and he clutched the towel rack for balance. It tore off the wall. As he staggered, Amalia dove into the bathroom and braced him from behind. Supporting him between us, Amalia and I pulled him over to the tub and tried to ease him down, but he was too heavy. He slipped backward and fell into the tub, his legs hooked over the edge and elbows smacking into the opposite side with hollow thuds.

"Sorry, Zylas," I panted. "Amalia, get the hot water on."

She spun the tap and water blasted from the showerhead, spraying across him. His dark eyes went wide.

"Cold!" he gasped, seizing the tub's edge. With sudden strength, he hauled himself up.

"It'll get warm in a minute!" I exclaimed. Amalia and I caught his shoulders and held him back. The last thing we needed was for him to collapse on the floor. "Just wait—"

He grabbed the front of my shirt and tried to pull himself out of the water—almost yanking me down on top of him.

"Idiot demon!" Amalia shoved him under the spray. He landed hard, water drenching him. "Would you toughen up for a damn sec—"

Zylas's head lolled back, half-lidded eyes emptying as though a light had been flicked off. He went limp.

My heart gave one panicked lurch and stopped. "Turn off the water!"

Amalia wrenched on the tap. The water cut off.

"Zylas?" Putting a knee on the tub's edge, I pressed a hand to his cheek, then patted it gently. No reaction. I held my fingers over his nose and mouth, lightheaded with relief when I felt his breath. "Zylas?"

Amalia leaned over his other side. "I think he's unconscious." Her stunned stare turned to me. "We just knocked out a demon with cold water."

Should we have realized that cold water would have the opposite effect to hot water? "Let's get him out again."

Together, we hauled the demon out of the tub, then ran the shower until the rickety pipes produced a steady stream of steaming water. We heaved him back under the flow, straining several muscles each.

I checked his head was safely away from the water, then reluctantly faced the bathroom mirror. No wonder the Good Samaritan who'd driven me home had suggested we go to the hospital. My clothes were singed black, smeared with blood, coated in dirt, and torn in several places.

Wincing with each movement, I tugged two of my three sweaters off, removed the infernus from around my neck, and pulled the notebook page and photo out of my last layer. I handed everything to Amalia.

"Can you please put those in my room, then run a spare blanket and some towels through the dryer on high?"

She nodded, took the objects, and left. With a peek to ensure Zylas was still out cold, I stripped down to my underwear, located a box of bandages and rubbing alcohol wipes, and cleaned the scrapes and scratches all over my body. Between my fall through a ceiling and the demon magic explosion, I was looking decidedly worse for wear.

I checked on Zylas again, then hurried into my bedroom. As I pulled on sweatpants and a soft sweater, Amalia stuck her head in. "You decent? Good. Tell me what happened."

Grimacing, I outlined our vampire nest infiltration and its depressing results.

"Another *demon* stole all the documents?" she repeated incredulously, following me back to the bathroom.

"Not just any demon." Sitting on the tub's edge, I checked that Zylas was still breathing. "Claude's demon."

"Guess he wanted his stuff back. Did you see the supreme asshole himself?"

"No, just the demon. I'm not sure what kind of contract Claude has with it, but that demon has way more autonomy than it should." Fighting my despair, I wet my hand in the steamy spray and rubbed the blood off Zylas's neck. "Chances are, Claude *and* the vampires now have enough information to find Uncle Jack."

"And we've got nothing." She tugged on her ponytail. "I still don't understand what vampires have to do with all this."

"Demon blood." I splashed water on the punctures in Zylas's arm. "Those vampires have been drinking demon blood, and it makes them as strong and fast as a demon. They said their 'lord' has promised them even more demon blood to feast on."

"Where are they getting demon blood from? Aside from Zylas." She gazed at him, nose wrinkled, then sighed. "Gotta say, I actually feel bad for him."

I felt worse than bad. Guilt dragged at my lungs.

She left me to babysit my demon, and I fretted over his unresponsive state. After my one vampire bite experience, the tranquilizing effect had worn off quickly, but who knew how much worse it affected demons? Either way, his blood loss was my bigger concern; until he recovered enough to heal himself with magic, he would be weak.

My guilt growing, I pushed his wet hair off his face, then combed my fingers through the tangles. I was considering grabbing my hairbrush when he stirred. His eyes cracked open, the faintest hint of scarlet glowing in their depths.

"Hey," I said softly.

"*Sahvē,*" he replied, equally quiet, his husky tones rougher than usual.

"I'm sorry about the cold water. I didn't realize ..."

Inhaling sharply, he pushed himself into a sitting position, the water pouring across his legs and lower torso. He angled his head away from the spray—away from me. "I did not tell you."

"Tell me what?"

"If I am very weakened, too much cold will kill me."

My stomach swooped in dread. How close had we come to accidentally snuffing out his life? "You should have warned me about that."

"Why would I tell you easy ways to kill me?"

Another swoop in my middle—a different kind. Jaw tightening, I reached down, heedless of the water misting my sleeve, and gripped his chin. I pulled his head toward me and growled, "Zylas Vh'alyir, you are *zh'ūltis*."

He bared his teeth and jerked away from my hand.

"I'm not your enemy," I told him angrily. "We're partners. We help each other. I can't fight like you, but I'll do everything I can to protect you like you protect me."

His anger faltered, his brow creasing.

"So don't be a stubborn idiot. *Tell me* important things like how not to kill you by accident!"

He snarled in answer.

I turned my back on him and folded my arms, fuming. If I was fuming, I didn't have to admit I was hurt that he still didn't trust me. Did he really think I would murder him the next time he was vulnerable?

"*Drādah*," he muttered.

I ignored him, nursing my righteous anger.

"*Drādah*." More insistent. Annoyed. Well, he could be annoyed. Served him right for so much as *thinking* I would—

His wet arm snaked around my waist and he pulled me backward into the tub. I yelped but his hand caught my head before it could hit the tiled wall, and I landed on his lap, the hot water drenching my clothes.

"Zylas!" I exclaimed furiously, hoping I wasn't blushing but knowing I was. "What are you doing? You—"

When my glare snapped to his face, I forgot what I was saying. He gazed at me with a deepening crease between his brows, as though I were a math equation he couldn't quite solve.

"What will you do, *drādah*, when you have the grimoire?"

"What do you mean?" I asked weakly, unable to look away from his probing stare. Our faces were much, much too close. "I'll translate it and see if it has answers about how to send you home."

"What if it doesn't?"

"I'll keep searching until I find a way."

He studied me, his dark eyes prying deep. "If I die, you will not have to do that."

My mouth fell open in disbelief. "If—"

"You said that, before me, you did not need protection. If I die, you will not be in danger. You will not need me. If I die, you will be free of these burdens."

"I don't—"

"You *want* me to die." His wet hand closed over my mouth, silencing my immediate protest. "I thought this, but then I was bitten and could not move. You could have run away. You could have left me."

I tugged on his wrist, forcing his hand off my mouth. "I would never have left you. You didn't leave me when I was bitten."

"I promised to protect you. You made no promise. You—"

"Then I'll promise right now. I'm not strong like you and I know it isn't worth much, but …" I stared hard into his eyes. "Zylas, I promise to protect you however I can, no matter what, until you return to your world."

He lowered his hand. "No, *drādah*, you cannot make that promise."

"Why not?" I asked fiercely.

"I cannot protect you if you are protecting *me*." He leaned in, bringing our faces closer. "Be smarter, *drādah*. Say this instead: 'Zylas, I promise to be your ally.'"

"Your ally?" I repeated, bemused.

"An ally helps and does not harm, but an ally is not …" He paused, searching for the right word. "An ally does not do stupid things and die."

A laugh bubbled in my throat. "So an ally isn't self-sacrificing, is what you mean. Okay, fine. Zylas, I promise to be your ally."

He blinked slowly. "*Hnn.*"

"What?"

"I have never had an ally." He shrugged one shoulder. "No demon will ally with my House."

"What about the demons *in* your House?"

"*Guh.* They have sworn to me, but they are useless. More useless than you."

"Thanks," I said dryly. "But even a demon with half your strength and skill would be better than me."

"No," he said confidently. "They are *zh'ūltis* and *nailēris.*"

"*Nah-ill-leer-iss?*"

"Easy to scare," he translated. "*Coward* is your word, *na?*"

"Haven't you called me that before?"

"I called you *nailis*. Weak. You are not *nailēris*."

He didn't think I was a coward? Well, that made one of us.

"But I am *zh'ūltis*," I reminded him. "You've told me about a hundred times."

"*Hnn*." He tilted his head. "Only sometimes, *drādah*."

My eyebrows rose and I smiled slowly. "Are you feeling okay, Zylas? You just told me I'm not stupid all the time and I'm less useless than some demons. I don't think you've ever said so many nice things."

His tail slapped the tub with a splash. "I have more insults if you want."

"I have just as many," I retorted. "We can start with how you thought I might try to kill you."

"Everyone tries to kill me, *drādah*."

My humor fizzled, an odd ache gripping my chest. I shoved the feeling away and slapped his shoulder lightly. "I'm not *everyone*, stubborn demon. I'm your contractor."

He snorted.

The dryer buzzed loudly, breaking the odd moment. My cheeks flushed and I hastily dragged myself out of the tub—and off his lap. Water dripped all over the bathmat and I sighed at having drenched the clothes I'd only put on ten minutes ago. Leaving Zylas to soak, I returned to my bedroom to change.

The water shut off, and a moment later, a soaking-wet demon walked into my room. His steps lacked his usual grace, but he was steady on his feet.

"Wait here," I ordered. "I'll be right back."

I returned with an armful of hot towels from the dryer. He stood at the foot of the bed, water running down his face, exhaustion clinging to him. I flipped a towel over his head, swung a second over his shoulders, then reached up and scrubbed his hair, careful not to catch the towel on his small horns.

"If you want to lie down on my bed," I said before he could complain, "you need to be dry first."

He grumbled something under his breath, then plucked at the straps over his shoulder. The buckles came undone and he pulled his chest armor off. It hit the floor with a *thunk*, just missing my toes.

I pulled the towel off his head, his hair mussed in every direction. Shedding the towel on his shoulders, he resumed stripping off his armor. Blushing all over again, I retreated to the laundry closet and pulled my spare blanket, reserved for the coldest winter nights, out of the dryer. A faint burnt smell clung to the overheated fabric. By the time I returned, Zylas was stretched across my mattress on his stomach, head pillowed on his arms and reasonably dry. Also, again, naked from the waist up.

Could he keep his clothes on for more than a few hours? Geez.

I flipped the warm blanket over him. "Are you going to heal yourself?"

"Later," he mumbled. "It is difficult *vīsh* and I am … what is the word for when the ground is moving but not moving?"

My eyebrows scrunched together. "Do you mean dizzy?"

"*Var.* I am too much dizzy."

I twisted my hands together helplessly. "Those vampires really had a thing for your blood, didn't they?"

"*Na*, of course." He peered at me with one eye. "*Hh'ainun* blood tastes terrible."

I giggled despite the fatigue weighing down my limbs. My back ached so badly I couldn't fully straighten my spine. I gazed at the demon in my bed, then sighed and climbed onto the mattress beside him, on top of the blanket while he was under it. He watched me, head resting on his folded arms.

Plumping a pillow, I propped it against the wall—I didn't have a headboard—and leaned into it, legs stretched out. The ache in my spine lessened slightly.

My gaze turned, seeking the object I'd been pointedly ignoring. The infernus lay on my bedside table, the chain curled neatly around the disc-like pendant. And beside it, crumpled and stained, were my graduation photo and the notebook page I'd found amidst the "garbage" the vampires had discarded.

Something akin to panic boiled through my chest. I sucked in a deep, shaky breath and steeled my heart. Ignoring the tremble in my fingers, I carefully lifted the lined paper off the table.

Dear Robin,

Hey there, little bird. If you're reading this, it means I can't say those words to you anymore. And it means, whatever happened, I didn't get to tell you some important things I needed to share. But I already told you the most important thing. I told you every day:

I love you, baby girl. Your father and I love you so much, and we're so proud of you.

The other things, they aren't as easy to say. They aren't pleasant to hear. There's so much I should have told you, and even as I write this letter, I know I should be saying all this right now, face to face. But how can a mother tell her daughter that her life and her dreams have to change? If I can spare you this burden for even one more day, how can I not?

It's because of our desire to protect you, Robin, that we've hidden so much.

I guess I should start at the beginning. The Athanas Grimoire. I've shown you this grimoire, but I never told you what it really is. To most of the mythic world, it's an ancient myth nearly forgotten. But for our family, it's our past, present, and future. It's our legacy and our burden—a burden that, if you're reading this letter, is now yours. And because of my shortsightedness, you're completely unprepared to shoulder it.

That's my fault, and my greatest regret. I should have prepared you. I should have nurtured your love of magic and Arcana, not pushed you away from all power. I thought if you could leave magic behind entirely, the grimoire would be even safer in your care than mine.

I was so wrong. Instead of keeping you safe, I've left you unarmed.

But Robin, I know how strong you are. How smart and capable. You're ready for this, little bird. Your inquisitive heart will lead you where you need to go. You'll find the answers I never could.

I've written so much and I still haven't explained the grimoire—what it is and what it means. It's among the most dangerous books to ever exist. That's why we've kept it hidden. Those who covet power nearly wiped our family *out of existence trying to get it, and only by fleeing to America and changing her name did your great-grandmother end the bloodbath.*

You see, Robin, our family aren't merely Arcana mythics. We're demon summoners— generation upon unbroken generation of summoners. We weren't just the best. We were the first

I stared at the last word. Her handwriting filled both sides of the paper, but the last sentence cut off, incomplete and unfinished. There must've been a second page, maybe several pages. Lost in the destruction, the fire, the collapsed ceiling.

My vision blurred, causing the final line to waver. *We were the first* … the first to do what?

A sob shuddered through me and I fought for composure. Zylas was watching me and I didn't want to break down in front of him. He'd already called me stupid for crying from grief, and I didn't want to hear it again. I rubbed my sleeve across my eyes and sniffed.

His gaze weighed on me, heavy and assessing. "What does it read?"

The quiet question caught me off guard. I glanced at his scarlet-tinged eyes and refocused on the page. Swallowing, I read the letter aloud. My voice trembled but I made it to the end without breaking.

"There's no more," I concluded. "The rest of the letter probably burned with everything else."

"What happened to the other papers?"

"The other demon … Claude's demon took them." I slumped miserably. "You knew he was there, didn't you? That's why you tried to call me back."

"I sensed his *vīsh*. I could have sensed it before he got so close but I was not paying attention."

"It isn't your fault. We weren't in a position to escape anyway." I glanced at my desk where the grimoire page and half-completed translation sat. "What kind of demon is he?"

"Dh'irath. Second House. He is very powerful."

"Do you know him?"

"No, but Dh'irath is always powerful. He will be the same to fight as Tahēsh."

Despair clung to me, filling my mind with doubts. Could we find Uncle Jack before either Claude or the vampires? Would I ever get the grimoire back? Maybe I could send Zylas home without it, but what other dangerous secrets did it contain?

"Well," I said heavily, "Claude and his demon have all the important documents the vampires collected, and everything else was destroyed. We have nothing."

"We have no less than we had before, *drādah*."

I absorbed that. He was right. We hadn't gained any ground, but neither had we lost any. It could've been worse.

My gaze drifted to the bite mark on Zylas's neck. It could've been much worse.

19

I WOKE UP WITH A DEMON in my bed.

Three seconds after I realized I must've fallen asleep curled up beside Zylas with only a thin blanket separating us, I was out of the bed, across the room, and through the door.

Maybe in the next century, the blush would finally fade from my hot cheeks.

Zylas noted my sprint from the room but didn't seem to care. Not that I could tell if he was embarrassed. With the reddish undertone of his skin, a blush would be difficult to notice, and besides that, he had yet to show the slightest hint of self-consciousness. Maybe he wasn't capable of embarrassment.

The thought occurred to me as I leaned against the kitchen counter ten minutes later, a spoonful of yogurt halfway to my mouth. What I would give to never feel embarrassed again. Shaking my head, I resumed eating my simple breakfast.

Amalia woke up half an hour later and we got to work discussing our next move. No matter how we looked at it, we had no significant leads to follow. Claude and his demon had all the information and we had no idea where to find them. Plus, if Zylas was right about the strength of Claude's demon, a Second House Dh'irath, we didn't want to chance a confrontation.

As much as I never wanted to see another vampire again, we didn't have much choice: we were going back to the tower.

While Amalia prepared cantrips on flashcards for self-defense—we weren't going near the vampire nest unarmed—I took a quick shower. Hair blow-dried, contacts in, and clothes on, I winced back to my room. I'd hoped the shower would ease the pain in my back from last night's intimate meet-and-greet with a wall, but the bruises flared with my every movement.

Red light glowed across my room. Zylas, back in his armor, lay in the middle of the floor. A spell surrounded his body, the twisting lines and spiky runes forming overlapping circles within a peculiarly oblong hexagon.

The light faded and the magic shimmered away to nothing. Zylas sat up with a grimace and examined his wrist. The vampire fang punctures were gone without a trace.

"Did you heal your blood loss too?" I asked as I moved stiffly to my bedside table.

"*Var*." He rolled his shoulders. "This time, they will not get my blood."

I lifted the infernus off my bedside table and looped the chain over my neck. The pendant settled on top of my thick, comfy sweater, the pale green cotton splashed with the logo of my favorite book convention. My mom had owned a matching one.

Warm breath stirred my hair.

Squealing in fright, I whirled around and lurched back, hitting the table and almost knocking the lamp over. Zylas frowned at my reaction. I hadn't noticed him stand up, let alone sneak up behind me.

"Go *sideways, drādah.*"

"Why are you testing me on that now?" I asked breathlessly, pressing a hand over my trembling heart and wishing he'd step back. "This isn't the time for—"

He laid his hands on the sides of my neck, palms warm and thumbs resting against my cheeks. I froze as he stared down at me. A sizzle of cool magic sparked over his hands and tingled across my nerves.

Releasing my neck, he seized my wrist and hauled me into the middle of the room. I huffed in confusion as he pushed me down to the floor and crouched, strangely focused on my face.

"Zylas, what—"

"You waste breath making noise when you are scared."

"Huh?"

He pushed against my upper chest, and the next thing I knew, I was lying flat on my back on the carpet, gazing at the ceiling. His fingers, splayed across my collarbones, lit with crimson power that veined over his wrist.

"You make too much noise," he repeated, his tone absent. Red lines spiraled across the floor on either side of me. "*Drādah ahktallis* is quiet when hunters are near."

"I don't intend to," I muttered, distracted by the zing of magic sinking into my chest. "It's reflexive. Zylas, what are you doing?"

"Making noise is not useful for escaping danger."

"I know but Zylas, what are you *doing*?"

His gaze flicked up to mine—and the cool magic drifting through my body flashed hot. The spell circle blazed brightly and burning pain flared down my spine. I went rigid, arching off the floor, but he pushed me down. After a moment, the agony subsided.

"You are injured. I am fixing you."

Yeah, I'd figured that out *now*. "You didn't have to do that … but thank you."

I started to sit up, but he forced me down yet again, his claws pricking me through my sweater. The spell circle twirled, runes fading and new ones forming as he adjusted its shape.

"I am not finished," he growled. "Your back is still damaged … *bruised*."

Relaxing into the floor, I watched the way concentration pulled at his mouth and tightened the line of his jaw. "Zylas … thank you. Really."

"You were moving too slow."

His words triggered a short but unpleasant slash of disappointment. "You're healing me because I'd be too slow against the vampires?"

"Why else?"

My cold disappointment deepened. I said nothing as he tweaked the spell, working through some unfathomable process required to heal my bruised back muscles.

"Zylas …" I drew in a slow breath. "You feel pain, don't you? When you're injured, does it hurt?"

"*Na*? Of course, *drādah*." He didn't add "*zh'ūltis*" because his disparaging tone said it for him. "But maybe not as much as the same wound hurts a *hh'ainun*? I do not know."

I had been reasonably sure he felt pain, but I'd wanted to know for sure. "If we weren't hunting vampires today, would you have healed me?"

"No."

He said it without thought, without consideration, without even looking away from his healing magic.

I swallowed against the lump in my throat. "Even though you know what pain feels like ... and you knew I was in a lot of pain ... you wouldn't have helped me?"

His head came up. His crimson eyes turned to mine, the slightest crease between his eyebrows.

"I see," I said softly, heavy sadness weighing down my lungs. It wasn't that he would have decided against helping me. The thought of easing my suffering hadn't even occurred to him.

The furrow between his eyebrows deepened. He glanced across me from head to toes, then swept his gaze back to my face. His mouth turned down, but it wasn't his usual irritated-by-the-stupid-human scowl.

"Is this part of *protect*? I am supposed to heal all your pain?"

"No ... it would be one of those 'nice things' I keep telling you about." I gave him a reassuring smile, concealing the quiet but unignorable ache in my chest. "It's okay, Zylas. Don't worry about it."

He canted his head, frowning, almost ... bewildered.

"Thank you," I added, "for getting me back into fighting shape."

Puzzlement written all over his face, he returned his attention to the healing spell. A new wave of cold washed over me, building up in my back muscles, then flared into scorching agony. A whimper scraped my throat, my limbs locked as I endured it.

As the pain and magic faded, I slumped into the floor, breathing hard. Zylas finally lifted his hand from my chest— and his thumb brushed across my cheek. He smudged away a tear that had escaped despite my efforts.

Then he was on his feet and walking away, his husky voice calling back to me, "Hurry up, *drādah*. It is time to go."

IT WAS A QUARTER AFTER ELEVEN by the time I opened the door to the Arcana Atrium on the Crow and Hammer's third level. As Amalia followed me inside, she let out an appreciative whistle.

"Starting small, eh?" she remarked.

Embarrassed but pleased, I grinned. "It should be charged and ready to go. I just have to complete the last stage."

I grabbed the textbook off the worktable, and after reviewing the next steps, I prepared the final quantities of sulfur and iron powder. Positioning myself in front of the array, I took a deep, calming breath.

"Remember," Amalia said, perching on the stool to wait, "if you fumble a single word, the spell will fail and you'll have to start all over again."

I shot her a glare, then focused on the incantation. Eighteen phrases in Latin, and I couldn't stumble, stutter, or mispronounce a single syllable. I could, however, take it slowly. No need to rush. Arcana was a patient magic.

"*Terra, terrae ferrum, tua vi dona circulum,*" I began in a slow, measured rhythm.

The pile of iron powder fizzed and blackened. I chanted the next line, and the copper blackened too. As I continued, the salt burned and the oil bubbled. Lastly, the sulfur burst into flame.

As the spell's ingredients were consumed, a faint glow imbued the white lines. I paused, as instructed by the text, and sprinkled my new measurement of sulfur across the rectangle of iron that would form the artifact. The powder puffed black and evaporated.

Standing, I chanted the next two lines. Heat waves rose from the array. A rainbow of colors rippled over the circle—yellow and gray where the sulfur and iron had rested, white and brown where the salt and copper had been consumed, and a shimmering swirl of pink and green where the oil had evaporated.

I flung the iron powder across the circle. It sizzled in the air and the colors brightened. I triple-checked the last line, then declared, "*Haec vis signetur, surgat vis haec iussu: eruptum impello.*"

The glowing magic and shimmering light rippled, then sucked down into the open triangle that directed the power into the artifact. The runes on the iron rectangle lit up and swirled with all the colors of the array. The spell circle darkened until only the artifact glowed brightly.

Then all the light and magic snuffed out like a candle flame in the wind.

I checked the book. Aside from a warning that the spell wouldn't affect any people or objects the caster was touching, it had no further instructions. The last line of text was the artifact's short "trigger incantation," which would activate the spell it now contained—assuming I'd done everything right.

Amalia leaned forward. "Did it work?"

"I'm not sure." I lifted the iron rectangle and weighed it on my palm. The runes I'd drawn on it were now etched lightly into its face. "I'll have to test it."

She waited a moment. "Then test it."

"Um." I glanced around the room. "Maybe not here. If it works, it might damage something."

Pulling my infernus off, I unclasped the chain and fed it through the hole at the top of the artifact. It settled beside the silver pendant like an oversized dog tag.

Amalia helped me clean up the room, then we hurried out of the guild and onto the downtown streets. Though we could've caught a bus, the wait would have taken almost as long as walking, so we set out at a quick pace—or rather, Amalia walked at a comfortable pace and I half-jogged on my much shorter legs.

The four- and five-story businesses surrounding the Crow and Hammer were swiftly replaced by thirty-story skyscrapers. Vehicles zoomed past as we walked along the sidewalk, the noon rush hour translating to increased foot traffic as well. It was the Friday before Christmas, and what seemed like half the downtown populace was taking advantage of a rare day without rain to escape their offices for lunch. I dodged people every twenty steps, but Amalia blazed straight ahead, forcing other pedestrians to leap out of her way. If I tried that, I'd get trampled. More short people problems.

We crossed a busy intersection and headed down an attractive street with trees along the boulevard. Ahead, the office tower loomed, slightly less intimidating in the daylight. As before, construction barriers were arranged in front, and the window I'd broken gaped accusingly.

"This is it?" Amalia asked.

I nodded, blinking against my dry contacts. "That's it. The alley goes around to the back where we can get inside."

My heart thrummed unhappily at the prospect of entering the building again, but at least I had a flashlight this time. I was getting the hang of this "combat mythic" thing. All I needed now was a fancy vest like the—

We rounded a corner and stopped dead.

—like the Crow and Hammer team standing around the very entrance Zylas and I had broken into last night. The doors of the guild's big black van hung open, and the mythics were unbuckling weapons and tossing them into the back. I spotted Drew, Cameron, and Darren, plus three other guild members whose names I couldn't remember.

"Robin?" Zora stepped around the van. "What are you doing here?"

My stomach dropped sickeningly. In the aftermath of my "infiltration" last night, I'd completely forgotten that Zora and her team had planned to investigate the building this morning. If I'd remembered, I would've warned Zora not to go. Even her experienced team was no match for *this* nest.

She approached Amalia and me, and two men broke away from the group to follow her.

"Um," I mumbled as the three mythics drew closer. "Hi Zora, and … uh …"

The older guy, with brown hair, fine laugh lines around his eyes, and a fatherly sort of look, held out his hand. "I'm Andrew."

I shook his offered hand, then shook hands with the other man, early thirties with short black hair and teak skin, who introduced himself as Taye in a pleasantly deep voice with a South African accent.

"I'm Robin. This is Amalia." I forced a smile for Zora. "We were just swinging by to see how things went."

She folded her arms and cocked a hip, her huge sword strapped to her back. "A total bust. They were definitely here, possibly right up until last night, but they've jumped ship. The place is abandoned."

I almost wilted with relief. Thank goodness everyone was safe.

"We found destroyed documents and a burnt computer," she continued. "It looks like this is where the contents of that summoner's townhouse ended up, but an explosion of some kind ruined everything."

"An explosion?" I repeated with innocent disbelief.

"We checked the entire building. Nothing. Andrew is taking the rest of the team back. Taye and I will give it one more thorough check for any hints on where they've gone, but …" She shook her head.

"How long will that take?" Amalia asked.

"A few hours, I expect."

"Damn, well, that sucks," Amalia said brusquely. "Guess we'll leave you to it. Come on, Robin."

My mouth was still hanging open when she grabbed my arm and hauled me back down the alley to the street.

"Amalia, that was *rude*," I hissed.

"What, did you want to stay and discuss the weather?" She dropped my arm and glared around at the busy street. "If they're going to be in there for hours yet, we'll have to wait to check it out."

"I was about to suggest we help them search the building."

She scowled. "Well, why didn't you say so?"

"You didn't give me a chance!" I huffed. "I'm pretty sure there's nothing to find inside. Zylas blew the room to smithereens. We need to know where the vampires are now."

"If we can get our hands on one, we can question them," Amalia agreed. "Find out what they're up to and what they know about my dad and the grimoire."

I wasn't as confident in our interrogation skills. "But how will we find them?"

We exchanged helpless looks as we strolled past the tower, feigning nonchalance. Pedestrians buffeted us as we passed a décor shop and a pizza joint.

"We need a way to track them," I muttered. "Zora's artifacts only work on nearby vampires. We need a spell that works like a bloodhound …"

"Or we need an actual bloodhound."

I stopped. A businessman shouldered past me, muttering angrily, and I shuffled closer to a shop window.

"*Zylas* can track them," I exclaimed in a whisper, amazed I hadn't thought of him immediately. "He can follow the blood scent."

Amalia's face brightened hopefully, then her scowl reappeared. She waved at the bustle around us. "It'll be the dead of night before these streets are empty enough for you to walk a demon around in the open."

The window beside me reflected my frustrated expression. I peered into the shop's interior, then swung to face Amalia, my pulse racing.

"I have an idea."

20

"OKAY." I STEPPED BACK, hands on my hips as I surveyed my work. "Amalia, what do you think?"

Beside me, she folded her arms and pursed her lips. In front of us, the narrow alley ended in a brick wall and a row of dumpsters, and beneath the heavy gray clouds, the shadows were dense—the perfect concealment for our task.

My demon stood in front of the dumpsters, but he didn't look very demony anymore.

A baggy black sweater featuring a blue sports logo with a killer whale covered his torso, and the hood hid his horns and shadowed his face. Equally baggy sweatpants covered his legs, pulled on over his armor. A pair of reflective sunglasses completed his disguise.

"Well," Amalia drawled, "he sure looks like a slob. Where's his tail?"

"He's got it looped around his waist under the hoodie."

Zylas tilted his head as though testing whether the sunglasses would fall off his face, then lifted his arms, the sleeves hanging to his fingertips. I'd bought an extra-large to ensure it would fit over his armor. He'd still had to unbuckle the shoulder piece, which was hanging against his side.

"Will this fool the *hh'ainun*?" he asked dubiously.

I tapped a finger against my lower lip. His skin was unusual—that reddish undertone to the warm brown—but nothing that would attract stares with only his lower face visible. The oddest thing about his appearance were his feet, bare except for the dark fabric wrapped around the arches and over the tops. He'd refused to put on the Crocs I'd bought.

Supposed I couldn't blame him for that. I wouldn't want to wear Crocs either.

"I think it'll work," I declared, tossing the bag from the sportswear shop into the nearest dumpster. "Let's give it a try."

Eyebrows raised skeptically, Amalia led the way out of the alley. I waved Zylas to my side and together we walked into the lunch-hour foot traffic. My pulse skipped in my throat but no one so much as glanced at us. Amalia did her "get out of my way" power walk, and Zylas and I strode in her wake.

I glanced at the demon to reassess his disguise and saw his wide grin. As unsuspecting humans walked right past him, he snickered quietly. Well, at least his disguise was working well enough to—

A passing woman did a double take, her brow furrowed and gaze locked on his mouth. Grabbing his sleeve, I hauled him past the lady.

"Stop grinning," I warned him. "People are noticing your teeth."

He pressed his lips together, hiding his pointed canines, but couldn't fully suppress his amusement. *Someone* sure found the obliviousness of the human race funny.

Not wanting to risk a run-in with any Crow and Hammer mythics—they wouldn't be as easy to fool—we wandered past the office tower's front entrance. I followed Amalia with half my attention on our surroundings and half on Zylas. The hood shadowed his features and his sunglasses reflected my face.

"Can you pick up anything?" I whispered.

His nostrils flared. "I can smell them but it is old. Circle the building and I will find the newest scent."

I passed that instruction on to Amalia and she angled toward an alley.

"*Drādah.*" His amused grin flashed as a group of young women in pencil skirts and high heels walked past us. "I have wondered … what are those?"

He flicked his fingers toward the street where traffic was slowing to a stop at a red light.

"Those are cars," I supplied, his question catching me off guard. Sometimes I forgot how foreign this world must be to him. "Or, 'vehicles' I guess is the better term."

"They are not alive," he mused. "But they are not *vīsh*. How do they move?"

"Uh, it's difficult to explain. They don't move on their own. Humans steer them. They have engines that you start with a key, and you have to put fuel in them. Lots of people own one and drive it from place to place every day."

He considered that. "They do this because *hh'ainun* are slow?"

"Yes," I said with a laugh. "Humans are slow and our cities are big, so we use vehicles to get around. Once we're finished searching for vampires, I'll take you on a bus ride." I pointed at a big gray bus rolling past. "One of those. You can see what it's like."

Stopping, he lifted the sunglasses above his eyes to peer at the bus. A middle-aged man in a custodian uniform stopped dead, staring at the demon's face, then hurried past us, looking over his shoulder with each step as though doubting what he'd seen.

I swatted Zylas's arm. "Sunglasses down!"

He resettled them on his nose, smirking. I rolled my eyes and tugged him into motion again.

We did a wide circle around the building, crossing as many streets and alleys as possible. Zylas chose what he thought was the most recent trail, which headed northwest toward the Coal Harbor neighborhood. He tracked the blood scent down an alley and onto another street. The vampires must've gone straight across but I had to steer Zylas to an intersection so we could cross the busy road at a traffic light, which required explaining why humans had created such an "annoying" system.

Needless to say, Zylas found the idea of humans running over other humans with their vehicles far too amusing. I was never letting him anywhere near the driver's seat of a car.

We safely crossed the road and found the trail. Amalia powered ahead of us, her bold attitude drawing attention away from Zylas's baggy, barefoot oddness. He tracked the scent for another half a block, then slowed. His hooded face turned to an alley too narrow for anything but a small car.

He rounded the corner and started down the alley. As Amalia looked back, I waved at her to wait and hastened after the demon. The light dimmed, blocked by the towering skyscrapers on either side, and the lunch-hour commotion grew muffled.

"Zylas," I whispered, "are they here?"

His steps shifted into a prowl, and his tail swept out from beneath his sweater. "The scent is strong."

I crept behind him, gripping the infernus and my new artifact through my sweater. A cold wind whipped down the alley, blowing in our faces as we ventured farther from the safety of the street.

Zylas reached back to push on my hip—his unspoken "wait" command. I halted and he continued forward, head swiveling. Wrapping my arms around myself, I peered into the shadows. Dumpsters and bins lined the strip of pavement, creating plenty of dark corners for a vampire or six to hide in.

As Zylas prowled past a row of blue recycling bins, something clattered behind me.

I whirled toward the sound. Ten paces away, a dumpster stood against the concrete wall. Grabbing my artifact again, I inched back a step. My skin prickled as I kept my gaze fixed on the shadows behind the dumpster. What had made that noise? Was it a vampire?

A warm hand curled around my throat. Hot breath brushed across my cheek and a husky voice whispered in my ear, "And now you are dead, *drādah*."

Gasping in fright, I tore free. Zylas stood behind me, his sunglasses reflecting my frightened face. "Zylas! What did you scare me for?"

"You are staring at one spot."

"Yes, because I heard a noise." I pointed at the dumpster. "I think there's—"

The wind gusted and a half-empty bottle of water rolled away from the dumpster—the noise I'd heard. I flushed in embarrassment.

"Be smarter, *drādah*."

My blush deepened. I started to turn away, but he caught my shoulder and pulled me in front of him, my back to his chest.

"When you hear a sound, do not stare in one spot. It is easy to ambush you."

I blinked, confused. I'd expected an insulting observation about my inability to detect an actual threat.

"You must always be looking everywhere. Side and side, up and down. Always move your eyes. Quick looks. Do not fixate."

With one hand gripping my shoulder, he turned me in a quarter circle and gestured across the alley. "Look for safe ground and dangerous ground. Look now so if you must run later, you know which way is best."

He pulled me in a sideways step. "Do not stand and wait for the hunter to attack. Look and search and *move*."

My heart thudded unsteadily as I moved my legs in the same pattern as his, our steps matching and his hands guiding me. We shifted down the alley, backs to the wall, and I understood what he was showing me—how to scan for danger while moving away from it at the same time.

A dozen paces from the main street, he stopped.

"Now you are safe." He leaned over my shoulder, his face beside mine. "Do not find the hunter, *drādah*. Escape the hunter."

I released a slow breath, strangely aware of his hands on my shoulders. "Someday, I want to fight the hunter like you do."

"You must learn to be hunted before you can learn to hunt."

Craning my neck to see him, our noses almost touching, I asked, "Did you learn to be hunted?"

"*Var*. When I was smaller than you."

I imagined a child-sized Zylas, small horns poking out of tousled black hair and big crimson eyes glowing in a boyish face.

"No horns, *drādah*. We do not have horns until much older."

I removed them from my mental picture. "How's that? Also, get out of my head."

"Do not throw your thoughts at me, then." He nudged me toward the sidewalk as he checked his tail was once again hidden under his oversized sweater. "The scent ends at nothing. They did not go this way."

We rejoined Amalia, and Zylas resumed tracking. After another block, his steps slowed again, but not because the trail had split. He cast back and forth on the sidewalk, annoying several passersby, then backtracked.

He relocated the trail and continued another fifty feet, only to lose it again. Three times we backtracked and each time he lost the scent. We made it another block, but even crouching to sniff at the ground—*that* earned us some strange looks—he couldn't get a hold on the trail.

"Too many *hh'ainun*," he complained, sitting on his haunches in the middle of the sidewalk. Confused pedestrians split to pass us on either side. "I cannot—"

"Out of the way," a man in a heavy winter parka snapped, hip-checking Zylas in the shoulder—or trying to.

Instead, he bounced off the sturdy demon, stumbled, and stepped off the curb. An oncoming car swerved away from him. A horn blared, then a loud bang as two vehicles collided.

Screeching tires, then a third car rear-ended the first one. Traffic slammed to a halt, both lanes blocked. A chorus of honking filled the street.

"*Na, drādah*," Zylas remarked, rising to his full height while I gaped at the accident, "maybe *hh'ainun* are too slow for this too."

I grabbed his wrist, Amalia grabbed his other arm, and we dragged him away from the collision as the drivers got out of their cars, shouting at each other. Zylas cackled under his breath.

"Don't you dare cause any more accidents," I warned him. "We need to focus."

"The scent is gone." He shrugged. "I can only smell *hh'ainun* and the stink of *vehicles*."

My shoulders drooped in defeat. "We can't just give up."

"Trying to do this at lunch hour was dumb," Amalia declared. "We should give the rush a chance to die down. Carlo's is near here, isn't it? I haven't eaten there in forever."

"Carlo's?" I echoed.

"Amazing calzones. Come on."

I followed her around the corner. Two blocks up the street, a red sign with white lettering announced Carlo's Calzones. As we neared, the mouthwatering scent of warm pizza permeated the chilly breeze. The restaurant's door swung open and closed with a steady stream of customers.

Gripping Zylas's sleeve, I slowed, searching for an alley or out-of-the-way corner where he could return to the infernus. A solid wall of skyscrapers lined the street, with ground-level businesses facing the sidewalk. People everywhere.

"Amalia," I called, "we need to go back and find an alley."

She turned, frowning impatiently. "But we're already here."

"We can't bring him *inside*."

Her frown deepened as she looked up and down the street. "But there's nowhere he can ..."

Nowhere he could dissolve into crimson power and possess a small pendant—a phenomenon we couldn't allow anyone to witness. My brow scrunched as I peered up at Zylas.

And that's how we ended up taking a demon out to lunch.

Five minutes later, I was sitting beside Zylas in a cramped booth in the back corner of the packed restaurant. Conversations buzzed all around us, but all I could think was that my *demon* was sitting in full view of a hundred people.

Hood up and sunglasses on, he took in the brick walls, cheesy red-checkered tablecloths, and open view of the kitchen. What if the server asked him to take his hood off? What if someone noticed the inhuman tinge to his skin or the dark claws that tipped his fingers? My only slight comfort was that Zylas seemed too curious to cause any trouble.

"Calm down, Robin," Amalia said, picking up a menu. "He looks like a weirdo, not a demon, and if anyone takes too much notice, we'll leave."

Right. Yes. No one could make him take his glasses or hood off. We would just leave. No big deal. Gulping back my panic, I opened my menu and held it up.

Zylas leaned into me to study the photos inside. "What is this?"

"The menu," I whispered. "It lists all the food they make. We'll tell the server what we want and she'll bring it to us in a few minutes."

"The spicy pesto calzone is excellent." Amalia lowered her menu enough to glare over the top. "Do *not* order him anything. He eats like a freak."

"It smells good," he growled. "I want to try it."

"Too bad."

"You can share mine," I said quickly. Zylas's good behavior wouldn't last if Amalia ticked him off. "I'll order the vegetarian one."

Despite his remorseless ability to kill, my demon was a hardcore, if temporary, vegetarian—though it seemed the olfactory appeal of hot pizza was winning out over his distaste for meat. Maybe I should see if he liked pepperoni.

I breathed easier once the waitress had hurried off with our orders. Fidgeting nervously, I scanned the nearest tables, ensuring no one was staring at us in shock or horror.

Amalia propped her chin on her palm. "We're getting nowhere searching for the vamps. We can give it another try after lunch, but what's our Plan B?"

"We don't have a Plan B," I muttered. "I don't even know what's most important anymore. The vampires and whatever is going on with them? Claude and his demon? Uncle Jack? There's too much we don't understand."

"The vampires are searching for my dad. I'm assuming they targeted Claude because he's searching for Dad and the grimoire too. Do the vampires also want the grimoire?"

"I think so. They're involved with Demonica somehow. They've been feeding on demon blood, and their leader promised them a steady supply. But how do any of them know that demon blood makes them stronger? I don't think they just stumbled across that knowledge."

Amalia shook her head, as stumped as I was. Zylas ignored our discussion, his attention on a nearby table where a woman was pulling apart her calzone, the golden crust flaking and steam rising from the melted cheese spilling onto her plate. I elbowed his side as he leaned into me, drawn toward the hot food like it was exerting a gravitational pull.

"Maybe they want the grimoire so they can ... summon demons themselves?" I suggested.

"That seems like the hardest possible way to summon a demon." Amalia tapped thoughtfully on the tabletop. "Zora said vampires aren't good at long-term planning, though, so maybe they don't realize the grimoire won't be any use without a summoner to do the work."

I rubbed my face, momentarily confused by the absence of my glasses. "We're missing something for sure. What—"

"Robin!"

I froze as the hailing voice cut across the loud conversations filling the restaurant. Horror seized my lungs like a steel clamp at the sight of two people moving purposefully through the bustle.

Zora was weaving through the tables. Zora and Taye, her teammate from earlier. They were heading straight toward us.

Oh no, oh no, oh no.

Amalia's expression was locked into a horrified stare, and I couldn't breathe as the two mythics reached our table. Zylas was unmoving beside me. His disguise could fool humans who had no clue demons were real, but not only was Zora perfectly aware of the existence of demons, but she'd also *seen* Zylas before.

"What are you doing here?" I blurted, my voice high and squeaky.

"Carlo's is the perfect dose of cheesy calories after a long, cold day on the job," Zora said cheerfully, missing my panic. "We come here all the time. Mind if we join you? Have you ordered yet?"

Not waiting for an answer, she swung a long black case that could only be her sword off her shoulder and dropped into the booth beside Amalia. Taye grabbed a free chair from another table and pulled it over. My panic ratcheted up a notch.

Zora's smile faltered at our tense silence—and she glanced at Zylas, probably wondering why we weren't introducing our "friend."

"Are we interrupting something?" she asked.

"Uh, no—but, uh, actually—bathroom!" I gasped incoherently. Before Taye could sit in his chair and block us in, I snatched Zylas's arm and dove away from the table. Dragging the demon behind me, I rushed to the front of the restaurant and ducked into the short hallway that led to the bathroom. Flinging the ladies' room door open, I checked it was empty.

"Come on," I hissed, pulling on Zylas's arm. "Get in here!"

He didn't move.

"Zylas, get in the bathroom! Once we're inside, you can return to the infer—"

His lips pulled back from his teeth in a viciously triumphant smile. "I can smell him."

"Smell who? The vampires?"

"No." He inhaled deeply through his nose. "The *hh'ainun*. The summoner." His head turned to me, my pale face reflected in his sunglasses. "I can smell Claude."

21

ZYLAS WAS OUT OF THE RESTAURANT in an instant, leaving me to rush after him. I cast a helpless look over my shoulder, meeting Amalia's surprised stare, then I pushed through the door.

"I have his scent," Zylas hissed as I joined him. "Not very old. Earlier this day he walked here."

"And you smelled him near the bathrooms?" I supposed it made sense. Fewer people walked down that hall than crossed the restaurant's dining room. But why had Claude been there in the first place? Unless he also enjoyed cheesy calzones after a hard day of plotting against his former business partner.

Zylas rounded a corner, his purposeful gait causing other pedestrians to hurriedly clear the way, and I was right behind him when a shout pulled me up short. Amalia ran to my side, puffing from her sprint. "What the hell?"

"Zylas caught Claude's scent."

"*Claude?*" She fell into step beside me. "No shit! I told Zora and that other guy they could have our food."

"Good. We don't want any company for this." I swallowed anxiously. "If we find Claude, we'll probably have to fight his demon."

"Unless his demon isn't with him. Seems like he sends it off on its own, doesn't it? You said there was no sign of Claude last night."

"That's true, but Claude could have been nearby."

Zylas turned into a gap between towers. Set back from the street, a nondescript entryway led into a vestibule with a security door and a panel of suite numbers and intercom codes. Zylas tried the door. When it didn't budge, crimson magic cascaded up his arm.

Three seconds later, he pushed the door open, the locking mechanism severed by his new burglary technique. He angled across the barren foyer and headed down the first hall. I tugged my infernus from under my sweater and settled it on my chest.

Zylas halted in front of a door. Nostrils flaring, he tilted his ear toward the wood.

"I hear nothing," he whispered, "but the *hh'ainun's* scent is strong. So is the scent of fresh blood."

"Vampires?" I mouthed silently.

With a quick spiral of glowing runes, he destroyed the bolt and pushed the door open on soundless hinges.

The interior was dim and unlit, heavy drapes covering the windows. Zylas glided inside and I inched in after him, scanning the unit. On one side, a bathroom. On the other, a dining nook converted to an office, a kitchen with a long island and modern finishes, and at the far end, a living room with a small sectional, a coffee table, and a wall-mounted TV.

Zylas ventured through a door into what I assumed was the bedroom, then reappeared. He pulled his sunglasses off. "There is no one here, but the scent of blood is everywhere."

"What is this place?" I asked Amalia. "Does it belong to Claude? I thought he lived in that townhouse."

"Crooks like him and my dad usually have a few homes," Amalia replied. "But based on *this*, it's safe to say this apartment definitely belongs to Claude."

She was standing at the kitchen island, where papers were laid out in a neat row. They were documents, all of them about or belonging to Uncle Jack. Tax records, electricity bills, a copy of his driver's license, lists of his relatives and business associates, and—my heart jumped—the page of emergency contacts I'd seen in the vampire's tower hideout last night. The one his demon had stolen from me.

Amalia tapped a lone page at the end of the row. Neat, masculine handwriting listed names and addresses, each one boldly crossed out.

"All places Claude has checked," she said. "Look, this one, that's a safe house we used three years ago. And that's my cousin's house. This one is my language tutor. Claude's looked *everywhere*."

"They're all scratched out." A flutter of satisfaction lightened my middle. "Wherever Uncle Jack has gone to ground, he's outsmarted Claude."

Amalia grinned ruefully. "Too bad he's outsmarting us as well. Where the hell could he be?" She ran her finger down the list. "Look here—Katrine Fredericks. Calgary, Alberta. Look what he wrote!"

Beside the Calgary address were five scrawled words: *Confirmed decoy. Kathy is alone.*

"My stepmom is in *Alberta*?" Amalia exclaimed. "And Dad isn't with her? Aunty Katrine is her sister, so I guess that makes sense. Well, at least I know where to find one of them now." She shuffled through a few more documents, then picked up a stack of photos. "Ha, look at this. I must be, like, four years old."

I leaned closer to see the photo of a blond girl staring aggressively into the camera. "Is that your mom with you?"

"Yep." Amalia smiled at the equally blond woman with a similarly intense stare. "She died when I was eight, and Dad married Kathy a year later. I hated him for that for a long time."

She flipped to the next photo. "That's my great uncle. Oh, and this one is a fishing buddy of dad's, but he died two years ago."

She turned the picture over. *"Deceased – illness"* was scrawled across the back in red ink.

"Has Claude checked all of these?" she mused as she shuffled through the stack. "He's been one busy …"

Trailing off, she stared at a snapshot of her dad beside an older man in camouflage and an orange vest, a rifle in one hand. A large, dead moose with a broad rack of antlers crowning its oblong head lay at their feet. Was it legal to hunt moose?

She checked the reverse side, which featured a single question mark in red ink, and whispered, "No way."

"Drādah!" Zylas barked.

My head snapped up. Red light lit his body, and he dissolved into crimson power that flashed toward me. The human clothes he'd been wearing dropped to the floor in a lumpy puddle of fabric.

The infernus was still vibrating against my chest when the apartment door swung open. I jerked back, expecting Claude to walk through—but it wasn't the summoner standing in the threshold.

Zora scowled at me, her sword case hanging over her shoulder and her leather jacket zipped up to her throat. Taye stood behind her, dark eyebrows arched high on his dusky face.

"Zora," I gasped. "How—how did you … find … us?"

"Taye is a telethesian."

My knees weakened with dismay. Telethesians were psychics with a supernatural ability to track people, especially mythics. Taye was the perfect partner for scoping the tower and searching out the vampires' new location. Also perfect for tracking a suspicious contractor and her suspicious friend after they'd ditched a restaurant and run off into the downtown streets.

"So," Zora drawled, hitching her sword case higher on her shoulder, "what's going on?"

My mind had gone completely, uselessly blank, and I was painfully aware of Zylas's abandoned clothes behind me. If Zora noticed them—and recognized them as my "friend's" outfit …

"Uh …" I mumbled.

"You haven't been part of this guild for long," she said coolly, "so maybe you don't know, but when we team up for jobs, we don't leave our teammates in the dark."

I blinked.

"Unless this isn't related to your summoner investigation?"

"Uh, it is," I stammered, "but it … it isn't *vampire* related, so I didn't think you—"

"It isn't?" Taye interrupted in his deep, accented voice. "There are vampire traces everywhere. Plus, Zora, you're glowing."

"I'm glowing?" she repeated blankly. "Oh!"

She stuck her hand in her jeans pocket, where a faint red glow shone through the fabric, and withdrew a blood-tracker artifact. I gasped fearfully. Vampires were nearby?

"Hmm." Zora turned in a slow circle. The faint light brightened as she aimed it toward the kitchen nook with Claude's desk. She strode closer and the glow increased. Taye, Amalia, and I followed cautiously.

Zora raised it higher, then lowered it toward the floor. The glow intensified as it drew level with the desk's bottom drawer.

"I don't think there's a vampire in there," she said dryly.

She tugged on the drawer and it slid open. Inside was a metal case similar to a safety deposit box. Kneeling beside her, I lifted it out. The latch flipped easily, no lock or spell sealing it shut. Inside, two heavy-duty steel syringes were nestled in a foam insert. A third slot in the foam was empty. Above them were three vials of clear liquid marred by tiny bubbles.

I stared at the syringes, cold recognition flowing through me. I remembered Claude's demon tossing one to Claude, the needle coated in Zylas's blood. I remembered Zylas collapsing to his knees, clutching my waist as he struggled to stay upright, and Claude's quiet, gloating words: *A good summoner knows how to safely neutralize a demon.*

"What on earth is this?" Zora asked, bewildered.

Amalia reached past me. She lifted a second metal case from the drawer and opened it. Instead of syringes, it held five sealed vials of dark liquid. She wiggled one out of the foam insert and held it up. Light refracted through the thick fluid, revealing its red tone.

Dark, thick blood. *Demon* blood.

"Zora," Taye said sharply.

As one, we all looked at the blood tracker she held. The gem-like end was glowing brighter by the second.

For an instant, none of us reacted, then Taye backpedaled toward the center of the room, facing the open door. Zora dropped the blood tracker and grabbed the zipper of her weapon bag. Amalia snapped the case of blood shut and shoved it on top of the desk as she backed away.

I didn't move, my mind spinning as pieces clicked into place—but the answers I now possessed had created more questions.

"Robin!" Amalia yelled in warning.

I looked up.

Three vampires filled the doorway. Red rings marked their eerie eyes and their fingers had elongated into deadly claws. The two males and a female, reflective sunglasses perched on top of their heads, wore jeans and jackets like every other pedestrian on the streets.

"Looky what we found," a male crooned.

Zora pulled her sword from its sheath with a rasp. The blade gleamed. "Out in the sunlight, bloodsuckers? How bold."

The female vampire leered delightedly. "Not a problem … not for us."

"We were waiting for a summoner." The creepy male licked his lips. "Not pretty ladies."

"Taye," Zora called. "Get out of here. Use the patio."

The telethesian rushed toward the sliding glass doors. Amalia shot me a questioning look and I nodded. She ran after the psychic and they disappeared outside.

Setting her feet in a defensive stance, Zora raised her sword confidently—but she had no idea these vampires were nothing like the ones she'd made her career exterminating.

The three vampires smiled. They knew we didn't stand a chance.

The creepy one stepped away from the others, his weird eyes on Zora. He strolled toward her, getting closer and closer to the shining blade of her weapon.

"*Ori torpeas languescas*," she said quietly. A faint shimmer ran down the sword.

He took one more step—then blurred almost out of sight as he lunged for Zora.

She wheeled sideways, saved by her combat reflexes. The vampire shot past her, spun, and halted, leering tauntingly.

"What the ..." She adjusted her grip on the sword. "This bastard is a fast one."

I grabbed my infernus. "They're all fast."

Red light flared across my pendant and all three vampires attacked at once.

The creepy one charged Zora again while the other two came straight for me. Zylas materialized with his dark claws slashing. He sprang between the two vampires, striking both simultaneously. A whirling kick sent one vampire flying past me. She hit the refrigerator headfirst and bounced off, the dented door swinging open.

Zylas exchanged swift blows with his second opponent. As the first one climbed to her feet, shaking her head back and forth as though stunned, I threw my full weight into the fridge door. It slammed shut on her head.

Across the living room, Zora darted side to side, frantically evading her adversary. A spell glowed on her left wrist, not doing anything as far as I could see. The vampire circled her, his attacks swift but playful. He was toying with the petite sorceress.

As the vampire pounced again, laughing nastily, she whipped her sword around. The tip of the blade nicked the vamp's arm—and a shimmer ran up the length of steel. Silver runes flashed across the vampire's arm and over his shoulder.

Beside me, the female vampire pushed backward off the fridge, wobbling unsteadily after the second impact to her skull. Before I could panic, Zylas slid across the island counter. He slammed both feet into the vampire, knocking her back into the open fridge. Condiment bottles tumbled to the floor.

He grabbed the door and swung it shut on her torso—but with exponentially more power than I had. Plastic shattered, metal warped, and bones crunched.

At the other end of the room, Zora's opponent was no longer playful. Silver runes glowed on his side and he kept lurching and stumbling, one half of his body moving much slower than the other.

The third vampire leaped over the counter. Zylas met him with open claws and tried to ram his fingers between the man's ribs. The vampire twisted away, then struck Zylas in the chest. The demon slammed into the fridge, crushing the female vampire all over again.

With a furious shriek, she flung the door open, throwing Zylas forward. Unhampered by her broken bones, she lunged for his back. The other vampire sprang at his front.

The terrifying memory of pointed fangs sinking into his skin flashed through me.

"*Ori eruptum impello!*" I yelled.

My new artifact flashed brightly and a dome of pale light burst from it. It expanded outward—and everything it touched was flung away from it: a toaster, a knife block, a drain tray full of dishes—

—and the two vampires and demon in front of me.

The vampires slammed into the counters on either side while Zylas was blasted across the length of the kitchen. He landed hard on his back, ten feet away. The fridge door slammed yet again and all the glass inside shattered.

My mouth hung open.

The vampires jumped back up, and Zylas rolled to his feet, shooting me his meanest glare. I winced guiltily.

Note to self: don't use spell *against* my demon.

Exchanging a look, the vampires split—one facing me and one facing Zylas. My face went cold. My artifact needed time to recharge before I could use it again. I was defenseless, and I couldn't even use the sidestep evasion technique Zylas had taught me because there was nowhere to go.

The two vampires charged.

Daimon, hesychaze!

Zylas dissolved into red light. The blaze of power streaked across the kitchen, passing right through the vampires, and hit the infernus. He reformed in front of me, claws flashing. He caught the vampire's reaching arm, planted his foot on the man's side, and wrenched.

I almost passed out on the spot when the vampire's arm tore off his body.

A shriek jerked my attention away from the bloodletting. I expected to see Zora on the floor, but it was the vampire scuttling backward, spitting with rage and bleeding from multiple wounds he seemed unaware of. The spell that had slowed him down had faded, but one of his legs was dragging awkwardly, half severed.

He shuffled backward and Zora, several spells glowing over her wrists, drove him into the bedroom. They disappeared inside. A heartbeat of silence—then a burst of golden magic. The wave of force caught the bedroom door and swung it shut with a bang.

I whirled back to Zylas and the remaining two vampires. *Now! Quickly!*

Crimson magic blazed up his arms. Six-inch talons extended from his fingers, and he buried them in the nearer vampire's chest. As the creature fell, the female vampire backpedaled in fright. Zylas stretched out his hand and two glowing triangles snapped around his wrist.

Power blazed and a spear of red light shot across the kitchen and struck the female vampire in the chest. She keeled over backward, a hole through her heart.

The bedroom door remained safely closed, and I let out a relieved sigh as Zylas banished the telltale glow of crimson from his hands. Stepping over the mess, I headed toward the bedroom to check if Zora was okay.

I got two steps and froze.

Zora was okay. I could see she was okay because she was standing in the bathroom doorway. The *bathroom*. Not the bedroom, even though I'd seen her go into the bedroom. The two rooms ... they must be connected.

She was standing in the doorway, sword in hand and her face deathly white. If I'd had any hope she hadn't seen Zylas's magic, her horrified expression immediately dispelled it.

22

ZORA'S GAZE DARTED between me and my demon, and her hands tightened on the hilt of her sword.

Zylas shifted his weight onto the balls of his feet, his fingers curling and claws glinting.

Daimon, hesychaze!

His head snapped toward me, disbelief and fury briefly touching his face before his body melted into glowing power. Crimson light leaped into the infernus and I closed my hand around the pendant.

Just stay there, I told him urgently. *Let me handle this.*

The silver buzzed under my hand, then went quiet. I exhaled shakily.

Zora slowly raised her sword. "So ... does this mean you *don't* plan to kill me now that I know you're an illegal contractor?"

"Of course I won't k-kill you." I wished my voice wasn't shaking. "Let me explain."

"Illegal contracts are *illegal*," she snapped. "Most of them come with a death sentence for the contractor. And yours isn't just a loose contract—your demon was using *magic*. How?"

She again shifted her grip on her sword, the long blade wavering, and I noticed the blood dripping from her elbow. The vampire had raked her upper arms with his claws.

I twisted my hands together. "Zora, please—"

"How did you fool Darius?" Her eyes blazed. "MagiPol is just *waiting* for an excuse to disband the Crow and Hammer. How dare you put our guild at risk?"

"I—I didn't—"

"A contracted demon with *magic*," she spat. "Now I know how you took down the unbound demon on Halloween. There's no way you can control your demon. There's no way you aren't a danger to *everyone* with that—"

The patio door banged open. Taye rushed in, Amalia right behind him.

"Zora," he said sharply. "You all right? The police are on the way. I put in a call to the MPD and they're sending agents and a cleanup crew, but we should leave the crime scene."

Her furious stare jerked back to me. "Are you waiting for the MPD?"

So they could arrest me on the spot? No thanks. "I—I should go."

"You can go for now," she said darkly, "but we aren't finished, Robin Page."

Taye's brow furrowed, whereas Amalia's expression flashed from confusion to alarm as she guessed what had happened.

Zora grabbed her sword case off the floor and crunched across the room to the patio. Amalia stepped back as the sorceress strode out the doors, Taye hurrying after her. As their footsteps retreated, the wail of police sirens drifted into the unit, growing louder by the second.

"Shit," Amalia muttered. "What does she know?"

"She saw Zylas use magic," I said heavily, fighting the nausea building in my stomach. "She knows my contract isn't legal, but not the full extent of it."

"Shit," she said again. "We need to get out of here."

Nodding grimly, I climbed over the fridge door—when had it fallen off?—and grabbed both the case of demon blood and the case of syringes from Claude's desk. Amalia scooped the papers and photos off the floor. Carrying our loot, we ducked out the doors.

The patio backed onto a courtyard shared by several apartment towers. We cut across it and joined the busy sidewalk. Three police cruisers with their lights flashing were parked on the curb, two officers directing pedestrians away while four more headed toward the condos. They were about to get a nasty surprise. The MPD agents would have fun smoothing over that bloodbath.

All in all, though, that didn't even rank on my list of worries.

I clutched the metal cases to my chest, breathing hard. Zora knew my secret. What would she do? Report me to the MPD? Report me to Darius? Both courses of action would have the same result. Darius had warned me that if anyone from the Crow and Hammer discovered the truth, he would turn me in to protect his guildeds.

No matter how I looked at it, I was doomed.

"Maybe she won't report you," Amalia said, her mind on the same worries as mine. "It's not like you're hurting anyone. Maybe …"

Faint hope sparked, but I didn't let it grow. Considering how furious and betrayed she'd appeared, I didn't think she'd ignore her discovery.

"I'll call her," I mumbled. "If I can explain the situation like I did with Darius, she might look the other way."

"Yeah … yeah, she probably will."

Silence fell between us. We both knew we were fooling ourselves.

"I grabbed all this stuff"—she hefted her armload of papers—"so the MPD wouldn't have a reason to look at my dad, but why'd you take those cases?"

"These are proof."

"Of what?"

"One holds bottled demon blood. The other … it has vials of vampire saliva. Last time we saw him, Claude used a syringe of it to bring down Zylas."

I couldn't believe I hadn't put the clues together before. The tranquilizing effect of a vampire bite was identical to Zylas's collapse after he'd been injected with the mysterious syringe. Vamp saliva was the perfect demon neutralizer, especially since it had an even stronger effect on demons than humans.

"You think Claude has been trading his demon's blood to the vampires in exchange for their saliva?" Amalia squinted. "But why did they trash his townhouse? And why did his demon steal back his documents from the vampires?"

"That part I don't get, but I suspect it has something to do with that Vasilii guy the other vampires are following. Maybe Vasilii isn't happy with their arrangement anymore."

We stopped at a crosswalk and waited for the light to change. The lunch rush had dispersed, leaving the streets much quieter.

"Hmm, well." Amalia cast me a sharp smile. "We might not know what's going on with Claude and the vampires, but we do have *this*."

She held up the snapshot of Uncle Jack and the bearded stranger standing over a dead moose.

"What's special about that?"

"This," she declared, waving the photo, "is where we're going to find my dad."

NOT EVEN A HOT SHOWER could calm the nerves churning through my gut. I rubbed a towel over my hair, watching my reflection in the foggy bathroom mirror. A thin white scar stood out against the smooth skin of my neck; the sight of it always chilled me. My blue eyes were tired and a seemingly permanent wrinkle of worry had formed between my eyebrows.

In less than twelve hours, I might finally reclaim my mother's grimoire.

According to Amalia, that photo was the clue she'd needed to figure out her dad's location. She'd booked a rental car so we could drive out to the property in the photo, owned by the bearded man whose identity Claude hadn't been able to uncover.

If she was right, my uncle would be there, and almost eight months after my parents' deaths, I would have in my hands their most treasured possession—a possession they might have died protecting. The two letters my mother had written, one to her brother and one to her daughter, sat on my bedside table. I would bring them with me tomorrow, and when I saw Uncle Jack, I would demand not only the grimoire, but answers. And, unlike our past confrontations, I wouldn't take "no" for an answer.

The girl he'd bullied and dismissed seemed like a stranger to me now. The new and improved Robin was a contractor. She regularly pitted her will against an ornery demon. She had faced an escaped demon from the powerful First House, a rogue guild, and unnaturally powerful vampires. She wouldn't be intimidated by her portly, middle-aged, cowardly uncle.

Or so I hoped.

I scrunched the water from my hair, considered blow-drying it, then decided I was too tired. Throwing my towel over the edge of the tub—the towel rack lay on the floor, ripped off the wall by Zylas—I pulled on a tank top and PJ shorts.

Cool air rushed into the steamy bathroom when I opened the door. Across the living room, a pair of green eyes reflected the dim light. Socks was curled up on the sofa, watching me, and I crossed the room to scratch her furry ears. The whir of Amalia's sewing machine accompanied the pattering of the rain against the window. I wasn't the only one having trouble sleeping tonight.

MPD agents hadn't knocked down our apartment door, so I assumed Zora hadn't reported my illegal contract yet. I'd tried calling her—six times—but my calls had all gone straight to voicemail. I didn't dare go to the guild to see if she was there.

All I could do was wait and see what happened. Would Zora pretend she hadn't seen anything illegal, or would the MPD be waiting for us when we returned from our outing tomorrow?

With a final pat for Socks, I wandered into my room. Only after I'd shut the door did I notice the dark shadow by my window.

Zylas sat on the floor, one shoulder leaning against the wall, his arm resting on the sill. His chin was propped on his forearm, crimson eyes gazing through the rain-streaked glass. Still and silent, he was a statue draped in shadow, the faint light from beyond the window tracing one edge of his jaw. His breath fogged on the glass, a white mist.

A memory slipped into my mind: Rose's crystal ball. The pale fog, the shadow of Zylas within it. Sitting still and silent, staring into nothing.

Uncertainty rooted my bare feet to the carpet, but I pushed myself forward. His gaze swept up to my face as I approached, his expression indecipherable.

"Are you going out tonight?" I asked softly.

"No." He returned his attention to the window. "Tonight I will stay."

He, too, was worried about what the morning might bring.

Another hesitation locked my muscles. Pushing away my inexplicable unease, I sank to the carpet beside him, pulling my knees up to my chest and wrapping my arms around them. I was dressed for bed and the air was cool on my exposed skin.

"Tomorrow, we might get the grimoire back," I murmured. "I don't know how long it will take me to translate it, but … it could have answers on how to send you home."

He said nothing.

"What's your home like?" The curious question slipped out thoughtlessly. I expected him to ignore it, but his head tilted slightly, gaze on the city street below.

"It is very different from here." His low, husky voice blended with the night and shivered across my skin. "There are many places we do not go where it is too hot or too cold. Where we live … the land is made of rock and sand. It is red, almost like me. The plants are darker, some red, some green."

My eyelids slid partway closed as I imagined it. A desert landscape of burnt maroon, the sand drifting among wind-carved rock. Dark foliage sprouted in nooks and crannies, clinging to life beneath a harsh, blazing sun.

"Some places, water runs deep and wide, and trees grow tall. Other places, there is no water for endless distances and we catch the rain at night to drink." His gaze drifted toward me. "The sun is hot in the day, but the land grows cold at night. Colder than here. You would not survive a night in my world."

"Does the cold bother you?" I whispered. I didn't know why I was whispering, only that I could almost *see* his words. I could imagine my head angled back, mouth open to the pouring rain, the liquid cool on my parched tongue.

"Only if we are weakened. During the day, we rest and recover our *vīsh*. At night, we hunt … or we are hunted. It is cold and very dark. The clouds come at night, and the rain. Great storms."

Roiling clouds lit by streaking white lightning. Earth-shaking thunder and torrential rain carving rivers of mud into the sand and rock. The powerful wind sweeping against me.

"We must conserve *vīsh* until the sun," he murmured. "It is a game and a hunt and a battle. Who is smartest? Who is strongest? They survive."

Glowing eyes in the darkness. A dim but distinct outline of heat and magic, curved wings spreading wide. A slash of fear in my chest.

I gave my head a sharp shake and absently rubbed my sternum as my heart rate kicked up. "You're hunted more because you're a demon king, aren't you?"

"I have always been hunted."

"Why?"

"Because I am Vh'alyir. I am Twelfth House. We are weak." His eyes glowed fiercely. "I have taught them to fear Vh'alyir."

Another zing of apprehension hit me, this one triggered by the savagery sliding across his features. "How?"

"They do not fear my strength, but the strike from the darkness." His tail lashed sideways, a quiet rustle across the carpet. "They call me *nailēris*, but they do not laugh at my House any longer."

Gooseflesh prickled up my arms, compounded by the chill air. The other demons called him cowardly ... but he had taught them to fear him anyway. For the first time, I saw a shadow of regal power in him, of unyielding command and ruthless authority.

"You're talkative tonight," I said weakly. "What were you thinking about before I came in?"

He let his head fall back, resting it against the window's edge. I saw no sign of his wolfish smirk, his contrary antagonism, or even his dangerous but semi-playful badgering.

"Maybe I will return soon to my world." His voice dropped, deeper and rougher, his accent thickening. "I will return not as *Dīnen* but as *Ivaknen* ... the Summoned."

The Summoned. I shivered again and rubbed my upper arms. His gaze followed the movement and he leaned forward with sudden interest. Warm hand closing over my wrist, he drew my arm up to peer at my skin.

"What is wrong with you?" he asked.

I rolled my eyes. "Nothing is wrong. It's how human skin reacts to cold."

"It is not cold."

"It is for me. The weather has to be much warmer than this for humans to walk around in as little clothing as you do."

He turned my hand over and his fingertips slid across my inner wrist. "This has not changed. Is this part of you not cold?"

I opened my mouth—but couldn't remember how to speak. He stroked the top of my forearm, exploring the texture of my skin as full-on gooseflesh made every fine hair stand on end.

He lifted my arm to his face and rubbed the lower edge of his cheek across my inner wrist. "This is smooth."

I didn't move, didn't utter a sound. Only my heart reacted, pounding erratically in my chest.

He ran his hand down my forearm, his palm hot as it passed over the scars from the first time he'd healed me. His fingers found the inner crease of my elbow, then traced up to my shoulder. My held breath rushed out between my parted lips.

His crimson eyes skimmed across me and found my bare legs—then his hand wrapped around my knee. He ran his fingers up the side of my thigh, his thumb rubbing across the slight bumps, his touch sliding higher.

Paralysis breaking, I scooted away from him. "Yes, my skin is different from yours. That's enough of—"

He stuck his hand under the hem of my tank top. His hot fingers brushed across my waist. "You are smooth here."

"Zylas," I snapped. "Stop—"

He pushed away from the wall, gaze fixed on my middle, intent on the mystery of gooseflesh. I pushed backward, feet slipping on the carpet. He followed, a graceful shadow with glowing eyes. His hand slid up my side, triggering a rippling shiver along my spine and causing a fresh wave of gooseflesh to rise in the wake of his touch.

I shoved away and my head bumped against my mattress. Nowhere left to retreat. His hands were on my waist, pushing up my shirt, and undiluted panic shot through me.

I grabbed his wrists. "*Zylas!*"

He stilled as my nails dug into his skin. The only sound was my quick, harsh breathing.

His mouth shifted into a frown—then he released my shirt, hands pulling free from my grasp. He sat back on his heels, his frown deepening into a scowl. "I did not hurt you."

The words were a question, a complaint, and an accusation all wrapped into one.

"No." I gulped down air. "But that doesn't mean you can do whatever you want."

"*Ch.*"

I shoved forward, glowering at him before I even realized how angry I was. "You aren't the only one who wants their autonomy respected, Zylas!"

He recoiled from my vehemence.

"You don't want me to use the infernus command unless absolutely necessary, and I'm respecting that. You need to respect me when I tell you to stop doing something I don't like."

His head tilted in a puzzled way. "You do not like it when I touch you?"

My stomach gave an odd, panicky flop. "I—I'm not …" My head spun. "Don't touch me under my clothes."

His nose scrunched like that was a bewildering stipulation. Heart beating uncomfortably fast, I pushed myself to my feet and tugged my shirt straight.

"I need to sleep." I flipped my blankets back. "We have a lot to do tomorrow. Uncle Jack, the grimoire … and we have to figure out what's happening with Zora."

"Figure out what?" he muttered. "It is easy to fix."

I glanced over my shoulder, eyebrows raised. "Oh really?"

"I will kill her."

"We're not killing her," I scoffed, climbing into bed. "We've discussed this before and—"

"*Drādah.*"

I hadn't heard him stand, but he was on his feet, his crimson stare fixed on me but not with the keen curiosity of a minute ago.

"She knows I am not enslaved," he growled quietly. "She will tell others, and they will come to kill you. I must kill her first to protect you."

Alarm buzzed across my nerves and I pushed my shoulders back, hands gripping my blanket. "Do *not* hurt her, Zylas."

"She knows—"

"We'll find another way. If you kill her, Darius will know it was you and he'll report us to the MPD anyway."

"I will make her disappear."

"No!" Panic rose through me again. "She's a guild member, she helped us, she—she's my *friend*, Zylas."

He curled his lip in disdain. "You will die so she can live?"

My mouth trembled and I clenched my jaw. "I won't kill her to save myself."

"*Nailis,*" he sneered.

"Cruel!" I retorted, pointing at him as tears stung my eyes. "Heartless! Barbaric! How can you even think about killing an innocent woman to save yourself?"

"To save *you*," he snarled. "I bound myself to protect you."

"We'll find a different way."

"What way? This is most safe. It is most easy."

"You want to kill her because it's *easy*?" My throat tightened with fear. I couldn't stop him from doing whatever he wanted. Even if I forced him back into the infernus, he would escape as soon as I fell asleep. "If you hurt her, Zylas, if you so much as lay a finger on her, I—I won't send you home."

His eyes widened. "You promised!"

He could tell if I was lying—and he knew my threat was deadly serious.

"I did, but if you go behind my back and hurt her, I won't do *anything* to help you."

He stared at me as though he'd never seen me before. Rage twisted his face, lips pulling back from his pointed canines. His hands clenched and glowing veins streaked up his wrists.

"Your promises mean nothing. Your words mean *nothing*."

As his furious snarl rumbled through the room, crimson power blazed across him. His body dissolved and the band of light leaped into the infernus on my bedside table. The pendant vibrated, then went still.

I flung myself onto my bed, face buried in my pillow to hide the tears streaking down my face. Zora had helped us, fought beside us, supported me—and he was perfectly fine with killing her. Perfectly willing. Perfectly remorseless.

No matter what he did, what he said … no matter how fiercely he protected me or how carefully he touched me … under the surface, he had no heart. He didn't care, didn't feel, didn't love. He could kill anyone and feel nothing. He could kill *me* and feel nothing.

Why had I ever thought he might be anything other than a monster?

23

"ROBIN," AMALIA HOLLERED, "would you hurry up?"

I hastily pulled the turtleneck sweater over my head, almost dislodging the small ponytail I'd forced my hair into—aided by half a pound of bobby pins. My hair was barely long enough to tie back.

My new black sweater was soft but the fabric didn't stretch and I had to wiggle my arms into the long sleeves. It fell to the tops of my thighs, the sleeves brushing my knuckles. I did up a row of buttons that ran over the shoulder and up the neck. Buttoned, the fabric hugged my throat.

Dropping the chain of my infernus and new artifact over my head, I hurried out of the room. Amalia stood near the door, her winter coat in one hand and car keys jingling impatiently in the other. She wore a turtleneck identical to mine—black with a dizzying pattern embroidered over every inch in matching thread. The effect was subtle but quite striking.

"Finally," she exclaimed. "How does it fit?"

I straightened the sweater's hem in annoyance. Considering how many times I'd waited for *her*, she could be more patient. "It's fine."

She nodded. "I prefer to use a knit fabric or even a cotton poplin stretch for shirts, but those wouldn't work with the embroidery."

I ran a fingertip over my sleeve, tracing a familiar shape hidden in the pattern. "A shielding cantrip?"

"Yep." She slapped her flat stomach. "The hexes cover the entire shirt. I've tested them with knives, though I doubt they'd stop a bullet. Still, every little bit helps, right? The effect lasts about half a minute."

I reexamined our sweaters. She'd finished both last night and insisted we wear them today—more because she was proud of her work than because we needed them. Uncle Jack, assuming we found him, wasn't likely to stab us.

Still, a shirt that could protect you from piercing attacks for thirty seconds was pretty amazing. The shield cantrip wasn't one I'd have thought to use. It was mostly useless because you had to draw a ridiculously huge rune to protect anything larger than a post-it note; the smaller the cantrip, the less magic it absorbed and released.

But covering an entire shirt in small cantrips was ingenious; they'd all trigger together with a single incantation. And the craziest part was that a sewn cantrip worked at all. Cantrips were normally drawn by hand because the process of creating them imbued the symbol with power. A regular human could draw runes all day long and not one would contain a smidge of magic. Only Arcana mythics could create them.

Amalia was watching me with a raised eyebrow—waiting for my approval.

"It's nice," I reiterated. Hadn't I already said it was good?

"Uh-huh. Let's get going, then."

I grabbed an extra sweater and followed her down to the parking lot where our rental car—which Amalia had picked up this morning—waited. I opened the dull gray door and climbed into the equally dull and gray interior. Amalia dropped into the driver's seat, started the engine, and we were off.

Time to find my uncle and get the Athanas Grimoire back. It was finally happening.

We made it out of downtown with little trouble and drove through the disreputable Eastside for twenty minutes. Crossing the harbor, we entered the significantly greener and more spacious neighborhoods of North Vancouver.

"So," Amalia began, "what's your problem this morning?"

I stared through the windshield at the mountain silhouettes filling the horizon. "No problem."

"Yeah, sure. How come I haven't seen your demon pal all morning, even though we should have run our plan past him before getting in this crappy rental car and driving to the middle of nowhere?"

"I told him the plan. In my head. He can hear me. Also, he's not my *pal*."

"What is he, then?"

"He's a demon."

She cast me a questioning look, then returned her attention to the road. An irascible frown settled onto her lips as she exited the freeway and merged onto a smaller thoroughfare.

Maybe … maybe I was a bit moody today. *She* wasn't the reason for my bad temperament.

"Thank you for the hex sweater," I said, properly sincere this time. "I can't believe you made something so beautiful and comfortable that's also stab-proof. It's really amazing."

Her frown eased. "Glad you like it. You're the first person besides me to wear one of my projects."

My smile softened into a more natural expression. "Thank you for sharing it with me. Do you have plans to sell your work? I bet guilds would love them."

"Maybe. I need to do more testing first. Fabrics and magic don't mix all that well and I'm not sure how quickly the hexes will deteriorate."

Falling silent, she concentrated on navigating a section of road construction that had closed one lane. The houses grew sparser.

"Oh, shit!" Amalia flipped on her signal light and zipped into the left lane. "This is our turn."

We made the corner on the yellow light, and the last signs of residential neighborhood disappeared. The road, hemmed in by green spruce and hemlock, slanted upward. Though the dense forest blocked our view, I knew we were ascending the sprawling slopes of Mount Seymour. Scattered vehicles drove with us, heading toward the ski resort near the peak.

"Where exactly are we going?" I asked. "Not to the resort, right?"

"Ha, no. The property isn't that high up the mountain. It's on the west side."

"And it belongs to the old guy from the photo—Kevin, you called him?"

"Kevin and Dad were hunting buddies, and my family used to come out here every summer. I always hated it. *So* boring.

Kathy thought so too, and she kicked up such a fuss about it that Dad quit going. He hasn't been in almost ten years."

I wrinkled my nose. "That sucks for your dad."

"If he wanted to enjoy life, he shouldn't have married Kathy." Amalia leaned forward as though encouraging the car onward up the incline. "Ugh, why didn't we get an SUV instead of this shit-mobile?"

"What makes you so sure your dad is out here?"

"First, Claude ruled out every possible option besides this one. And second, it's perfect. Kevin doesn't own this property. He borrows it from his cousin. And as far as I—or anyone else— knows, Dad and Kevin haven't talked in years, and there's no paper trail to tie either of them to this location. It's private, isolated, and totally safe."

Sounded plausible. "I hope Uncle Jack has answers."

"Yes," Amalia agreed fiercely. "First, I want to know why he couldn't get a message to me. Second, I want to know what the hell is up with Claude. And third, all this weirdness with vampires."

I pressed my lips together. "What I want is the grimoire."

"We won't learn *anything* if your demon goes berserk and kills my dad. Zylas won't have any warm, fuzzy feelings for his summoner. You sure you've got him under control?"

"He won't lay a hand on your dad," I confirmed grimly. "I already warned him."

"Yeah, but since when is he obedient?"

"He'll behave. If he doesn't, I won't send him home."

She steered the car around a tight bend. A few snowflakes swirled past the windows. "But you *want* to send him home so you can be rid of his demonic ass."

"I do, but if he kills people …" I folded my arms across my chest. "I'm not helping him with anything if he kills people."

"He's a demon. Killing is what they do." She paused. "Didn't you *promise* you'd send him home?"

"I did, but—"

"And you told him you'll rescind that promise if he doesn't do what you want?"

"Yes, but—"

"Oh hell." She shot me a disbelieving look. "No wonder he's in a snit."

A guilty, anxious squirm awoke in my belly. "What do you mean?"

"You have to ask? Come on. You two made a deal, and you can't just add new terms or conditions to it on a whim."

"How else am I supposed to stop him from murdering people?"

"I don't know, but Robin …" She shook her head, her blond ponytail swinging. "That horned asshole is going to be complete misery to deal with now. Your promise to send him home was the only thing keeping him in check."

"But I *will* send him home as long as he—"

"Yeah, but he won't trust you anymore." At my confused look, she sighed. "It's a power thing, Robin. If you have the power to change the deal and he doesn't, that makes the deal worthless. Changing your promise is the same as breaking it."

Your promises mean nothing. Zylas's furious accusation.

Deep, icy cold settled in my gut, making itself right at home like it intended to stay awhile.

"Ah, here's the turn off!" She slowed the car as the highway doubled back on itself in order to continue up the side of the mountain. On our left, a short gravel offshoot split in a Y-shape, with one track heading uphill and one descending the mountainside.

She waited a minute with her signal on, craning her neck to watch the oncoming cars. When a gap in the traffic opened, she gunned it across the highway and angled toward the downhill road where a gate, bolted with a chain and boldly marked with a Private Property sign, blocked our passage.

She shifted into park, hopped out, and jogged up to the gate, leaving the car door hanging open. A moment of fumbling with the chain, then she shoved the gates open.

"Wasn't even locked," she announced as she dropped back into her seat and shut her door. "Great security. At least it isn't snowed in up here."

The car bumped along the gravel, the vibrations rattling my teeth. My nerves grew, my stomach twisting unhappily and that pit of ice unchanged. Once we were done here, I would make Zylas understand that I hadn't betrayed my promise. I'd only wanted to …

… to control him by leveraging the one thing he really wanted.

Oh crap. That's what I'd done, wasn't it? No wonder he was furious.

The gravel road went on and on, the car's constant bouncing shaking me down to my bones. Towering conifers stretched toward the gray sky, the forest dotted with bare-branched deciduous trees awaiting spring, and snow-dusted grass bordered the road.

Amalia slowed, then turned onto an even narrower, bumpier track. Tree branches smacked the car's sides as we rolled deeper into the wilderness.

The track ended abruptly. An old pickup truck with a Yukon license plate was parked in front of a log cabin with a steeply peaked roof. The blinds were drawn across the small front windows and a pile of rusting junk was stacked against a sagging shed. Once, the cabin's log walls had been stained dark but weathered patches spotted the wood like a disease.

Amalia pulled up beside the truck and cut the engine. I pushed my door open and climbed out. The mixture of dirt and stunted grass masquerading as a lawn was frosted white, and a blast of icy wind blew snow into my face.

Tugging my sweater over my hands, I shut my door with my elbow and faced the cabin. My heart hammered, fear competing with anticipation.

Amalia joined me, and together we marched up four rotted steps to the crumbling front porch.

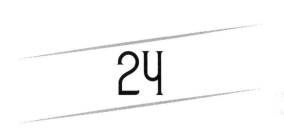

SILENCE ANSWERED AMALIA'S KNOCK. She waited a moment, then hammered the door again. Were we wrong? Was no one here? But the truck ...

A thump from inside, then a clatter against the door. "Who's there?"

Even muffled by the door, I recognize that slightly wheezy voice.

"Oh, no one important," Amalia called sarcastically. "Just your *daughter.*"

Another clatter, the clack of the bolt, then the door cracked open. The first thing I saw was the muzzle of a gun. Uncle Jack flung the door open the rest of the way, his beady eyes darting past us.

"Are you alone?" he barked. "Were you followed?"

"I'm not an idiot, Dad. Would you mind *not* pointing that thing at us?"

He raised the large hunting rifle, the stock braced against his shoulder, and squinted at his daughter. "How did you find me?"

"Ugh." Amalia bulldozed forward, forcing him to backpedal. "We're coming in."

I crossed the threshold after her, my nose wrinkling at the lingering odor of sweat, stale coffee, and damp mold that permeated the musty air. Though the blinds on the tiny front window were closed, the space was bright and open—one huge room with a kitchen, dining table, and living area, all arranged to face huge windows that filled the back wall, rising all the way to the twenty-foot vaulted ceiling.

Once, it had been a beautiful cabin, but years of poor maintenance had weathered the comforts it offered. However, no amount of neglect could dim the view beyond those windows. The mountainside dropped away, revealing a sea of snow-dusted green that swept down toward the distant city.

"You're disgusting." Amalia's furious rant broke into my awed staring. "Look at you. Look at this place. Ugh. What have you been doing these last five weeks? Lying around like a fat slob?"

Uncle Jack, still holding the rifle, flinched under his daughter's admonishment. Unshaven and greasy, he looked like the most likely source of the old sweat smell hanging in the air. A stained t-shirt hung off him, and despite Amalia's "fat slob" remark, he seemed to have lost weight. His infernus hung around his neck, an unfamiliar emblem etched in its center. All summoners were also contractors; as I'd learned during my research, summoning a demon required a demon.

"Amalia," he began cautiously, "I'm—"

"Your next words better be a damn good explanation for why you haven't contacted me in weeks. I didn't even know if you were alive!"

Another flinch, which surprised me as much as his slovenly appearance. The Uncle Jack I remembered had been domineering and superior, even with his kids.

"I didn't contact you for your safety, Amalia," he muttered. "I ... I made a terrible mistake."

I slid my hand into my coat pocket. Withdrawing my mother's two letters, I unfolded the one she'd written to Uncle Jack, strode up to him, and stuck the letter under his nose.

"Does your 'terrible mistake' have anything to do with this?" I demanded coldly.

He took the letter, surprise crossing his features before they crumpled with unmistakable grief. "We ... we should sit down."

Amalia opened her mouth, took another look at her father's expression, and stomped to the sofa. She unzipped her coat, threw it over the armrest, and dropped onto a cushion, legs crossed and arms folded. She glowered expectantly.

I removed my top layer and sat beside her. As we faced him, our solidarity was enforced by our matching turtlenecks, the hex-patterned fabric running from just below our chins to mid-thighs.

Leaning the gun against the armchair across from us, Uncle Jack lowered himself into the cushions. His stare was fixed on my chest, where my infernus lay atop my shirt, gleaming silver.

"You ..." he whispered. "*You* stole the Twelfth House demon?"

"I didn't *steal* it." I rubbed my thumb across the pendant. The Vh'alyir emblem was emblazoned across it, and since

Uncle Jack had seen the grimoire page, he must have recognized the symbol. "I made a contract with the demon after your Red Rum clients tried to use me as a bargaining chip."

"A bargaining chip?"

"I'd been talking to the demon almost since the day I arrived," I revealed baldly. "But let's not get off track. You're going to explain that letter. Right now."

Uncle Jack frowned at me—taken aback by my assertiveness, maybe?—then looked down at the letter.

"Did you even care?" The furious accusation burst from me. "Or did you sit back and wait for her to die so you could have the grimoire? She *begged* you for help!"

"I called her the moment I finished reading this letter," he whispered. "I thought she was wrong. How could anyone have found her? But she was asking for help and ..." His shoulders bowed forward. "I thought, if we started talking again, then maybe this time I could convince her to show me the grimoire."

My fists squeezed so tightly my fingernails cut into my palms.

"But I wanted to help too!" he added quickly. "If she was right, then we were all in danger. We talked for over an hour that night, and we agreed to meet the next evening. I was there, right at seven like we'd planned, and I waited at the restaurant all ... all night, Robin. I waited ..."

The same icy pain as that horrible night washed over me. "But they never arrived."

He blinked, his eyes shining wetly. "It was almost midnight when I got the call from the police ... about the accident ..."

"And you finally got what you wanted." Venom coated my voice. "You had the grimoire all to yourself. And you didn't waste any time summoning the demon names from it, did you?"

He didn't even deny it, merely nodded.

Amalia slumped back in the sofa, one hand pressed over her mouth. "My god, Dad."

I unfolded the second letter and held it out. He heaved himself out of his chair and took it, already reading as he sank back down. He turned the page, glancing over the back, showing no surprise.

"You've seen that before," I said quietly. "It was in your safe in your garage, wasn't it?"

"Where's the rest of the letter?"

"Destroyed before I could read it. Where did it come from, Uncle Jack?"

"It was tucked in the front of the grimoire." He stared down at the two pages of his sister's handwriting. "I guess I'll start from the beginning, so you can understand."

"The beginning of what?"

"Demonica."

Amalia and I exchanged bewildered looks.

"Your mother wrote it right here. *We were the first* ... the first summoners."

Silence settled across the room.

"Anthea Athanas." He leaned back in his chair. "The very first sorceress to ever summon a demon, and the mother of all Demonica magic. Our family has carried the grimoire for millennia, recopying it every few centuries. All twelve demon names are from her original grimoire. All summoning rituals are based on her original spells."

The first summoners ... my ancestors were the original summoners? We had *invented* Demonica?

"Anthea trained her children and several apprentices in summoning and gave them each a demon name. Over the generations, her descendants spread Demonica to other sorcerers, revealing more names but keeping the best, most powerful names to themselves. These days, only a handful of summoners know the Second and Third House names, and the First House was lost in the early 1900s …"

"Until *you* got the grimoire," I growled.

"The widespread use of the other names devalued them overtime—as much as a demon name can be devalued," he continued as though I hadn't spoken, "and acquiring the rare first three Houses became a Holy Grail for other summoners. The Athanas family was too famous, reputed to be the only summoners with all twelve names. The others hunted us, and the Athanas summoners began to die out."

Those who covet power nearly wiped our family out of existence, my mother had written in her letter.

"By the second World War, the Athanas family was down to three. Diandra, your great-grandmother, fled Albania and dropped the Athanas name. She emigrated to North America, married a sorcerer, and decided the only way to hide the grimoire was to give up summoning entirely."

"But *you're* a summoner," Amalia blurted. "And you want me to be one too."

"By the time Sarah and I were born, our family had shifted away from not just Demonica, but Arcana too. Sarah could barely create a simple artifact and devoted her time to translating grimoires for other mythics." He sat quietly, the seconds sliding into a full minute. "I wasn't satisfied with that. I wanted to be a powerful summoner like our ancestors. I wanted riches and recognition, not obscurity. We didn't need to bring back the Athanas name or flaunt all twelve Houses, but we could still become summoners.

"Our parents wouldn't even consider it, but Sarah and I used to talk about it. She didn't care about money, but she wanted to translate the entire grimoire—which hasn't been done since before Diandra's time—and learn our family's history. We imagined summoning a demon from each House and being the first humans in centuries to see all twelve lines."

My head spun, my mouth dry and heart thudding loudly.

"When your grandma died, Sarah inherited the grimoire. I was already secretly apprenticing with a summoner, and Sarah began translating it the day she got it."

He let out a long breath. "I don't know what changed her mind. A few months later, she told me we couldn't use it. She said we couldn't summon demons, any demons, and that we had to lie low and protect the grimoire.

"I was furious … this was my dream. I asked her to give me a name, any name, so I could start my career. She refused. She wouldn't explain why, only that the grimoire was too dangerous and we couldn't attract attention to ourselves. She switched to a sleeper guild a few weeks later and stopped practicing magic entirely."

"You always told me she was a summoner and had cheated you out of your fair inheritance," Amalia said accusingly.

"Every Athanas descendant is a summoner, whether they practice or not. And I *did* feel like I'd been cheated." His guilty stare turned to me, and I frowned back at him—then realized why he looked so ashamed.

"You …" A sick feeling washed over me. "You kept my inheritance from me as *revenge*, didn't you? You were punishing me for what you thought my mom had done to you."

He cringed, then sighed bitterly. "Sarah and I were no older than you two girls are now when we went our separate ways. She said as long as I insisted on practicing Demonica, she couldn't associate with me. I said as long as she refused to share the grimoire, I didn't want anything to do with her. We went on with our lives for years and years, then …"

"Then you got her letter," I guessed.

"And she died." He rubbed a hand over his greasy forehead and stubbly hair. "The grimoire was finally mine. I could take my career to the next level and become a famous summoner like I'd always wanted. And, of course, I would protect the grimoire too. It would be safe with me …"

"You tried to sell the First House name to *Red Rum*," I pointed out angrily. "How was that protecting the grimoire?"

"That was a mistake. A stupid, greedy mistake. Robin, I thought the grimoire had been forgotten. I never thought anyone would tie me and your mother to the legends." He exhaled unsteadily. "But I'd already made my biggest mistake, long before I ever touched the grimoire."

I stared at him coldly. "What was that?"

"Claude," he whispered.

My heart felt like a block of lead, weighed down by sickening trepidation that had no outlet; the terrible consequences had already played out.

"I don't know if he was already searching for us when he befriended me years ago, or if he heard me complain about my sister cheating me out of our family's priceless Demonica grimoire." He gripped the arms of his recliner, knuckles white.

"He never asked about the grimoire or Sarah. How could I have guessed it? Even after ... even after Sarah ..."

Uncle Jack buried his face in his hands and a hoarse sob wheezed in his throat.

"He killed my parents, didn't he?" My throat was so dry the words hurt. "Claude killed my parents."

Uncle Jack lowered his hands from his face, his eyes damp and haunted. "I never suspected him, not until the demon escaped last month. He demanded the grimoire, and when I refused, he tried to force me to give it up."

Amalia folded her hands together in her laps, fingers squeezing tightly. "I'm surprised he didn't kill you."

"He didn't know where the grimoire was. I never let him near it, you see. I copied individual pages and sent them to him. He's never seen the actual book."

Well, at least Uncle Jack had been smart about *one* thing. I unclenched my jaw before my molars cracked, pain and grief and fury forming a maelstrom in my lungs.

"I've been hiding here ever since," Uncle Jack said heavily. "I knew he'd be watching you, Amalia. I didn't want to give him any reason to think you knew where to find me."

"Who is Claude?" she demanded. "His demon is in an illegal contract."

"His demon is Second House," I added darkly. "He has all the demon names now, because of you."

"Not all of them," he corrected. "A demon name is made up of three parts: the name written in the demonic language, the House's sigil, and the proper pronunciation. Claude only has two of the three for the Twelfth House. I never let him see how the name is written."

Claude had told me he had all the names, but maybe he'd been stretching the truth. If he couldn't summon the Twelfth House himself, that explained his offer from weeks ago—the invitation to join with him. He'd wanted access to Zylas.

"I don't know who he is," Uncle Jack admitted. "I can't investigate from here, but I've confirmed 'Claude Mercier' is a fake identity. He appeared about six years ago. That's all I know."

I squeezed my eyes shut, drowning in a torrent of emotions. Claude had murdered my parents. That knowledge shifted the axis of my world. Suddenly, my grief wasn't alone. It had been joined by an equally powerful, scorching need for justice. For revenge.

"What about the Twelfth House?" I asked him hoarsely.

"What about it?"

"Why is it special? Claude told me his goal is to get his hands on a Vh'alyir demon."

Uncle Jack tensed. "How do you know that name?"

"I found the scanned page on your computer before the house burned down."

"Oh." He drummed his fingers on his knee. "There are rumors—or legends, I should say, about the Twelfth House. Some say Vh'alyir is the most powerful, while others say it's a uselessly weak House. One legend says the House is cursed."

I tensed. "*Cursed?*"

"I don't know what it means. The answers are probably in the grimoire."

My spine stiffened even more. I braced myself. "Where is the grimoire?"

He gazed at me, and I didn't look away. Didn't blink. Didn't cower.

"Here," he replied quietly. "I have it here. Are you sure, Robin?"

I had to unlock my jaw to speak. "Sure about what?"

"That you're ready for it."

"It's mine."

"Yes," he agreed. "But are you ready to protect it? I read your mother's letter—the whole letter she wrote for you. Do you understand what she meant when she said she left you unprepared?"

I pressed my palms against my thighs. "I haven't learned much magic."

"That was the mistake she regretted most. She told me in our phone call ... she'd realized abandoning all magic had been the wrong choice. Obscurity could only protect them until it failed, and once it did, she—and you—had no skills to protect yourselves. That's why she needed my help."

Was I ready to take on this burden? Was I ready to hold the history, the origin, of Demonica in my hands and protect it with my life? Was I ready to sacrifice my future and my dreams to safeguard a book?

"Bring me the grimoire."

Uncle Jack pushed to his feet. He disappeared down a short hall. A door opened and his footsteps thumped down a flight of stairs. A long minute passed, then he reappeared, a flat metal box in his hands.

I'd seen that box before. Seen it in my mother's office on the rare occasions she would bring the grimoire home to work on the translation for a few precious days.

He set the box on my lap. "The spell on it will only respond to sorcerers of our bloodline. The incantation is '*Egeirai, angizontos tou Athanou, lytheti.*'"

I pressed my hand to the box and repeated the Ancient Greek command. "*Egeirai, angizontos tou Athanou, lytheti.*"

White runes blazed across every inch of the steel. Swallowing against my racing pulse, I lifted the lid. Brown paper covered the precious package within, and I unwrapped it with gentle care, my hands surprisingly steady. The crinkling sheath opened and I gazed down upon the Athanas Grimoire. My mother's treasure.

The leather was dark and worn, the stitching neat but the threads stained. In places, it had been carefully repaired with bright, sturdy stitches. A brass buckle on the front cover held an encircling strap in place, binding the covers shut. Crisp, modern paper poked out the top, the edge of my mother's handwriting visible on the topmost page.

"I don't know where she kept her translation work," Uncle Jack murmured. "There are only a few pages in there."

I touched the buttery smooth cover, the ancient leather webbed with tiny cracks. The Athanas Grimoire. It was mine ... almost mine. Setting the box aside, I rose to my feet with the grimoire cradled in my hands. My mind turned inward.

Zylas? Please come out?

Uncle Jack gasped when the infernus on my chest lit up. Crimson light spilled from it and pooled upward. The demon took form, glowing eyes staring down at me, cold and unforgiving.

Shoving out of his chair, Uncle Jack gawked with a mixture of amazement and terror. Neither Zylas nor I looked away from each other, ignoring my uncle's reaction. My fingers tightened on the grimoire and I drew in a deep breath. Exhale. Inhale again. Steady.

I lifted the grimoire. Extended it. Held it in the space between me and the demon.

Zylas. His name formed in my mind, clear and strong. *This is the grimoire. It is the thing I want most. It's the most important thing to me in the entire world.*

He listened to my silent words, unmoving, expressionless.

I was wrong to hold the thing you want most against you. I promised to send you home. With this, I think I can do that. Without it, I'll still find a way. No matter what, no matter what you do or don't do, I will. I promise.

"What is she doing?" Uncle Jack whispered.

Zylas held my stare, waiting.

Doubt shivered through me, but I clamped it down. I'd broken the fragile trust between us, but more than that, I wasn't sure if I'd ever really trusted him. How much faith had I put in the uncertain contract that bound him to protect me, and how much had I put in *him*?

He'd admitted his fears to me—his secret worry that I might want him dead—but in what ways had I shown him *my* trust?

"I want to give this to you," I whispered. "Until I send you home, it belongs to you. That way, we each have power over the other's most precious desire. When I send you home, you can give it back to me."

His tail slid slowly across the floor as he considered my words. He reached up, but his hand passed over the grimoire and instead settled on top of my head. His fingers curled into my hair, his gaze breaking from mine to sweep across the room.

He pulled me into his chest, squashing the ancient grimoire between us. As I squeaked in dismay, his husky voice whispered above my head, almost too quiet to hear.

"*Drādah*, I smell fresh blood."

25

COLD FEAR SHOT through my gut—then Zylas threw me backward.

I sailed through the air and crashed into Amalia, knocking her to the floor. Zylas was already whirling as the windows behind him exploded into shimmering shards. Three men in dark clothes leaped into the cabin, their fingers extending into long claws and mouths gaping hungrily.

Fangs exposed. Black-and-white eyes marked with bright red rings.

The vampires charged Zylas and he leaped to meet them. Crimson magic spiraled up his arms and glowing talons extended from his fingers. He ducked a vampire's grabbing hands, rammed another with his shoulder, and slashed his claws across the third's stomach.

Blood spilled down the vamp's front but he scarcely stumbled. Blurring with speed, the vampires encircled Zylas.

He spun through them, grace and power. They were fast and strong, but he was experienced.

Another slashing exchange. Two vampires flew back, thrown by powerful blows, and Zylas rammed his talons into the chest of the third, stopping the creature's heart. He ripped his talons out and whirled, but not toward the remaining vampires.

Toward me.

A blur interrupted my line of sight. The new vampire, attacking from my left, snatched at the grimoire and I frantically twisted away. His claws caught on my infernus chain. Sharp pain cut into my neck, then the chain snapped.

Zylas lunged for my attacker and the vampire darted out of reach. A flash of motion behind him.

Between one instant and the next, a man appeared. Arms clamped around Zylas. A hand seized his jaw and twisted his head sideways.

The vampire bit into Zylas's neck.

As a horrified scream rang through my head, someone grabbed me and hauled me backward—Amalia, her breath coming in fearful pants. She dragged me away from the vampire and Zylas.

Daimon, hesychaze! I silently shouted.

Zylas didn't ignite into a crimson glow. The magic on his hands dissolved, his body limp in his assailant's hold, his eyes darkening by the second. I looked down. My new artifact was tangled on the broken chain of my infernus, still hanging off my neck, but the silver pendant was missing.

The vampire pulled his fangs from Zylas's neck and lifted his head.

Vasilii, the vampires' leader. As his slow gaze moved across me, I met his eyes. They weren't white on black like the other vampires. They were solid, unbroken black.

Red light flared—but not Zylas's magic. The power leaped from the infernus around Uncle Jack's neck. His demon materialized beside him, towering at eight feet tall with scaled patches over its arms and legs. A long tail hung, unmoving, behind it, its stare eerily blank in an apelike face crowned by four long horns.

As the demon turned with robotic steps to face the vampires, Uncle Jack swung his rifle toward Vasilii.

"No!" I cried, lunging forward. I shoved the gun sideways.

Uncle Jack shouldered me out of the way and raised the gun again, pointing it at the vampire's heart—except the vampire was holding Zylas in front of him, heart over heart. To kill the vampire, Uncle Jack would have to shoot the rifle's unstoppable bullet right through Zylas.

Vasilii glanced dismissively at Uncle Jack before returning his attention to me. His tongue slipped between his thin lips and licked at the blood smearing his mouth.

"Exquisite," he rasped. "Rich with power and ... superbly fresh. Her infernus?"

Another vampire moved, and Uncle Jack jerked his rifle as though unsure who to aim at. The vampire stooped, picked something off the floor, and handed it to Vasilii. Rejoining the vampire lord's other two lackeys, who waited off to one side, he resumed staring at Zylas's bleeding neck with ravenous hunger.

Vasilii examined the small object—my infernus—then tucked it in his pocket. Smiling faintly, he slid a hand across Zylas's shoulder. A twist of his fingers, a quiet tear, and Zylas's small armor plate fell, its straps severed. It hit the floor with a clang, leaving the demon's chest exposed.

Vasilii turned his inky eyes on Uncle Jack, silently daring the man to shoot.

Panic screamed through my head. Holding Uncle Jack's rifle with one hand, I clutched the grimoire to my chest. "Let my demon go."

"An interesting proposition," Vasilii replied in his dry monotone.

I shivered involuntarily. My gaze darted to Zylas, lifeless and unmoving, with Vasilii's arm curled around his unprotected chest, thin fingers gripping the demon's throat.

"Robin," Uncle Jack growled, "get your hand off the gun. A shot through the heart will kill him."

"And my demon too!"

"You can summon another demon," he snapped.

Vasilii's black eyes stared right through me. "Robin Page, daughter of Sarah Page, owner of the Athanas Grimoire. Would you like to bargain?"

Tension burned in my muscles. "Why would I trust a vampire's word?"

"I am not a vampire." The slightest smile. "I am … as you call us … a fae."

That took a moment to sink in. "But fae spirits create vampires by infecting humans, so …"

"I am not as they are," he countered, each sound measured carefully in his toneless voice. "They are lowly, bodiless shades, ruled by their basest nature, and I am … how to explain so you might understand?" He paused thoughtfully. "I am to my brethren as the wolf is to the flies that crawl upon its kill."

Not the best analogy, but it got his point across.

"I prefer my kin—other fae—as my quarries, but I enjoy the power I gain from these ... demons." He pulled Zylas's head back, the wound on his neck reopening with another trickle of dark blood. "Now, Robin Page, that you know I am of honor, I ask again: Would you like to bargain?"

Fae. I didn't know enough about fae for this. I'd read about them, that bargaining and exchanges were part of their mysterious culture, similar to negotiating with a demon, but I had no idea what the rules were. They were known for keeping their word, weren't they? But I suspected Vasilii, whatever he was, might be a far less trustworthy *darkfae*.

"What's your offer?" I asked cautiously.

"The grimoire. I will claim it regardless, but should it be damaged ..." His black eyes bored into me. "Give me the grimoire, Robin Page, and I will release your demon to you, no further harm inflicted."

The rifle twitched as Uncle Jack tried to pull it out from under my hand. Amalia stood rigid on my other side, her gaze darting from the three vampires to Vasilii to Uncle Jack's unmoving demon as though calculating our odds.

"Why do you want the grimoire?" I asked, my voice cracking with suppressed panic. "What use would a fae have for it?"

"A trade, Robin Page. An item of value to be exchanged for that of equal value." He twisted Zylas's neck a little further, threatening to break it. "I will answer no more questions. My offer is given. Do you agree?"

I swallowed hard. Vasilii was our greatest threat, but even a super-speed fae wasn't as fast as a bullet from fifteen feet away. Uncle Jack's demon, with its armored skin and large size, could probably kill the remaining vampires—or buy us enough time to run to the car and escape.

All we had to do was sacrifice Zylas.

One shot. Vasilii and Zylas would both die, and Uncle Jack, Amalia, and I could escape. The grimoire would be safe. I could go home, no longer a Demonica mythic, no longer in danger of being found out as an illegal contractor. Zora could report me to the MPD and it wouldn't matter. I would have no demon for them to investigate.

Or I could give up the grimoire and save Zylas's life.

I looked down at the grimoire pressed to my chest, to my heart. My mother's treasure. The origin of Demonica. Priceless, precious, dangerous—but just a book. How could I trade a life for a book?

Zylas …

Eyes burning, I drew in a shaky breath—and a memory of his husky voice whispered, *Be smarter, drādah.*

Just yesterday, alone in a cramped alley. I could almost feel his heat behind me, his hand on my shoulder as he murmured in my ear. *You must always be looking everywhere.*

I pulled my gaze off Vasilii's unnerving eyes for the first time. The three waiting vampires stood near the kitchen. I skimmed across the room, picking out the shadowy corners, glancing across the broken windows, whisking past the large raised deck outside—

A shape ducked backward out of sight, hidden around the corner just outside the window. Another vampire outside. Why would that one be outside?

Unless there was more than one. Unless more vampires were positioned to ambush us.

Be smarter, Zylas had told me. If he were standing behind me right now, as he had in that alley, I knew what he would whisper in my ear. Vasilii had more vampires waiting out of sight. He wasn't bargaining with us because we had any chance of survival. He wanted to secure the grimoire before he killed us.

Raising my chin, I looked into Vasilii's black eyes. "I accept your offer."

Amalia gasped. Uncle Jack's grip on the rifle spasmed, a hoarse groan catching in his throat.

Vasilii's lips formed that faint, emotionless smile. "Bring me the grimoire."

I tightened my hand on the barrel and turned, giving my uncle the most meaningful stare I could manage. Releasing the rifle, I hastily knotted my broken infernus chain, then slowly approached the fae. Vasilii waited, his arm hooked around Zylas, slender hand gripping the lifeless demon's throat.

One long step away from them, I stopped. Vasilii stared unblinkingly into my eyes as he extended his other hand, fingers spread.

My heart slammed into my ribs as though it were trying to ram through me and grab onto the grimoire. I placed the book in the fae's waiting hand. He curled his fingers over the cover, his expression faintly pleased.

He released Zylas. The demon crumpled—and I dove to the floor with him.

The rifle went off with an earsplitting bang. Vasilii jerked backward. Dead center in his chest, a dark hole the size of a golf ball had shredded his shirt. Sprawled on the floor beside Zylas's prone form, I waited for the fae to collapse.

Grimoire cradled in one hand, Vasilii lightly touched his chest as though surprised by the wound. A small smile curved his lips.

He wasn't falling. He wasn't dying. He'd been *shot in the heart* with a bullet big enough to kill a bull moose. *Why wasn't he dead?*

Uncle Jack clutched the rifle, his hands shaking. Amalia stood beside him, her face stamped with horrified disbelief.

Still smiling, Vasilii reached for me.

"*Ori eruptum impello!*" I screamed.

Silvery light burst from the artifact around my neck. The dome rushed outward, hurling Vasilii away, along with two kitchen chairs and the other vampires. The sofa flipped onto its face with a muffled thud. Only Zylas, safe with my hands on him, was unaffected.

The three vampires crashed down, but Vasilii landed neatly on his feet, unhampered by the hole in his chest. He stroked the grimoire as though to ensure it was undamaged, then turned. He stepped over the windowsill, broken glass grinding under his shoes, and ambled into the blowing snow.

Ravenous eyes glowing, his minions advanced on us to clean up the loose ends while their master whisked away the precious grimoire.

The precious grimoire I had *handed* to him. What kind of monster could survive a shot through the heart?

My hands tightened on Zylas's shoulders, but he didn't stir. The vampires prowled closer, drool running down their chins as they homed in on the helpless demon and his intoxicating blood.

A loud, metallic clack. The vampires looked up.

Uncle Jack pushed his rifle's bolt forward and pulled the trigger. The ear-rupturing bang exploded again and the bullet tore through two vampires, taking them both out with one shot. As they keeled over, Uncle Jack threw the rifle aside and grasped his infernus. His demon lumbered forward, powerful arms swinging. The remaining vampire bared his fangs and took a cautious step backward.

But he wasn't alone. Glass crunching, the vampires who'd been lurking outside, hidden from view, stepped over the windowsills—four of them, their eerie eyes staring and mouths curved eagerly. One laughed at the sight of our helpless group.

Despair closed over me. *Zylas?*

Uncle Jack sent his demon charging at the vampires. He and Amalia backed toward the door, calling for me, but I knew it was pointless. There were too many and they were too fast.

I heaved Zylas's limp form onto his back. His dark eyes were empty, but his chest rose and fell in shallow breaths. Vasilii's bite had sent the demon into a coma-like state.

Three of the vampires leaped on Uncle Jack's massive but slow demon, and the other two advanced on the father and daughter. Amalia thrust out a flashcard and yelled an incantation, but the vampire barely stumbled from the cantrip. Uncle Jack gripped his infernus. His demon turned, called toward its master, but the three vampires dragged it to a halt.

"Zylas," I whispered, pressing my hand to his face. "Please wake up."

A flicker deep in his eyes.

With a crash, Uncle Jack's demon collapsed, the three vampires pinning it to the floor as they attempted to bite through its scaled skin.

I leaned down and touched my forehead to Zylas's, eyes squeezed closed and terror quivering through my limbs. *Zylas, help us.*

Amalia was screaming, her voice piercing my ears.

A quiet rasp sounded in Zylas's throat. His cool fingers fumbled against my wrist, then closed tight. I looked into his dark eyes, our foreheads still touching.

Drādah.

An image formed in my mind. Spiky red runes, tangled lines and circles. An arching spell in his glowing magic burned brightly inside my head. I recognized it—the same explosive spell he'd cast in the tower basement. His fingers tightened around my wrist and he pushed my hand off his face, raising it above us.

I didn't know why, but I opened my fingers, spreading them wide.

My fingertips tingled. Heat grew—inside my hand, inside my chest. The image of the spell seared my mind. All around me, the room darkened. The temperature dropped.

Cast it.

I closed my eyes, my face pressed to his. Hotter and hotter, my chest burned. The fire was in my arm, in my hand. The spell was inside my head but it was outside my head too. It arched over us in glowing lines, demonic runes, and deadly spirals of power. The air crackled, hissed.

The vampires were coming for us. They were rushing forward, fangs bared, rings in their eyes glowing scarlet with fury and hunger.

But my eyes were closed, so how could I see that?

Zylas's other hand was curled over the back of my neck, palm against my cheek, his shallow breath warm on my skin. I could feel his touch, his physical closeness—and I could feel more than that. I could feel *him*. A fierce presence inside my mind, bright crimson with an inky black core.

Finish it!

My eyes flew open and for an instant, I saw the crimson power lighting my hand, the twisting veins crawling up my arm, glowing through my sleeve. I saw the spell arching over us and the vampires lunging toward it, claw-like fingers reaching for my exposed back.

"*Evashvā vīsh!*"

As my voice rang out, I heard his voice in my head, speaking the same alien words. Scorching heat rushed through my body—and the room exploded.

Zylas pulled me down on top of him, arms wrapped over my head, my face crushed against the side of his neck. Light blazed through my eyelids, the roar deafening, arctic cold stabbing my skin in a frigid gust. Crashing, shattering—then a second detonation.

A fireball erupted from the kitchen. Zylas pushed off the floor, flipping our bodies, covering me. The roaring inferno blasted outward—and cold swept in to consume it. The heat and light sucked into Zylas's body as he pulled in the power.

A wave of shrinking fire danced across us, then faded. The acrid stench of burnt plastic singed my nose.

Zylas braced his elbows on either side of me and raised his head. Our stares met, inches between our faces. Bright, hot power glowed in his eyes, replenished by the flames.

My eyes were wide, my lips parted in disbelief. I didn't remember moving my hand, but my fingertips were resting against his jaw.

I could *feel* him. He was there, inside my head, a shadowy presence that tasted of everything he was—power and brutality, cunning and intelligence, resolve and breathtaking intensity. A steely will. The tang of his sharp humor. And a quiet, hollow despair.

"What …" I breathed, awed and terrified.

"You always could hear me, *drādah*." His husky whisper sounded in my ears and in my mind at the same time. "You were not listening."

A hoarse wail broke into my confusion. Zylas pushed himself up and sat on my legs, scanning the room. The furniture was no more than shredded fabric and splintered wood. The kitchen had been demolished, its remains burnt black and the gas range a twisted husk. Uncle Jack's demon stood unmoving amid the destruction, but the five vampires lay dead on the shattered floor.

"Dad," Amalia rasped, her voice quavering from behind the heavy dining table, lying on its side and peppered with shrapnel. I pulled my feet from under Zylas and clambered up. Breathing hard as though I'd run a mile, I stumbled toward the table. The feeling of Zylas inside my mind faded.

Sheltered behind the table, Amalia knelt beside her father, hands pressed to his stomach. He lay on his back, his mouth open in pain and horror. Blood flowed over Amalia's hands and pooled around him. The wounds from a vampire's claws raked his belly.

"Dad," Amalia choked. "Hold on, Dad."

The strength left my legs and I sank to my knees, gripping the edge of the overturned table, still on the wrong side of it. Uncle Jack panted for air, his hands weakly grasping Amalia's. Tears streamed down her cheeks, her face contorted.

"Don't leave me, Dad," she whispered. "Please. Please don't."

Suffocating pain rose in my chest. Grief, sharp and fresh, pierced me—anguish for my lost parents, reawakened, and anguish for Amalia, who was about to lose the only parent she had left.

She pushed on Uncle Jack's stomach, trying desperately to stop the bleeding. A sob shook her body, high-pitched and agonized.

With a soft scuff of a footstep, Zylas appeared beside me. He gazed down at the dying man, expressionless. I bowed my head, unable to watch, my heart breaking for Amalia.

A brush against my arm—Zylas moving. My head came up as he stepped over the barrier of the table. He stood for a moment, then crouched beside Uncle Jack, narrowed eyes watching his summoner, the man who'd torn him from his home, imprisoned him, and tried to enslave him.

The demon's gaze shifted to Amalia's tear-streaked face, to mine, and back to Uncle Jack.

"*Zh'ūltis*," he muttered.

Then he placed his hand on Uncle Jack's chest and crimson magic streaked up his arm.

ZYLAS'S POWER FADED. As his luminescent spell dissolved, the demon lifted his hand from Uncle Jack's chest. Wrinkling his nose, he wiped his bloody palm on the man's pant leg.

Uncle Jack drew in a trembling breath and released it. Amalia clutched her father's hand, but her disbelieving stare was on Zylas.

"You healed him," she whispered hoarsely.

Zylas rose to his full height, tail snapping irritably, and hopped over the table. Catching my elbow, he swung me off my feet. I yelped in surprise as I thudded against his back, automatically clamping my arms and legs around him.

"What—" I began.

He leaped the length of the living room, nearly dumping me off his back, and sprang out the broken window. Thudding down on the deck, he paused, head swiveling as he scented the breeze.

"Zylas," I tried again, "what—"

"This is not over. Hold on."

As I squeezed my legs more tightly around his waist, he shot to the end of the deck and launched off it. He hit the ground and dashed into the forest. Towering spruce trees flashed past, snow swirling down and the icy wind cutting through my shirt.

He ran at full demon speed—fast enough to outstrip the best human sprinter. Tail lashing for balance, he cut past trees, branches whipping against our sides. The ground sloped down, the mountainside sweeping for miles to the city below. I had no idea where he was going or what he was chasing.

Then I saw the flare of crimson light through the trees.

Zylas slowed to a slinking prowl, his steps silent on the snowy leaf litter. The forest opened into a wide swath of dirt and pebbles—an old rock slide. At the edge of the trees, he stopped.

Vasilii stood in the center of the clearing, the grimoire held casually in one hand.

Claude's demon stood ten paces from the darkfae, his reddish-brown skin contrasting with the dusting of snow. Wings curled against his back, tail snaking across the ground, dark hair tied back from his sharp-featured face. His magma-red eyes glowed with power.

Vasilii slowly canted his head to the right—toward Zylas and me. He returned his attention to Claude's demon.

"My ability to track my prey surpasses that of even my fae brethren," he said in his slow, dry voice. "I did not expect you to possess similar skills, Nazhivēr. How did you arrive here so soon after me?"

Claude's demon smiled coldly. "You have underestimated us from the beginning."

I shuddered at his deep, rumbling growl. His English wasn't as heavily accented as Zylas's but the guttural inflection was the same.

"Have I?" Vasilii whispered. "I ascribed your master only the intelligence he has displayed. He thought me a mere vampire. He thought, by peddling your blood to my nest, he could win their loyalty. He thought me too simple a creature to discover what he searched for, or to seek it myself."

The demon flicked his tail across the ground, an angry tic that Zylas possessed too.

"Such great boons have come to me, Nazhivēr. Did you know I came here seeking a druid? Instead, I found his territory abandoned."

I gripped Zylas's shoulders. A druid? I'd never heard of a druid in Vancouver.

"An unprotected hunting ground," Vasilii continued, "which I have now claimed. No sooner did I draw the city's vampires under my control than you and your master so freely handed me even greater power." Vasilii caressed the grimoire's leather cover. "And now I have claimed this as well."

"You think we did not see your betrayal well before you acted?" Nazhivēr rumbled, satisfaction pulling at his dusky lips. "What you have done is save us a great deal of time."

"You presume to take this from me?" Vasilii mused. "I see. Take it, then, demon. With but one hand, I will slay you."

The darkfae cradled the grimoire safely against his chest and raised his other hand, fingers casually curled. The slender digits darkened to black and extended into rigid claws.

Nazhivēr raised his hands in turn, scarlet glowing across his wrists and up his arms. Before the demon's talons could finish forming on his fingers, Vasilii vanished.

Blood sprayed and Nazhivēr lurched backward, his chest raked with wounds. Vasilii slashed again and the demon darted sideways, scarcely evading. As Nazhivēr swung his glowing talons, Vasilii reappeared behind the demon. Blood splattered the ground.

Vasilii was so fast I couldn't follow him. So fast he seemed to disappear as he moved.

Zylas pushed on my legs and I dropped off his back. Deepening his stance, he cast me a silent, commanding look—*stay there*—then slunk into the clearing. Motions blurring, Claude's demon and the vampiric darkfae circled and slashed. Only Nazhivēr bled.

Cautiously, Zylas closed in, and when Vasilii blurred beyond my vision, Zylas launched forward. His glowing talons struck Vasilii's lower back, tearing through his dark shirt and ripping deep into the fae's flesh.

Zylas leaped sideways, evading Vasilii's counterstrike, and Nazhivēr smashed his fist into Vasilii's stomach. The darkfae flew backward, landed on his feet in a graceful skid, and straightened.

He gazed emotionlessly at the two demons, standing side by side as though they'd planned to ally against him all along. He blinked his charcoal eyes and lifted the ragged bottom of his shirt.

Zylas's talons had torn deep, revealing dark, inhuman flesh beneath his humanlike skin—but the bloodless wounds were shrinking. The skin drew back together, the injury melting away. As the slices disappeared, the fae's skin dimmed. His flesh grew darker and darker—and as it blackened, his body changed.

Limbs lengthened as though stretching out, thin and wiry. His spine stretched up, tattered shirt rising above his waist to reveal black skin clinging to prominent bones and rangy muscle. His face sunk in, inky eyes largening until they dominated his face. His bulky jaw opened, gaping wider than it should've, to reveal inch-long fangs.

With that horrifying grin, the seven-foot-tall darkfae vaulted toward the demons.

Zylas and Nazhivēr split, spun, and came at Vasilii from opposite sides. The three adversaries flashed across the clearing, too much speed and agility for my human eyes and slow human brain to comprehend. Crimson magic flashed in brief spurts, but even Zylas's swift demonic magic required a few uninterrupted seconds to cast.

Vasilii was so swift that neither demon could produce a powerful spell. None of their attacks, even the ones that connected, slowed the fae—while bleeding gashes marred both demons. The fae's long limbs, despite their fragile appearance, struck with crushing power, and through it all, he held the grimoire to his chest like a mother cradling an infant.

Zylas broke free of the lethal dance, skittering sideways on nimble feet.

"*Adināathē izh*," he barked. "*Ittā rēsh!*"

Nazhivēr lunged in. His tail caught Vasilii's legs, interrupting his movements for the barest instant, and his fist struck the fae's head.

Zylas angled across the clearing, opening a space between him and his enemy. Crimson power raced up his arms. Runes formed across his limbs in their wake and spell circles surrounded him like satellites orbiting a planet.

Vasilii broke away from Nazhivēr and whirled toward Zylas, the length of the clearing separating them. Nazhivēr grabbed his arm, halting him—and Vasilii rammed his claws into the demon's gut, sinking them six inches deep.

Crimson light blazed.

Vasilii tore away from the wounded demon and flashed toward Zylas, inconceivably swift.

The rune circles spun around Zylas, all six aligning atop one another, facing the oncoming fae. Before Vasilii could change course, a fiery beam exploded from the spell, struck the fae, and hurled him backward. Vasilii flew thirty feet and smashed into a tree trunk, shaking the fifty-foot hemlock. Pine needles rained down as Vasilii slumped to the dirt, his left hand empty— the grimoire gone from his hold.

Silence fell, broken only by gusts of wind whining through the trees and my pulse thundering in my ears.

Nazhivēr, one hand pressed to his punctured gut, walked forward. He stopped in the center of the clearing. From out of the snow, he lifted the grimoire.

A quiet scrape. Vasilii raised his head, then pushed off the ground, clothes torn and smoking. The wounds in his black flesh shrank to nothing. In the time it took him to straighten, his injuries had healed.

He craned his head one way then the other, rolling his narrow shoulders as though working out a mild cramp. His ebony eyes found Nazhivēr.

The demon spread his wings and leaped skyward. As he took flight, he tore open the belt that held the grimoire closed.

The loose pages containing my mother's translations fluttered down.

In a flash, Vasilii leaped after the flighted demon. The fae grabbed Nazhivēr's legs and shoved his talons through the demon's knee.

Nazhivēr flung the grimoire away.

It flew end over end, arcing through the air—and Zylas caught it. Vasilii released the winged demon and dropped back to the ground. Wings pumping, Nazhivēr soared above the treetops and disappeared from sight, fleeing the indestructible fae—which left Zylas to battle Vasilii alone.

Zylas took one wide-eyed look at the grimoire he held, then tossed it high into the branches of the nearest tree. He'd barely completed the motion before Vasilii slammed into him.

Tearing free with a splatter of blood, Zylas skittered sideways with rapid steps. Vasilii paused, gazing up into the tree where the grimoire was caught on a branch, then pivoted to face Zylas. He opened his other hand, the one with which he'd been holding the book, and his fingers morphed into long, rigid claws. Now both hands were deadly weapons instead of just one.

Zylas took a slow, cautious step backward—and I realized he was afraid. He'd taught me not to step backward, and he'd only do it himself if he wasn't thinking clearly.

The darkfae vanished—and reappeared in a blur, already striking. Zylas whirled away, but blood misted the air as those claws shredded his arm. He and Nazhivēr together couldn't stop the fae. Alone, Zylas had no chance.

But he wasn't alone. I was still here—but what could I do?

Vasilii slashed again, his long reach far greater than the demon's. His claws tore across Zylas's thigh. The demon staggered and caught the fae's next strike on his armored left forearm. His glowing talons struck the fae's right hip, tearing deep, but the wounds healed immediately.

Was Vasilii truly unkillable? Did he have a weakness? He must have a weakness! I tried to think. Vampires. Fae. I must know something. My brain was full of useless facts, stories, and ancient legends.

Vasilii sank his claws into Zylas's upper arm. The demon ripped free with another splatter of blood, crimson magic shooting up his other arm.

Vampires. Vasilii wasn't a true vampire, but maybe he had the same weaknesses. What had I read? Sunlight—stake through the heart—beheading—garlic? No, that was a stupid myth. What else?

Zylas fell, his cast interrupted. Rolling, he shot to his feet again, tail whipping out. Vasilii smiled.

Holy water? No. Silver? Maybe. Was there anything else? In the story of the famous vampire hunters who'd exterminated hundreds of vampires, how had they done it? A sorcerer and a—

Vasilii grabbed Zylas and pulled the demon into his chest like a passionate lover.

—and a *heliomage*.

Crushing Zylas against him, Vasilii opened his deformed jaw, fangs gleaming. Fear flashed across Zylas's face. One touch of those fangs and he'd be paralyzed.

I flung myself out of the trees and sprinted toward the fae and demon.

"A shame," Vasilii whispered, "to waste such a delicacy."

He brought his mouth down, fangs reaching hungrily for Zylas's shoulder.

I leaped into them, my arm thrust out as I screamed, "*Indura.*"

Vasilii's teeth met my arm with bruising pain—but no piercing agony. His long fangs were caught on my shirt, the fabric patterned with Amalia's careful hexes.

Yanking my arm free, I clutched Zylas and shouted, "*Ori eruptum impello!*"

A silvery dome exploded from the artifact. It struck Vasilii and hurled him backward—but the spell hadn't had time to fully recharge and the burst of force wasn't as strong as before. It was still enough to send Vasilii crashing down on his back.

Holding me tight, Zylas sprang away, opening a wider gap. Vasilii rose with uncanny grace, unharmed. Nothing we did could damage him.

Except, maybe, fire.

We needed an inferno and we needed it right this moment—but how? There were no gas cans for me to ignite with an otherwise harmless flame cantrip.

Zylas, can you light him on fire?

As my mind turned inward, I felt the demon again—that dangerous, shadowy presence inside my head. I could feel his urgency, his fear. He didn't know how to stop this creature. He could heat things up but he didn't have a spell to burn Vasilii. That was human magic. That was—

My magic.

No time to draw a cantrip large enough to do any damage. My magic wasn't fast enough. Fast spells were—

My magic, Zylas whispered in my head.

He raised his hand—and I raised mine. His palm pressed to the back of my hand, our fingers aligned. Crimson power streaked up his arm—and hot scarlet magic blazed over my wrist in twisting veins. In my mind was the fire cantrip, the smooth lines of the rune bold and crisp. Simple. So simple compared to the complex tangles of Zylas's spells.

Crimson light ignited before my eyes. The Arcana cantrip appeared on the ground in glowing lines of demon magic, spanning three long yards—with Vasilii in its center.

An instant for the fae's black eyes to narrow. An instant for the creature to lunge toward us.

"*Igniaris!*"

Zylas's snarl and my cry rang out together, the sounds melding into one—and the giant cantrip erupted into roaring flames. The boiling fire surged skyward, towering thirty feet. Blistering heat blasted my face, then swirling cold engulfed me as Zylas pulled the fire's energy into his body. His fingers curled down, gripping my hand as the glow of his magic faded from our arms.

The inferno crackled and rippled for twenty long seconds, then the flames shrank and shrank until only burning embers remained, smoldering on the blackened grass. The snow was gone from the clearing, evaporated in seconds.

In the center of the charred circle, a burnt husk lay, unmoving. A fitful wind blew down the mountainside and the corpse crumbled, ash blowing across the ground. Something silver glinted in the debris—my slightly blackened infernus.

All the strength left my limbs and I slumped in Zylas's arms. "It worked. I can't believe it worked."

"Which part?" Zylas asked. "The fire or the *vīsh?*"

"Both?"

His arms loosened, my only warning. I braced my feet just before he let go, but I wobbled unsteadily. Deciding it was all-around safer, I sank onto the damp earth.

Fire. I hadn't been sure it would work, but one of the two legendary vampire hunters from my history book had been a heliomage. One of the most destructive Elementaria combinations: air and fire.

I stared at the fae's crumbling corpse. We'd defeated Vasilii. Not with demon magic or Arcana but with a union of the two. Just as we had somehow cast a demonic spell together while he'd been too weak to move, we had cast an Arcana spell together—merging his ability to instantaneously create a rune with the swift, simple power of my cantrip.

Later, I would freak out over both those occurrences, but not now. My brain was already threatening to implode.

With a rustle of branches, Zylas dropped out of a nearby tree. Heedless of his bleeding wounds, he crouched beside me and held out the grimoire. Fighting back tears, I took it in both hands.

It ... well, it had survived. The clasp was torn but the cover was intact. A few pages were on the verge of falling out, and some had partially torn, but overall, not too much damage. Awe slid through me as I carefully flipped page after page of Ancient Greek handwriting in faded ink. So much archaic knowledge, so much forgotten history.

I turned the last page and my heart lurched painfully.

At the back of the book were the torn stubs of a dozen pages. The ripped edges were white—recently torn.

I remembered Nazhivēr snapping the enclosing belt off the book. Remembered the open book in his hands as he sprang skyward.

"He stole pages," I whispered, horror muting my voice. "He ripped pages out."

And he'd escaped with them, leaving the rest of the grimoire behind, knowing Vasilii would go after the book. Nazhivēr had taken what he'd wanted most and fled, leaving Vasilii to claim the vandalized grimoire and kill Zylas. Furious tears stung my eyes.

"We will get the pages back," Zylas said, "when we kill them."

"Will we?" I mumbled despairingly.

A slow smirk curved his lips. "I cannot let them steal from *my* grimoire."

I blinked in confusion—and he plucked the book out of my hands. Then he was on his feet and walking away with a jaunty snap of his tail. I blinked again, then shoved to my feet and rushed after him, unsure if I should laugh, scream, cry—or smack that smartass demon right in his smug face.

27

I PEERED OVER THE TOP of the thick textbook with concentration so fierce my head ached.

On the other side of the coffee table, Zylas was sprawled across the sofa, ankles propped on one end and his head cushioned on the opposite armrest. As I peered intently at him, he reached over his head for the small bowl on the side table, filled with chocolate-dipped grapes rolled in crushed almonds, flaky caramel, and butterscotch chips.

He plucked a grape and held it above his mouth. One eye opened and his dark pupil, nearly invisible in the glowing crimson, turned to me.

I narrowed my eyes to slits, straining my brain as hard as I could.

"That is not how to hear inside my head, *drādah*."

Damn it.

His husky laugh rolled through the room—as usual, he had no problem hearing *my* thoughts—and he dropped the grape in his mouth. His jaw moved as he chewed through the chocolate layer before swallowing.

Sighing, I returned my attention to the textbook. The coffee table was spread with old leather tomes, textbooks, and scattered papers. In the center was the grimoire, open to page sixteen. That was as far as I'd gotten in the last week.

In a neat stack beside the grimoire were half a dozen pages of my mother's translations, the paper crinkled and the ink smudged. Zylas and I had searched the mountainside for half an hour to find them, but not knowing which grimoire pages they went with, I hadn't yet made much sense of them.

I peered at the textbook again—an exhausting, brain-destroying breakdown of the Arcane jargon used in Ancient Greek—then gave up. As I stacked my reference books, my attention returned to the demon hogging my sofa. Or, actually, the demon and the kitten.

Now that she'd recovered from her injuries and the shock of a new home, Socks was friendly enough with me and Amalia, but she did not deign to cuddle with us, probably because we were intolerably inferior to her favorite sleeping spot.

That spot being anywhere on or beside Zylas.

At the moment, she was curled into a furry donut right in the middle of his stomach, blissfully dreaming cat dreams. When his magic was fully charged, he ran a couple degrees hotter than a human, so it didn't surprise me that she'd want to sleep on him. What surprised me was Zylas's tolerance of it.

I hid my smile and continued packing up my work. Looking back on it now, I wasn't sure Zylas had ever intended to *torment* the injured kitten, even when he'd perched on top of her crate. A cruel demon terrifying her for his own twisted satisfaction?

Or a curious demon who had no idea how to interact with a small, easily frightened creature of another species?

In some ways, that applied to me as much as it did to Socks. Small, easily frightened … and he had no idea how to handle either of us. He was figuring it out as he went along, just as I was figuring out how to interact with him.

As I scooped up a stack of books, the grimoire resting on top, he opened his eyes again.

"Where are you taking my grimoire?" he asked with a sly gleam in his gaze.

"To its usual spot." I rolled my eyes. "You don't need to ask me every time I move it."

An amused flash of pointed canines. I rolled my eyes again to make sure he'd noticed, then stalked into my room. At every *possible* opportunity, he pointed out that the grimoire was his. I had given it to him and he got to decide when and where and how I got to use it. He'd even tried to convince me that I had to ask his permission to take it out of its box, but I'd put my foot down on that one. He'd settled for constant reminders.

Annoying demon.

"*Drādah mailēshta,*" he called from the living room.

"Get out of my head!" I yelled back. The grimoire's case lay open on my bed—the metal box that only an Athanas sorcerer could open. I wrapped the book in brown paper, settled it in place with my mother's translations resting on top, and closed the lid. White runes flickered across it as magic sealed the box shut.

I slid it under my bed, then sat on the mattress and heaved a long sigh. In the week since we'd killed Vasilii and reclaimed the grimoire—or rather, *most* of the grimoire—we'd found no sign of Claude. Not that we'd really searched. Christmas had been on Tuesday, and it was hard to worry about a dangerous summoner and his demon with all the holiday cheer going on.

Amalia and I had decided that, since neither of us had available family members to celebrate with, we would skip all the traditional Christmas activities. Instead, we'd gone for a double feature at the cinema, then ordered enough Chinese food to last us a week.

Since then, I'd been spending hours every day on the grimoire despite the disappointing lack of revelations. What I'd translated so far wasn't even Demonica but other Arcana that Anthea Athanas had recorded thousands of years ago. I might have to skip ahead.

My wandering gaze fell on the book on my bedside table: *The Complete Compilation of Arcane Cantrips*. The vivid memory of the fire cantrip in Zylas's crimson magic rushed through my head—followed by the equally vivid memory of his power flowing over my hand and up my arm.

Pushing to my feet, I returned to the living room. At my approach, Socks uncurled from her ball and stood on Zylas's stomach, back arching in a luxurious stretch. Hopping onto the floor, she wound around my ankles and meowed demandingly.

I wasn't worthy of cuddles, but when dinnertime came around, she expected me to provide.

Hands on my hips, I peered down at Zylas, again trying to pry open his head and see his thoughts underneath. I wanted another glimpse of the mind behind those crimson eyes. Of the keen, cutting intelligence, the brutal determination to survive, the dizzying expanse of experiences I couldn't begin to imagine.

He gazed up at me, impassive.

"How do I hear your thoughts the way you can hear mine?" I demanded.

"Why would I tell you?"

"Because it's more fair that way." I pointed at him accusingly. "You were hiding it all this time, that we could speak to each other in our heads. Don't you think that might've been *useful* before now?"

"*Ch*," he scoffed, closing his eyes lazily.

"How did we combine our magic?" I'd asked him this question half a dozen times, and his answer was always the same. At my feet, Socks meowed loudly, then stalked off with her tail held high.

Zylas stretched his spine, then relaxed into the sofa. "I don't know."

"Guess, then."

"*Kūathē gish.*"

"Huh?"

"Go away. You are noisy."

I squinted one eye, then turned around. Instead of walking away, I dropped onto the sofa. He might be super strong and halfway to invincible, but even a demon couldn't ignore a hundred pounds landing on his diaphragm.

His breath whooshed out. Eyes snapping open, he glowered at me. I flopped against the back cushion, sitting on his stomach where Socks had been, my feet dangling above the floor.

"As you can see, I'm not going away," I declared. "So let's talk about the whole 'magic sharing' thing."

His nose scrunched in annoyance, then he resettled his head on the cushion, grabbed a chocolate-and-butterscotch grape, and ate it.

I waited a minute, my chagrin growing, then growled, "Zylas."

"*Drādah.*"

"You can't just ignore me sitting on you."

He pointedly closed his eyes again.

"Tell me about the magic. You must have *some* idea."

"I do not know." He reached blindly for another grape. "I did not *think*. I just did."

During the fight, I hadn't stopped to think about it either. It had felt … natural. Instinctive. As simple and easy as raising my arm and spreading my fingers.

I gazed at my hand, held before my face with my fingers stretched wide. I remembered his presence inside my head, dark and ferocious.

Sitting forward, I aligned myself to face him. Jaw tight with focus, I pressed my palms against his cheeks, my fingers resting on his pointed ears and tangled hair.

Staring intently into his eyes, I strained to hear his thoughts. To find his alien presence. To reform that bizarre, breathtaking connection. I wanted to hear him again. I would make it happen. Catching my lower lip in my teeth, I brought our faces—our minds—closer. *Where are you, Zylas?*

He stared up at me, then took my face in his hands, fingers catching in my hair. His crimson eyes searched mine, his lips parting.

"*Na, drādah,*" he whispered.

My breath caught in my lungs. "Yes?"

"This"—his hands tightened on my cheeks and a laughing grin flashed over his face—"will not work either."

I growled furiously. "You—"

With a clatter, the apartment door swung open. Amalia breezed in, her cell phone against her ear and a bag from her favorite fabric store hanging off her arm.

"Yeah, hold on, Dad," she said, her gaze sweeping across the room to find me. "I'll ask her—*ah!*"

Her shriek rang out and she flung both arms up like she was being assaulted by an invisible burglar. Her phone flew out of her hand, her face stamped with horror.

She pointed at me and yelled, "What are you *doing?*"

I blinked. Looked down. Realized what I was doing.

"*Ah!*" I shrieked. I released Zylas's head and threw myself off his chest—which I'd been *straddling*. Stumbling wildly, I bolted away from him. Amalia stared at me like I'd sprouted my own horns and tail.

"It wasn't—I didn't mean to—I was just—" I babbled, my face flaming.

She took in my embarrassment, then barked a laugh. "Let me guess. It was for science."

My blush deepened and I peeked at Zylas. He was nonchalantly eating grapes and ignoring the human dramatics a few yards away. Socks poked her whiskers out from under the coffee table.

Shaking her head, Amalia searched around the floor and found her phone.

"It's okay—somehow. Didn't even crack." She raised it to her ear. "Sorry, Dad. Robin was being a weirdo again. Repeat that … right." She refocused on me. "Dad asked if the missing pages from the grimoire are all from the back?"

I nodded.

Another pause as she listened, then she asked me, "Are there any drawings of sorcery arrays in the back?"

Frowning, I recalled my examination of the book. "I don't think so."

"She doesn't think so." Amalia listened for a moment. "Hold on, switching to speakerphone. Okay, say that again."

"Robin." Uncle Jack's tinny voice sounded from the phone. "If the arrays from the final pages were still there, you'd know it. The spells …" He cleared his throat. "I told Claude about those pages. I'd been planning to scan a few to see if he could decipher them, but I never got around to it."

My worried gaze met Amalia's. "I think Claude might already have an idea what those arrays are," I said. "Otherwise, he wouldn't have had his demon steal them."

"I think so too," Uncle Jack agreed grimly. "And I think we need to know what those arrays are, and what magic Claude now has. Get translating that grimoire, Robin."

"Already working on it. Are you all settled in?"

"Yes. This safe house is much more comfortable than the last one. I don't think Claude has any more use for me, but just in case …" Another awkward cough. "You girls stay safe now."

Amalia gave her phone an exasperated look. "We'll be fine, Dad. You're the one who almost died."

"Yes, well …" A third cough. "Let me know if you need anything."

"Yep. Talk to you later." She disconnected the call, her attention swinging onto Zylas, reclined on the sofa. I saw the question in her eyes—a question I'd been dwelling on too.

Uncle Jack had almost died … and he was only alive because Zylas had healed his mortal wounds. The demon had barely glanced at the man afterward. He didn't seem to care. Hadn't acknowledged his summoner in any way since.

Why had he healed Uncle Jack?

Amalia and I both gazed at the demon, then looked at each other. Her tiny, hopeful smile reflected mine. Maybe our hope was silly. Maybe we were being ridiculous, naïve humans, but we both suspected the same thing: Zylas had acted not because he cared about Uncle Jack living or dying, but because Amalia and I cared.

She dropped her shopping bag on the counter. "Have you changed your mind about our evening plans?"

I ignored the swoop of nerves in my gut. "Nope."

"Then I'd better get changed." She shrugged off her coat. "I'm not dressed properly for Grand Theft Library."

"COAST IS CLEAR," Amalia whispered.

Leaving her to stand guard, I slipped down the short hall to a door marked *Guild Members Only*. Two weeks ago, Zylas had broken through it while tracking the scent of old demon blood, but the librarian had caught us before he could find the source.

We were here to fix that.

The Arcana Historia's library closed to the mythic "public" in twenty minutes, so we didn't have much time. *Okay, Zylas.*

Crimson light bloomed and the demon took shape beside me. He glanced up and down the hall, then used his burglary spell to sever the locking mechanism—a far quieter option than smashing through the door. I followed him into the room.

As before, the worktable was stacked with the achingly familiar tools of book restoration, the scents of leather, paper, and harsh glue permeating the dusty air. The same cabinets lined the wall, one bolted with a rune-engraved padlock.

Zylas glanced at me, nothing but trouble in his eyes. "I am allowed to break it this time, *na?*"

"Yes." I urged him on with a wave. "Hurry up and do it."

Crimson magic swirled over his hand, tiny runes mixed into the glow. He grasped the padlock and its defensive spell lit up, but he clenched his hand. Power flared and the padlock deformed as though he were squeezing putty instead of steel.

He pulled it off the cabinet doors and dropped it. I cringed at the clatter.

Pushing in beside him, I opened the doors. Plain cardboard boxes were stacked on the shelves inside, each labeled neatly … in Latin. My Latin wasn't good enough to decipher more than a few.

Zylas inhaled through his nose. Leaning down, he sniffed again and pointed to a box on the bottom shelf. I crouched and squinted at the label. *Magia Illicita.* Even I could figure out what that one meant.

I tugged the box out. Inside were book-shaped packages wrapped in brown paper and tied with twine. Zylas squatted beside me and lifted the first one. He sniffed at the paper, then handed it to me. Picking up the next, he checked it for the scent of blood.

My nerves wound tighter as he smelled each bundle. This was taking too long.

Zylas picked up the sixth package and sniffed. "This one."

I set the others back in the box. With a worried glance at the door, I pulled the paper apart, revealing a grimy grimoire, maybe fifty years old, with a cheap leather cover and a revolting brown stain darkening the pages. A piece of crisp white paper was tucked inside the cover and I slid it out.

Someone's neat handwriting, in English, laid out the basics of the book—that it had belonged to a Demonica summoner named David Whitmore, who'd died in 1989, as well as where the book had been found and in what condition. The final paragraphs described its contents, and I pushed my glasses up my nose as I read.

David Whitmore engaged in methodical experimentation involving demon blood. He initially tested various theories that combined demon blood with sorcery arrays and alchemic transmutations. Later, he began conducting dangerous and unethical experiments on unwitting subjects, in and out of the mythic community. Despite the continual sickening and/or deaths of his subjects, Whitmore persisted with these trials. Whitmore resisted arrest and was killed by MPD agents.

The Analyst notes that this grimoire is among the most disturbing he has ever evaluated.

The Analyst further notes that, by his own assertion, Whitmore's experiments were largely failures. However, he references the work of sorcerers for whom we have no records, whose details have now been logged in the MPD database.

Recommendation: Grimoire to be transferred to MPD Illicit Magic Storage.

I looked again at the *Magia Illicita* box. Its contents must be destined for internment in MagiPol's strictly guarded storage facilities for dangerous or illegal magic and magical knowledge.

"This book smells of blood and death," Zylas muttered.

Even I could smell it—a musty, moldy tang that coated my nose like oil. I wanted to wash my hands. I wanted to throw this grimoire into a fire and watch it burn.

Nose wrinkled, I rewrapped the book and set it in the box. Zylas watched me slide the box back onto its shelf.

"You are not taking it?"

"No." I stood up and closed the cabinet. "We don't need it, and it's better that it be sent to the MPD for safekeeping."

"*Hnn*." He canted his head. "I hear footsteps."

I jolted away from the cabinet and opened my mouth to order Zylas back into the infernus, but he was already dissolving into crimson light. I burst into the hallway as Amalia rushed to meet me. I swung the door shut, then we both dashed into the washroom at the end of the hall and locked ourselves in.

"The librarian was coming this way," Amalia whispered. "Not sure if she'll come over here, though."

"Let's hope not," I muttered, leaning against the sink.

Amalia scanned me. "Weren't you stealing a book?"

I described what I had found and how I'd decided I didn't want to take it. "We don't need to know the details of that guy's messed-up experiments."

"No …" Amalia agreed, her gaze distant.

I figured she was thinking the same thing as me. "Claude must've gotten the idea to feed demon blood to vampires from *somewhere*, right?"

"Yeah, from sickos like that Whitmore quack and his idols. Who knows what other ideas Claude has gotten from their experiments?"

Silence settled over us, broken by the slow drip of water from the faucet.

"There's something really weird about Claude," Amalia murmured, her words slow and thoughtful. "Something really …"

"Insidious?" I suggested.

"Yeah. He—"

The loud *bing* of my phone interrupted her. I dug my cell out of my pocket and tapped the screen. At the sight of the new message, my face went cold.

When I stared at my phone, saying nothing, Amalia huffed. "What is it?"

"It's … it's from Zora."

Over a week had passed since Zora had discovered I was an illegal contractor. I'd tried to explain myself, but she'd only responded once to my messages. Her reply: *Do the right thing and turn yourself in.*

That had been six days ago, and I'd heard nothing since. With no other options, I'd avoided the guild at all costs and hoped against hope Zora would wash her hands of it—maybe even pretend she hadn't seen anything and didn't know my secret.

But now her number glowed on my screen with a new message: *Meet me in the Arcana Atrium at the guild. Right now.*

Losing patience, Amalia pulled my phone closer to read it. "Oh, shit."

"She wants to see me," I whispered. "Do you think she wants to talk?"

"Or she's luring you in for the MagiPol agents." Amalia tugged nervously at her sleeves. "I don't know, Robin."

Exhaling, I pushed my phone back into my pocket. "I guess we should go."

"But—"

"If she hasn't reported me, then not showing up might be the last straw for her. And if she *has* reported me—" I gulped back a surge of panic. "Then it's already too late. I can't survive as a wanted rogue, Amalia."

She rubbed her forehead. "Yeah, you're right. You wouldn't last a day. It seems weird she'd wait so long to report you. She must've been waiting for something else. I guess we should find out what."

I managed a smile at her "we," glad I wasn't going into this alone.

The downtown streets were dark and icy cold, the blustery wind blowing fitful rain in our faces. We bundled up tight and braved the trek on foot. The sidewalks were busy, Vancouver's citizens too accustomed to the winter rain to let it hamper their Saturday night plans.

The Crow and Hammer's windows glowed invitingly as we trudged the final block, our heads down and hands tucked in our coats. Zylas had warned me that his world's temperatures dropped below anything he'd experienced here—every night—and I was extremely glad I didn't live in his realm.

When Amalia shoved the guild door open, a notch of painful tension in my spine eased. The pub was busy, half the tables full and voices swelling with cheerful conversation. No MPD agents. No bounty hunter ambush.

Amalia and I shared nervous looks, then she headed for an empty table in the corner to wait. Delaying the moment I had to face Zora, I walked to the bar, passing three different discussions about New Year's Eve plans on my way. The atmosphere couldn't have been more different from my inner apprehension.

Despite the hubbub, only one customer stood at the bar: a woman with silvery hair in a shoulder-length bob, her glare mean enough to melt steel beams.

"I did *not* short your whiskey, Sylvia," a familiar voice growled, "and if you whine about it again, I'll mix your next Manhattan with our shittiest beer. Now get lost!"

The silver-haired woman snatched up her drink and whirled away from the bar, almost mowing me down as she stormed back to her table. Behind the counter, the red-haired bartender smacked a washrag down on the bar top.

"What do you want?" Tori snapped at me.

I flinched, my eyes wide and mouth too dry to respond.

She straightened from her aggressive posture and blew out a long breath, several long curls fluttering around her face. Between her holiday trip and my avoidance of the guild, I hadn't seen her since the monthly meeting.

"Sorry." She slid a bottle of vermouth off the counter and returned it to her well. "Having a bad day."

"Is ... is everything all right?" I asked hesitantly, afraid to trigger her temper again. "How was your trip?"

Her hazel eyes clouded. "It was ... okay. I'm just stressed out, that's all. I'll figure it out. I just ... unless *you* could ..."

"Unless I could what?" I asked, my brow furrowing.

She stared at me strangely, then gave her head a single sharp shake. "Never mind. Want anything to drink?"

"Um, actually, I was just wondering ... do you know if Zora is upstairs?"

Tori glanced around. "I think I saw her, but I'm not sure where she is."

"Oh. Okay. I—um—I'll just …"

When I trailed off, she arched an eyebrow. "You're paler than me, and that's saying something. What's wrong?"

"N-nothing."

"Nothing, eh? In that case, how about …" She reached under the counter, produced two shot glasses, and smacked them down. Next thing I knew, she held a silver bottle and was splashing clear liquor into the glasses.

I stepped back. "Oh, no. I don't—"

"This is the good vodka and it's on the house," she said with a grin that didn't quite reach her worried eyes. "I think we could both use a dose of 'calm the hell down.'" She picked up a glass. "You with me?"

With a mental shrug, I picked it up. We clinked our glasses together in a wordless toast, then tossed the shots back. The liquor burned down my throat.

"That was … good," I wheezed.

"Damn right." She gave me a friendly wave of dismissal. "Now go find Zora. I need to get back to work."

Worrying my lower lip between my teeth, I crossed to the stairs and started up them. Zora hadn't reported me. I chanted the reassuring words with each step. She hadn't reported me and she wanted to talk. This was a good thing. This was what I'd wanted all along—a chance to explain myself. A chance to make her understand that I was an illegal contractor by necessity, not choice.

Despite my inner pep talk and Tori's dose of liquid courage, nerves fluttered in my stomach as I reached the third floor. I turned down the side hall and paused at the atrium door, its sign turned to its blank back. Zora was giving me a chance. I would find a way to convince her.

As I gingerly knocked on the door, I dredged up the memory of the unlocking rune, but the door swung silently open. The atrium's interior was black and almost no light leaked in from the hall. I took a step inside, hesitating. Was I early? Or late? Where was—

Light bloomed. *Fire*light.

The orange glow swept across Zora, who stood in the middle of the white circle on the floor. She was dressed in full combat gear, and her hands rested on the pommel of her huge sword, its point resting between her feet.

She wasn't alone.

On her left was a man with dark hair, dark eyes, and two katana sheathed at his hip, his fingers hooked on the hilt of the longer one. On her right stood a man with coppery red hair, bright blue eyes, and a broadsword even larger than hers, already unsheathed. His palm was raised, flames dancing above it.

Aaron and Kai. Pyromage and electramage. They had been at the park on Halloween when Zylas had killed Tahēsh, and they'd fled with Tori and Ezra afterward.

They also represented two-thirds of the Elementaria trio that Zora had called the guild's strongest combat team outside of leadership.

"Close the door," Zora said quietly.

I didn't know what else to do. Fear sizzling in my blood, I pushed the door closed.

"This room is reinforced with the best magical protections possible." Her voice, like her face, was grim. "No amount of force or magic can break the walls. Nothing that happens in this room can harm anyone outside it."

A deeper cold chilled my limbs.

"Aaron and Kai," she continued, "have volunteered to support me. I figure that makes the odds about even, so if you plan to kill us, you can go ahead and call your demon out."

My head spun. I slid one foot sideways, widening my stance so I wouldn't sway where I stood. The two mages, towering head and shoulders above the petite sorceress, watched me without expression. Well, now I knew why Zora had delayed confronting me; she'd been waiting for Kai and Aaron to return from their trip.

Slowly, her words sunk in. If I planned to …

"*Kill you?*" I whispered. My disbelief cracked, a flicker of anger lighting in my chest. "I'm not going to kill you! Don't you think that's pretty obvious?"

Zora raised her eyebrows. "True. You had a much better opportunity back in that apartment. You could've blamed my death on the vampires."

I clenched my jaw, waiting to see what she would say next.

"I haven't told anyone what happened that afternoon. Not even these two." She indicated the mages. "They're here purely on faith."

They didn't react, their silence bordering on threatening. No sign of Kai's charming smile or Aaron's boisterous laughter, which I'd seen and heard often during the last guild meeting, touched their impassable faces.

"Here's the deal, Robin," Zora said flatly. "From now on, you don't do anything or go anywhere without telling me. I will be your shadow. If you sneak around behind my back or break one more MPD law …" An ominous pause. "You know what will happen."

I tensed.

"Should any sort of 'accident' befall me," she went on, "you'll answer to these two. You can imagine how that will go."

Frigid anxiety fluttered through me.

"If you're the person I think you are, this shouldn't be a problem. If you're not, well ..." Zora stared hard into my face. "So, you have three options: you can accept my terms, you can surrender, or we can fight it out right now."

My gaze shifted from the sorceress's unforgiving stare to Kai's glacial eyes to Aaron's stony expression, his face lit by the flickering fire in his hand. I had no intention of breaking any laws beyond the ones my illegal contract had already trampled over. I was a good person. I wanted to *be* a good person.

But it wasn't *my* morality that had my stomach twisting into knots.

It was my not-so-good, not-so-law-abiding, and all-too-disobedient demon that made me think this would probably end very, very badly.

ROBIN'S STORY CONTINUES IN

HUNTING FIENDS FOR THE ILL-EQUIPPED

THE GUILD CODEX: DEMONIZED / THREE

I thought I understood power.

My parents taught me that magic attracts equal danger, and everything I've seen since becoming a demon contractor confirms it. I've witnessed how power twists and corrupts—and I've tasted power no human should wield.

I thought I knew greed.

Ambition and avarice drove my family into hiding. My parents died for someone else's greed. I've never hunted anything in my life, but now I'm hunting their killer—with Zylas's help.

I thought I'd seen evil.

But with each step closer to my parents' murderer, I'm uncovering a different sort of evil, piece by hidden piece. I've stumbled into an insidious web that silently, secretly ensnares everything it touches. Zylas and I came as the hunters …

… but I think we might be the prey.

www.guildcodex.ca

ABOUT THE AUTHOR

Annette Marie is the author of YA urban fantasy series *Steel & Stone*, its prequel trilogy *Spell Weaver*, romantic fantasy trilogy *Red Winter*, and sassy urban fantasy series *The Guild Codex*.

Her first love is fantasy, but fast-paced adventures, bold heroines, and tantalizing forbidden romances are her guilty pleasures. She proudly admits she has a thing for dragons, and her editor has politely inquired as to whether she intends to include them in every book.

Annette lives in the frozen winter wasteland of Alberta, Canada (okay, it's not quite that bad) and shares her life with her husband and their furry minion of darkness—sorry, cat—Caesar. When not writing, she can be found elbow-deep in one art project or another while blissfully ignoring all adult responsibilities.

www.annettemarie.ca

SPECIAL THANKS

My thanks to Erich Merkel for sharing your exceptional expertise in Latin and Ancient Greek. Any errors are mine.

THE
GUILD CODEX
DEMONIZED

Robin is ready to become a hunter, her sights set on Claude and his demon, but the web of his secrets is far more insidious than she imagined. This mission is too much even for Zylas to take on alone … but who from the Crow and Hammer can they turn to for help?

THE
GUILD CODEX
SPELLBOUND

Meet Tori. She's feisty. She's broke. She has a bit of an issue with running her mouth off. And she just landed a job at the local magic guild. Problem is, she's also 100% human. Oops.

Welcome to the Crow and Hammer.

DISCOVER MORE BOOKS AT
www.guildcodex.ca

SPELL WEAVER

*The only thing more dangerous than the denizens of the
Underworld ... is stealing from them.*

As a daemon living in exile among humans, Clio has picked up some
unique skills. But pilfering magic from the Underworld's deadliest
spell weavers? Not so much. Unfortunately, that's exactly what she has
to do to earn a ticket home.

A destiny written by the gods. A fate forged by lies.

If Emi is sure of anything, it's that *kami*—the gods—are good, and *yokai*—the earth spirits—are evil. But when she saves the life of a fox shapeshifter, the truths of her world start to crumble. And the treachery of the gods runs deep.

This stunning trilogy features 30 full-page illustrations.